The zanzibar cat
Joanna Russ

WITH A FOREWORD BY MARGE PIERCY

AND DRAWINGS BY DENNIS NEAL SMITH

ARKHAM HOUSE PUBLISHERS, INC.

ACKNOWLEDGMENTS

"Corruption," copyright © 1976 by Fawcett Publications, Inc. for *Aurora: Beyond Equality*, edited by Susan Janice Anderson and Vonda N. McIntyre.

"The Extraordinary Voyages of Amélie Bertrand," copyright © 1979 by Mercury Press, Inc. for *The Magazine of Fantasy and Science Fiction*, September 1979.

"A Game of Vlet," copyright © 1973 by Mercury Press, Inc. for *The Magazine of Fantasy and Science Fiction*, February 1974.

"Gleepsite," copyright © 1971 by Damon Knight for *Orbit 9*, edited by Damon Knight.

"How Dorothy Kept Away the Spring," copyright © 1976 by Mercury Press, Inc. for *The Magazine of Fantasy and Science Fiction*, February 1977.

"My Boat," copyright © 1975 by Mercury Press, Inc. for *The Magazine of Fantasy and Science Fiction*, January 1976.

"My Dear Emily," copyright © 1962 by Mercury Press, Inc. for *The Magazine of Fantasy and Science Fiction*, July 1962.

"The New Men," copyright © 1965 by Mercury Press, Inc. for *The Magazine of Fantasy and Science Fiction*, February 1966.

"Nobody's Home," copyright © 1972 by Robert Silverberg for *New Dimensions 2*, edited by Robert Silverberg.

"Old Thoughts, Old Presences" appeared originally as "Daddy's Girl," copyright © 1975 by Cornell University for *Epoch*, Winter 1975, and as "Autobiography of My Mother," copyright © 1975 by Cornell University for *Epoch*, Fall 1975.

"Poor Man, Beggar Man," copyright © 1971 by Terry Carr for *Universe 1*, edited by Terry Carr.

'The Soul of a Servant," copyright © 1973 by Roger Elwood for *Showcase*, edited by Roger Elwood.

'There Is Another Shore, You Know, Upon the Other Side," copyright © 1963 by Mercury Press, Inc. for *The Magazine of Fantasy and Science Fiction*, September 1963.

"Useful Phrases for the Tourist," copyright © 1972 by Terry Carr for *Universe 2*, edited by Terry Carr.

"When It Changed," copyright © 1972 by Harlan Ellison for *Again, Dangerous Visions*, edited by Harlan Ellison.

"The Zanzibar Cat," copyright © 1971 by Coronet Communications, Inc. for *Quark 3*, edited by Samuel R. Delany and Marilyn Hacker.

Published by arrangement with Pocket Books, a Simon & Schuster Division of Gulf & Western Corporation.

Copyright © 1983 by Joanna Russ

Library of Congress Cataloging in Publication Data
Russ, Joanna, 1937–
The Zanzibar cat.
I. Title.
PS3568.U763Z23   1983   813'.54   83-3874
ISBN 0-87054-097-1

contents

Foreword

Here is a rich and diverse collection from an exceptional writer, better known as a novelist, although first published and recognized as an author of short stories. Joanna Russ is one of the most intelligent writers we have operating in the States now. I do not qualify this comment with "for a science fiction or speculative fiction writer"; I am speaking of all writers now on deck.

In her novels Russ is concerned with survival, loneliness, community, violence, sex roles, the nature of oppression, the necessity of further civilization, and what is gained and what is lost by its progress. (I have written two essays on Joanna Russ's novels, both contained in my collection of essays *Parti-Colored Blocks for a Quilt*, part of the University of Michigan's Poets on Poetry series.) Some of her concerns are evident in these short stories, yet different passions also emerge.

She is as much the master of characterization in her short fiction as in her longer. Dorothy of "How Dorothy Kept Away the Spring," the protagonist of "When It Changed," the eponymous heroine of "The Extraordinary Voyages of Amélie Bertrand," Alpha in "Corruption," the mother and daughter in "The Autobiography of My Mother," Emily of "My Dear Emily," and twenty others are memorable, believable characters.

Russ is also the same master of narrative and action. Never does she loiter or dwell on her effects. She never overdevelops some idea or scene past its function in the whole. Things move along, sometimes with a sense of giddy speed.

We have also learned to expect wit from Russ. Her humor is wonderfully varied, sometimes earthy, sometimes close to vaudeville or slapstick (as in her novel *The Female Man*), sometimes rich with an intellectual and bodily sense of the absurd. "Useful Phrases for the Tourist" is essentially a stand-up comic routine, drawing its humor from the absurdities of guidebooks with their assumption, on the one hand, of a universal bourgeois politeness (How do you do, sir or madam, how delightful to make your acquaintance) and, on the other hand, the listing of disasters: Help! Police! Fire! Doctor! Nurse! I have lost my purse, my wallet, my passport, my way, my wife, my husband, my glasses, my life. But Russ is concerned equally with the absurdities of our attempts to imagine actual contact between species of different evolutionary lines and vastly different configurations. Either all the aliens are bipedal and speak American, or you may be in for a lot of trouble when you try to use the public restrooms.

One surprise for me is the number of fantasy stories in this collection, as opposed to the sterner speculative fiction of Joanna Russ's novels. (Although *Kittatinny: A Tale of Magic* comes to mind as an example of book-length fantasy.) Sometimes she works consciously close to the fairy tale, as in the title story, a dissertation on the empowerment of the female imagination. "The Zanzibar Cat" is a short and delightful tale about an evil Duke and the Miller's daughter who should, of course, be a victim or prize, but who turns out instead to be the author and sole creator of the story.

Another surprise is the number of vampire stories in this volume. Why does this myth occupy women's imaginations? As you read Russ's "My Dear Emily," you realize that, given the boredom and powerlessness of many women's lives, being transformed into a vampire is a not entirely unattractive alternative to wife-and-motherhood and housewifery. Emily, a turn-of-the-century heroine, not permitted any unladylike adventure or exploration, is not so much seduced or victimized by the vampire as she is empowered by him. Like the character Ernst in the novel *The Two of Them*, the vampire is a means of escape and empowerment for the bright but frustrated young heroine. "The New Men" is an entirely different vampire story, set in Communist Poland, where a Russian bureaucrat suffering from leukemia is forced to spend the night with an aristocrat of the ancien régime who turns out to be a vampire.

Not a tale of vampirism but a ghost story, "There Is Another Shore, You Know, Upon the Other Side," concerns a wistful spectral tourist, a young girl who died without having lived enough to relinquish existence.

Two of the other fantasies center on some kind of relinquishment. Russ remembers childhood with extreme and unsentimental clarity, how frightening it often was, how lonely, how passionate, how frequently mysterious, how violently willful and blocked. She remembers with equal clarity adolescence, especially the adolescence of the bright nonconformist, the intellectual in high school, the girl who will not play proper girls' games, the kid with pimples the size of Crater Lake who reads science fiction and builds rocket models in her or his room. "My Boat" again concerns empowerment, fantastic empowerment on the one hand and the refusal of it on the other. "How Dorothy Kept Away the Spring" is a chilling meditation on the loneliness and alienation of a child whose mother has died.

One of Russ's strong themes is negation: "The New Men," in which commissar and vampire negate each other; Dorothy, who of course must recall to us as she journeys with her fantastic hunter, clown, and gnome the other Dorothy of *The Wizard of Oz*, but whose spirit and intent are so extremely contrary; Emily, who finds in vampirehood more fulfillment than in ordinary womanhood; "Corruption," in which an agent penetrating a bleak regimented society is destroyed by assimilation, finally killing the people he had once cared about even as he accomplishes his mission of mechanical sabotage—alienation produces inner and outer negation.

Occasionally we find in the work of a novelist that a particular story is a study, a preliminary sketch or trial run, for an idea that will later become a novel. "When It Changed" bears such a relationship to the novel *The Female Man*, even to the extent that the entirely female world is called Whileaway. This is a far gloomier rendering of the prospects of that society, although the society itself I find as sprightly if not as detailed as it is in the novel. This female society has been produced by accident, however, not by choice, and as it is in another space rather than another time, it is thus far more vulnerable to invasion and interference. In some ways the world of "When It Changed" resembles the world of the mother in the story "Daddy's Girl," an extremely brilliant piece that is as much prose poem or essay as story; much of its considerable power lies in its imagery.

One unavoidable observation as I read through these stories is the growth of Russ's feminism. In a story like "The Soul of a Servant," rape is used as male writers use it, half decoratively, in passing, without any sense of its physical reality. As often in male writing it stands for something rather than being a concrete act, although it is clearly an act of hostility rather than an act of desire. But the story buys the male rationalization, in its viewpoint character, that a young woman being flirtatious, which may be the only form of friendliness she has been allowed to express, is asking for it. Similarly, I doubt if "The New Men" or "Poor Man, Beggar Man" would be in any interesting way different if written by a man. I find that distinctively untrue, however, of the other stories.

Russ's most powerful works often concern empowerment and powerlessness, aggression and negation, but "A Game of Vlet" is caught somewhere midway between such changes of consciousness. The Lady who appears to engage in the game and force the revolution forward seems powerful and then is revealed not to be, finally, in a story that apparently promises more than it ultimately delivers. The metaphor is more meaningful than the use to which it is put in this tale.

If I seem to find Russ's more feminist stories more successful than her less feminist stories, it is not only, or I believe even chiefly, because I agree with her politics, although of course with any writer that always helps. It is because her imagination is more liberated to follow through on the narrative premises. Stories like "The Autobiography of My Mother," "When It Changed," "Daddy's Girl," are wilder, freer in their forward momentum. They are fully achieved.

These stories exhibit a satisfying range of tone and style, from the calm sunny homage to Jules Verne, "The Extraordinary Voyages of Amélie Bertrand," to the surrealistic nightmare of "Gleepsite," the bustling languors of "My Dear Emily," the realistic creation of myth in "The Autobiography of My Mother," the icy dream landscape of "How Dorothy Kept Away the Spring." Russ's exciting fictional worlds are of two sorts, which share honors. One world is very like our own, although bleeding at the edges into surrealism, dream, or fairy tale, often clearly the United States of the fifties, the sixties, the seventies, or the eighties with some interesting variable or power relationship surfaced. In the other worlds, as in "Nobody's Home," a whole social and economic structure is sketched in casually, at breakneck speed.

I very much admire the sense of speed that Russ often gives the reader, of eliminating intermediate steps and decisions. When you start one of her stories, it is not at all like an Ibsen play. You do not begin with the slow exposition, the first act with the maid dusting the parlor and telling the butler all about the curse of the family, which of course the butler knows as well as she does: "Today Per Lagersholm comes to visit his wife for the first time in forty-two years, so we must dust the entire house carefully, my Eric." "Why is it, Olga, that Per Lagersholm hasn't come to visit his wife in forty-two years, which must be about the day that they married, unless I am hideously mistaken." Joanna is not so kind to the slow reader. She has the habit of starting in medias res and in medias place. It's your job as the reader to work and try to figure out what's going on and where we are in earth or elsewhere, or far more importantly, what essentially is going on among all these articulate people.

It is a very jazzy style that she has in several of the short stories, a feeling of clever and controlled improvisation. I am in no wise suggesting that the stories are, in fact, improvisations; what I am trying to describe is a sense in them of much occurring and of bright people trying to understand what is happening and to enjoy it or control it or exploit it. I am thinking in particular of that short story "Nobody's Home." Nothing is explained and everything is given us. We find a large family taking in a new member who turns out to have the fatal character flaw for that time of not being exceptionally intelligent. In this story Russ has created a utopia of the bright. We shall not be lonely, we shall not be alone, we shall inherit the earth—not the lovers of power, not the big daddies with their nukes, not the controllers or the comptrollers, but the bright and the curious shall inherit the earth and create a society of multiple options and quick responses and large polymorphous perverse warm families in which art and child care and scientific curiosity and games are all intermingled.

She is seldom a self-indulgent writer, however, and thus sees even that society as one that fails some of its members through no fault of their own. What you finally carry away from these stories is a sense of possibilities, both negative and positive. Russ is one of our best novelists of ideas because she has all the traditional fictional virtues. She creates full-fleshed characters, full of quirks and odd memories and hot little sexual nodes that make them believable. She embodies her ideas in a fast-moving arc of action. Finally, she has effective emotional range, all the way from savage indignation to vaudeville routines, from the bleak to the lush, from extreme alienation to a warm and powerful projection of community. What Russ does not create is a world where love conquers all, certainly not her women. The push toward freedom, appetite, curiosity both intellectual and sensual, the desire to control and expand their own existence, figure far more importantly in the lives of her female characters than does traditional romance. Here then are a number of adventures of the mind that I commend to your enjoyment.

MARGE PIERCY

The Zanzibar Cat

ШНЕП ІЬ СНаПФЕd

Katy drives like a maniac; we must have been doing over 120 kilometers an hour on those turns. She's good, though, extremely good, and I've seen her take the whole car apart and put it together again in a day. My birthplace on Whileaway was largely given to farm machinery and I refuse to wrestle with a five-gear shift at unholy speeds, not having been brought up to it, but even on those turns in the middle of the night on a country road as bad as only our district can make them, Katy's driving didn't scare me. The funny thing about my wife, though: she will not handle guns. She has even gone hiking in the forests above the forty-eighth parallel without firearms for days at a time. And that *does* scare me.

Katy and I have three children between us, one of hers and two of mine. Yuriko, my eldest, was asleep in the back seat, dreaming twelve-year-old dreams of love and war: running away to sea, hunting in the North, dreams of strangely beautiful people in strangely beautiful places, all the wonderful guff you think up when you're turning twelve and the glands start going. Someday soon, like all of them, she will disappear for weeks on end to come back grimy and proud, having knifed her first cougar or shot her first bear, dragging some abominably dangerous dead beastie behind her, while I will never forgive for what it might have done to my daughter. Yuriko says Katy's driving puts her to sleep.

For someone who has fought three duels, I am afraid of far, far too much. I'm getting old. I told this to my wife.

"You're thirty-four," she said. Laconic to the point of silence, that one. She flipped the lights on, on the dash—three kilometers to go and the road getting worse all the time. Far out in the country. Electric-green trees rushed into our headlights and around the car. I reached down next to me where we bolt the carrier panel to the door and eased my rifle into my lap. Yuriko stirred in the back. My height but Katy's eyes, Katy's face. The car engine is so quiet, Katy says, that you can hear breathing in the back seat. Yuki had been alone in the car when the message came, enthusiastically decoding her dot-dashes (silly to mount a wide-frequency transceiver near an IC engine, but most of Whileaway is on steam). She had thrown herself out of the car, my gangly and gaudy offspring, shouting at the top of her lungs, so of course she had had to come along. We've been intellectually prepared for this ever since the colony was founded, ever since it was abandoned, but this is different. This is awful.

"Men!" Yuki had screamed, leaping over the car door. "They've come back! Real Earth men!"

We met them in the kitchen of the farmhouse near the place where they had landed; the windows were open, the night air very mild. We had passed all sorts of transportation when we parked outside, steam tractors, trucks, an IC flatbed, even a bicycle. Lydia, the district biologist, had come out of her Northern taciturnity long enough to take blood and urine samples and was sitting in a corner of the kitchen shaking her head in astonishment over the results; she even forced herself (very big, very fair, very shy, always painfully blushing) to dig up the old language manuals— though I can talk the old tongues in my sleep. And do. Lydia is uneasy with us; we're Southerners and too flamboyant. I counted twenty people in that kitchen, all the brains of North Continent.

Phyllis Spet, I think, had come in by glider. Yuki was the only child there.

Then I saw the four of them.

They are bigger than we are. They are bigger and broader. Two were taller than me, and I am extremely tall, one meter, eighty centimeters in my bare feet. They are obviously of our species but *off*, indescribably off, and as my eyes could not and still cannot quite comprehend the lines of those alien bodies, I could not, then, bring myself to touch them, though the one who spoke Russian—what voices they have!—wanted to "shake hands," a custom from the past, I imagine. I can only say they were apes with human faces. He seemed to mean well, but I found myself shuddering back almost the length of the kitchen—and then I laughed apologetically—and then to set a good example (*interstellar amity*, I thought) did "shake hands" finally. A hard, hard hand. They are heavy as draft horses. Blurred, deep voices. Yuriko had sneaked in between the adults and was gazing at *the men* with her mouth open.

He turned *his* head—those words have not been in our language for six hundred years—and said, in bad Russian:

"Who's that?"

"My daughter," I said, and added (with that irrational attention to good manners we sometimes employ in moments of insanity), "my daughter, Yuriko Janetson. We use the matronymic. You would say patronymic."

He laughed, involuntarily. Yuki exclaimed, "I thought they would be good-looking!" greatly disappointed at this reception of herself. Phyllis Helgason Spet, whom someday I shall kill, gave me across the room a cold, level, venomous look, as if to say: *Watch what you say. You know what I can do.* It's true that I have little formal status, but madam president will get herself in serious trouble with both me and her own staff if she continues to consider industrial espionage good clean fun. Wars and rumors of wars, as it says in one of our ancestors' books. I translated Yuki's words into *the man*'s dog-Russian, once our *lingua franca*, and *the man* laughed again.

"Where are all your people?" he said conversationally.

I translated again and watched the faces around the room; Lydia embarrassed (as usual), Spet narrowing her eyes with some damned scheme, Katy very pale.

"This is Whileaway," I said.

He continued to look unenlightened.

"Whileaway," I said. "Do you remember? Do you have records? There was a plague on Whileaway."

He looked moderately interested. Heads turned in the back of the room, and I caught a glimpse of the local professions-parliament delegate; by morning every town meeting, every district caucus, would be in full session.

"Plague?" he said. "That's most unfortunate."

"Yes," I said. "Most unfortunate. We lost half our population in one generation."

He looked properly impressed.

"Whileaway was lucky," I said. "We had a big initial gene pool, we had been chosen for extreme intelligence, we had a high technology and a large remaining population in which every adult was two-or-three experts in one. The soil is good. The climate is blessedly easy. There are thirty million of us now. Things are beginning to snowball in industry—do you understand?—give us seventy years and we'll have more than one real city, more than a few industrial centers, full-time professions, full-time radio operators, full-time machinists, give us seventy years and not everyone will have to spend three-quarters of a lifetime on the farm." And I tried to explain how hard it is when artists can practice full-time only in old age, when there are so few, so very few who can be free, like Katy and myself. I tried also to outline our government, the two houses, the one by professions and the geographic one; I told him the district caucuses handled problems too big for the individual towns. And that population control was not a political issue, not yet, though give us time and it would be. This was a delicate point in our history; give us time. There was no need to sacrifice the quality of life for an insane rush into industrialization. Let us go our own pace. Give us time.

"Where are all the people?" said that monomaniac.

I realized then that he did not mean people, he meant *men*, and he was giving the word the meaning it had not had on Whileaway for six centuries.

"They died," I said. "Thirty generations ago."

I thought we had poleaxed him. He caught his breath. He made as if to get out of the chair he was sitting in; he put his hand to his chest; he looked around at us with the strangest blend of awe and sentimental tenderness. Then he said, solemnly and earnestly:

"A great tragedy."

I waited, not quite understanding.

"Yes," he said, catching his breath again with that queer smile, that adult-to-child smile that tells you something is being hidden and will be presently produced with cries of encouragement and joy, "a great tragedy. But it's over." And again he looked around at all of us with the strangest deference. As if we were invalids.

"You've adapted amazingly," he said.

"To what?" I said. He looked embarrassed. He looked inane. Finally he said, "Where I come from, the women don't dress so plainly."

"Like you?" I said. "Like a bride?" for the men were wearing silver from head to foot. I had never seen anything so gaudy. He made as if to answer and then apparently thought better of it; he laughed at me again. With an odd exhilaration—as if we were something childish and something wonderful, as if he were doing us an enormous favor—he took one shaky breath and said, "Well, we're here."

I looked at Spet, Spet looked at Lydia, Lydia looked at Amalia, who is the head of the local town meeting, Amalia looked at I don't know who. My throat was raw. I cannot stand local beer, which the farmers swill as if their stomachs had iridium linings, but I took it anyway, from Amalia (it was her bicycle we had seen outside as we parked), and swallowed it all. This was going to take a long time. I said, "Yes, here you are," and smiled (feeling like a fool), and wondered seriously if male Earth people's minds worked so very differently from female Earth people's minds, but that couldn't be so or the race would have died out long ago. The radio network had got the news around-planet by now and we had another Russian speaker, flown in from Varna; I decided to cut out when *the man* passed around pictures of his wife, who looked like the priestess of some arcane cult. He proposed to question Yuki, so I barreled her into a back room in spite of her furious protests and went out on the front porch. As I left, Lydia was explaining the difference between parthenogenesis (which is so easy that anyone can practice it) and what we do, which is the merging of ova. That is why Katy's baby looks like me. Lydia went on to the Ansky Process and Katy Ansky, our one full-polymath genius and the great-great-I-don't-know-how-many-times-great-grandmother of my own Katharina.

A dot-dash transmitter in one of the outbuildings chattered faintly to itself: operators flirting and passing jokes down the line.

There was a man on the porch. The other tall man. I watched him for a few minutes—I can move very quietly when I want to—and when I allowed him to see me, he stopped talking into the little machine hung around his neck. Then he said calmly, in excellent Russian, "Did you know that sexual equality has been reestablished on Earth?"

"You're the real one," I said, "aren't you? The other one's for show." It was a great relief to get things cleared up. He nodded affably.

"As a people, we are not very bright," he said. "There's been too much genetic damage in the last few centuries. Radiation. Drugs. We can use Whileaway's genes, Janet." Strangers do not call strangers by the first name.

"You can have cells enough to drown in," I said. "Breed your own."

He smiled. "That's not the way we want to do it." Behind him I saw Katy come into the square of light that was the screened-in door. He went on, low and urbane, not mocking me, I think, but with the self-confidence of someone who has always had money and strength to spare, who doesn't know what it is to be second-class or provincial. Which is very odd, because the day before, I would have said that was an exact description of me.

"I'm talking to you, Janet," he said, "because I suspect you have more popular influence than anyone else here. You know as well as I do that parthenogenetic culture has all sorts of inherent defects, and we do not—if we can help it—mean to use you for anything of the sort. Pardon me; I should not have said 'use.' But surely you can see that this kind of society is unnatural."

"Humanity is unnatural," said Katy. She had my rifle under her left arm. The top of that silky head does not quite come up to my collarbone, but she is as tough as steel; he began to move, again with that queer, smiling deference (which his fellow had shown to me but he had not), and the gun slid into Katy's grip as if she had shot with it all her life.

"I agree," said the man. "Humanity is unnatural. I should know. I have metal in my teeth and metal pins here." He touched his shoulder. "Seals are harem animals," he added, "and so are men; apes are promiscuous and so are men; doves are monogamous and so are men; there are even celibate men and homosexual men. There are homosexual cows, I believe. But Whileaway is still missing something." He gave a dry chuckle. I will give him the credit of believing that it had something to do with nerves.

"I miss nothing," said Katy, "except that life isn't endless."

"You are—?" said the man, nodding from me to her.

"Wives," said Katy. "We're married." Again the dry chuckle.

"A good economic arrangement," he said, "for working and taking care of the children. And as good an arrangement as any for randomizing heredity, if your reproduction is made to follow the same pattern. But think, Katharina Michaelason, if there isn't something better that you might secure for your daughters. I believe in instincts, even in man, and I can't think that the two of you—a machinist, are you? and I gather you are some sort of chief of police—don't feel somehow what even you must miss. You know it intellectually, of course. There is only half a species here. Men must come back to Whileaway."

Katy said nothing.

"I should think, Katharina Michaelason," said the man gently, "that you, of all people, would benefit most from such a change," and he walked past Katy's rifle into the square of light coming from the door. I think it was then that he noticed my scar, which really does not show unless the light is from the side: a fine line that runs from temple to chin. Most people don't even know about it.

"Where did you get that?" he said, and I answered with an involuntary grin, "In my last duel." We stood there bristling at each other for several seconds (this is absurd but true) until he went inside and shut the screen door behind him. Katy said in a brittle voice, "You damned fool, don't you know when we've been insulted?" and swung up the rifle to shoot him through the screen, but I got to her before she could fire and knocked the rifle out of aim; it burned a hole through the porch floor. Katy was shaking. She kept whispering over and over, "That's why I never touched it, because I knew I'd kill someone, I knew I'd kill someone." The first man—the one I'd spoken with first—was still talking inside the house, something about the grand movement to recolonize and rediscover all that Earth had lost. He stressed the advantages to Whileaway: trade, exchange of ideas, education. He too said that sexual equality had been reestablished on Earth.

Katy was right, of course; we should have burned them down where they stood. Men are coming to Whileaway. When one culture has the big guns and the other has none, there is a certain predictability about the outcome. Maybe men would have come eventually in any case. I like to think that a hundred years from now my great-grandchildren could have stood them off or fought them to a standstill, but even that's no odds; I will remember all my life those four people I first met who were muscled like bulls and who made me—if only for a moment—feel small. A neurotic reaction, Katy says. I remember everything that happened that night; I remember Yuki's excitement in the car, I remember Katy's sobbing when we got home as if her heart would break, I remember her lovemaking, a little peremptory as always, but wonderfully soothing and comforting. I remember prowling restlessly around the house after Katy fell asleep with one bare arm flung into a patch of light from the hall. The muscles of her forearms are like metal bars from all that driving and testing of her machines. Sometimes I dream about Katy's arms. I remember wandering into the nursery and picking up my wife's baby, dozing for a while with the poignant, amazing warmth of an infant in my lap, and finally returning to the kitchen to find Yuriko fixing herself a late snack. My daughter eats like a Great Dane.

"Yuki," I said, "do you think you could fall in love with a man?" and she whooped derisively. "With a ten-foot toad!" said my tactful child.

But men are coming to Whileaway. Lately I sit up nights and worry about the men who will come to this planet, about my two daughters and Betta Katharinason, about what will happen to Katy, to me, to my life. Our ancestors' journals are one long cry of pain and I suppose I ought to be glad now but one can't throw away six centuries, or even (as I have lately discovered) thirty-four years. Sometimes I laugh at the question those four men hedged about all evening and never quite dared to ask, looking at the lot of us, hicks in overalls, farmers in canvas pants and plain shirts: *Which of you plays the role of the man?* As if we had to produce a carbon copy of their mistakes! I doubt very much that sexual equality has been reestablished on Earth. I do not like to think of myself mocked, of Katy deferred to as if she were weak, of Yuki made to feel unimportant or silly, of my other children cheated of their full humanity or turned into strangers. And I'm afraid that my own achievements will dwindle from what they were—or what I thought they were—to the not-very-interesting curiosa of the human race, the oddities you read about in the back of the book, things to laugh at sometimes because they are so exotic, quaint but not impressive, charming but not useful. I find this more painful than I can say. You will agree that for a woman who has fought three duels, all of them kills, indulging in such fears is ludicrous. But what's around the corner now is a duel so big that I don't think I have the guts for it; in Faust's words: *Verweile doch, du bist so schön!* Keep it as it is. Don't change.

Sometimes at night I remember the original name of this planet, changed by the first generation of our ancestors, those curious women for whom, I suppose, the real name was too painful a reminder after the men died. I find it amusing, in a grim way, to see it all so completely turned around. This too shall pass. All good things must come to an end.

Take my life but don't take away the meaning of my life.
For-a-While.

The Extraordinary Voyages of Amélie Bertrand

HOMMAGE À JULES VERNE

In the summer of 192- there occurred to me the most extraordinary event of my life.

I was traveling on business and was in the French countryside, not far from Lyons, waiting for my train on a small railway platform on the outskirts of a town I shall call Beaulieu-sur-le-Pont. (This is not its name.) The weather was cool, although it was already June, and I shared the platform with only one other passenger: a plump woman of at least forty, by no means pretty but respectably dressed, the true type of our provincial *bonne bourgeoise*, who sat on the bench provided for the comfort of passengers and knitted away at some indeterminate garment.

The station at Beaulieu, like so many of our railway stops in small towns, is provided with a central train station of red brick through which runs an arch or passageway, also of red brick, which thus divides the edifice of the station into a ticket counter and waiting room on one side and a small café on the other. Thus, having attended one's train on the wrong side of the station (for there are railroad tracks on both sides of the edifice), one may occasionally find oneself making the traversal of the station in order to catch one's train, usually at the last minute.

So it occurred with me. I heard the approach of my train, drew out my watch, and found that the mild spring weather had caused me to indulge in a reverie not only lengthy but at a distance from my desired track; the two-fifty-one for Lyons was about to enter Beaulieu, but I was wrongly situated to place myself on board; were I not quick, no entrainment would take place.

Blessing the good fathers of Beaulieu-sur-le-Pont for their foresight in so dividing their train depot, I walked briskly but with no excessive haste towards the passage. I had not the slightest doubt of catching my train. I even had leisure to reflect on the bridge which figures so largely in the name of the town and to recall that, according to my knowledge, this bridge had been destroyed in the time of Caractacus; then I stepped between the buildings. I noticed that my footsteps echoed from the walls of the tunnel, a phenomenon one may observe upon entering any confined space. To the right of me and to the left were walls of red brick. The air was invigoratingly fresh, the weather sunny and clear, and ahead was the wooden platform, the well-trimmed bushes, and the potted geraniums on the other side of the Beaulieu train station.

Nothing could have been more ordinary.

Then, out of the corner of my eye, I noticed that the lady I had seen knitting on the platform was herself entering the passage at a decorous distance behind me. We were, it seems, to become fellow passengers. I turned and raised my hat to her, intending to continue. I could not see the Lyons train, but to judge by the faculty of hearing, it was rounding the bend outside the station. I placed my hat back upon my head, reached the center of the tunnel, or rather, a point midway along its major diameter—

Will you believe me? Probably. You are English; the fogs and literature of your unfortunate climate predispose you to marvels. Your winters cause you to read much; your authors reflect to you from their pages the romantic imagination of a *réfugié* from the damp and cold, to whom anything may happen if only it does so outside his windows! I am the product of another soil; I am logical, I am positive, I am French. Like my famous compatriot, I cry,

"Where is this marvel? Let him produce it!" I myself do not believe
what happened to me. I believe it no more than I believe that
Phileas Fogg circumnavigated the globe in 187- and still lives today
in London with the lady he rescued from a funeral pyre in Benares.

Nonetheless I will attempt to describe what happened.

The first sensation was a retardation of time. It seemed to me
that I had been in the passage at Beaulieu for a very long time, and
the passage itself seemed suddenly to become double its length, or
even triple. Then my body became heavy, as in a dream; there was
also a disturbance of balance as though the tunnel sloped *down*
towards its farther end and some increase in gravity were pulling
me in that direction. A phenomenon even more disturbing was the
peculiar *haziness* that suddenly obscured the forward end of the
Beaulieu tunnel, as if Beaulieu-sur-le-Pont, far from enjoying the
temperate warmth of an excellent June day, were actually melting
in the heat—yes, heat!—a terrible warmth like that of a furnace,
and yet humid, entirely unknown to our moderate climate even in
the depths of summer. In a moment my summer clothing was
soaked, and I wondered with horror whether I dared offend
customary politeness by opening my collar. The noise of the Lyons
train, far from disappearing, now surrounded me on all sides as if a
dozen trains, and not merely one, were converging upon Beaulieu-
sur-le-Pont, or as if a strong wind (which was pushing me forward)
were blowing. I attempted to peer into the mistiness ahead of me
but could see nothing. A single step farther and the mist swirled
aside; there seemed to be a vast spray of greenery beyond—indeed,
I could distinctly make out the branches of a large palm tree upon
which intense sunlight was beating—and then, directly crossing it,
a long thick sinuous gray serpent which appeared to writhe from
side to side, and which then fixed itself around the trunk of the
palm, bringing into view a gray side as large as the opening of the
tunnel itself, four gray columns beneath, and two long ivory tusks.

It was an elephant.

It was the roar of the elephant which brought me to my senses.
Before this I had proceeded as in an astonished dream; now I turned
and attempted to retrace my steps but found that I could hardly
move *up* the steep tunnel against the furious wind which assailed
me. I was aware of the cool, fresh, familiar spring of Beaulieu, very

small and precious, appearing like a photograph or a scene observed through the diminishing, not the magnifying, end of an opera glass, and of the impossibility of ever attaining it. Then a strong arm seized mine, and I was back on the platform from which I had ventured—it seemed now so long ago!—sitting on the wooden bench while the good bourgeoise in the decent dark dress inquired after my health.

I cried, "But the palm tree—the tropical air—the elephant!"

She said in the calmest way in the world, "Do not distress yourself, monsieur. It was merely Uganda."

I may mention here that Madame Bertrand, although not in her first youth, is a woman whose dark eyes sparkle with extraordinary charm. One must be an imbecile not to notice this. Her concern is sincere, her manner *séduisante*, and we had not been in conversation five minutes before she abandoned the barriers of reserve and explained to me not only the nature of the experience I had undergone, but (in the café of the train station at Beaulieu, over a lemon ice) her own extraordinary history.

"Shortly after the termination of the Great War," (said Madame Bertrand) "I began a habit which I have continued to this day: whenever my husband, Aloysius Bertrand, is away from Beaulieu-sur-le-Pont on business, as often happens, I visit my sister-in-law in Lyons, leaving Beaulieu on one day in the middle of the week and returning on the next. At first my visits were uneventful. Then, one fateful day only two years ago, I happened to depart from the wrong side of the train station after purchasing my ticket and so found myself seeking to approach my train through that archway or passage where you, monsieur, so recently ventured. There were the same effects, but I attributed them to an attack of faintness and continued, expecting my hour's ride to Lyons, my sister-in-law's company, the cinema, the restaurant, and the usual journey back the next day.

"Imagine my amazement—no, my stupefaction—when I found myself instead on a rough wooden platform surrounded on three sides by the massive rocks and lead-colored waters of a place entirely unfamiliar to me! I made inquiries and discovered, to my unbounded astonishment, that I was on the last railway stop or terminus of Tierra del Fuego, the southernmost tip of the South

American continent, and that I had engaged myself to sail as super-cargo on a whaling vessel contracted to cruise the waters of Antarctica for the next two years. The sun was low, the clouds massing above, and behind me (continuing the curve of the rock-infested bay) was a jungle of squat pine trees, expressing by the irregularity of their trunks the violence of the climate.

"What could I do? My clothing was Victorian, the ship ready to sail, the six months' night almost upon us. The next train was not due until spring.

"To make a long story short, I sailed.

"You might expect that a lady, placed in such a situation, would suffer much that was disagreeable and discommoding. So it was. But there is also a somber charm to the far south which only those who have traveled there can know: the stars glittering on the ice fields, the low sun, the penguins, the icebergs, the whales. And then there were the sailors, children of the wilderness, young, ardent, sincere, especially one, a veritable Apollo with a broad forehead and golden mustachios. To be frank, I did not remain aloof; we became acquainted, one thing led to another, and *enfin* I learned to love the smell of whale oil. Two years later, alighting from the railway train I had taken to Nome, Alaska, where I had gone to purchase my *trousseau* (for having made telegraphic inquiries about Beaulieu-sur-le-Pont, I found that no Monsieur Bertrand existed therein and so considered myself a widow), I found myself, not in my Victorian dress in the bustling and frigid city of Nome, that commercial capital of the North with its outlaws, dogs, and Esquimaux in furs carrying loads of other furs upon their sleds, but in my old familiar visiting-dress (in which I had started from Beaulieu so long before) on the platform at Lyons, with my sister-in-law waiting for me. Not only that, but in the more than two years I had remained away, no more time had passed in what I am forced to call the real world than the hour required for the train ride from Beaulieu to Lyons! I had expected Garance to fall upon my neck with cries of astonishment at my absence and the strangeness of my dress; instead she inquired after my health, and not waiting for an answer, began to describe in the most ordinary manner and at very great length the roast of veal which she had purchased that afternoon for dinner.

"At first, so confused and grief-stricken was I, that I thought I had somehow missed the train for Nome, and that returning at once from Lyons to Beaulieu would enable me to reach Alaska. I almost cut my visit to Lyons short on the plea of ill-health. But I soon realized the absurdity of imagining that a railway could cross several thousand miles of ocean, and since my sister-in-law was already suspicious (I could not help myself during the visit and often burst out with a *'Mon cher Jack!'*), I controlled myself and gave vent to my feelings only on the return trip to Beaulieu—which, far from ending in Nome, Alaska, ended at the Beaulieu train station and at exactly the time predicted by the railway time-table.

"I decided that my two years' holiday had been only what the men of psychological science would entitle an unusually complete and detailed dream. The ancient Chinese were, I believe, famous for such vivid dreams; one of their poets is said to have experienced an entire lifetime of love, fear, and adventure while washing his feet. This was my case exactly. Here was I not a day—nay, not an hour—older, and no one knew what had passed in the Antarctic save I myself.

"It was a reasonable explanation, but it had one grave defect, which rendered it totally useless.

"It was false.

"Since that time, monsieur, I have gone on my peculiar voyages, my holidays, *mes vacances,* as I call them, not once but dozens of times. My magic carpet is the railway station at Beaulieu, or to be more precise, the passageway between the ticket office and the café at precisely ten minutes before three in the afternoon. A traversal of the passage at any other time brings me merely to the other side of the station, but a traversal of the passage at this particular time brings me to some far, exotic corner of the globe. Perhaps it is Ceylon with its crowds of variegated hue, its scent of incense, its pagodas and rickshaws. Or the deserts of Al-Iqah, with the crowds of Bedawi, dressed in flowing white and armed with rifles, many of whom whirl round about one another on horseback. Or I will find myself on the languid islands of Tahiti, with the graceful and dusky inhabitants bringing me bowls of *poi* and garlands of flowers whose beauty is unmatched anywhere else in the tropical portion of

the globe. Nor have my holidays been entirely confined to the terrestrial regions. Last February I stepped through the passage to find
myself on the sands of a primitive beach under a stormy gray sky;
in the distance one could perceive the roarings of saurians and
above me were the giant saw-toothed purple leaves of some
palmaceous plant, one (as it turned out) entirely unknown to
botanical science.

"No, monsieur, it was not Ceylon; it was Venus. It is true that I
prefer a less overcast climate, but still one can hardly complain. To
lie in the darkness of the Venerian night, on the silky volcanic
sands, under the starry leaves of the *laradh*, while imbibing the
million perfumes of the night-blooming flowers and listening to the
music of the *karakh*—really, one does not miss the blue sky.
Although only a few weeks ago I was in a place that also pleased
me: imagine a huge whitish-blue sky, a desert with giant mountains
on the horizon, and the lean, hard-bitten water-prospectors with
their dowsing rods, their high-heeled boots, and their large hats,
worn to protect faces already tanned and wrinkled from the intense
sunlight.

"No, not Mars, Texas. They are marvelous people, those
American pioneers, the men handsome and laconic, the women
sturdy and efficient. And then one day I entrained to Lyons only to
find myself on a railway platform that resembled a fishbowl made
of tinted glass, while around me rose mountains fantastically
slender into a black sky where the stars shone like hard marbles,
scarcely twinkling at all. I was wearing a glass helmet and clothes
that resembled a diver's. I had no idea where I was until I rose, and
then to my edified surprise, instead of rising in the usual manner, I
positively bounded into the air!

"I was on the Moon.

"Yes, monsieur, the Moon, although some distance in the future,
the year two thousand eighty and nine, to be precise. At that date
human beings will have established a colony on the Moon. My carriage swiftly shot down beneath one of the Selenic craters to land in
their principal city, a fairy palace of slender towers and domes of
glass, for they use as building material a glass made from the native
silicate gravel. It was on the Moon that I gathered whatever theory
I now have concerning my peculiar experiences with the railway

passage at Beaulieu-sur-le-Pont, for I made the acquaintance there
of the principal mathematician of the twenty-first century, a most
elegant lady, and put the problem to her. You must understand that
on the Moon *les nègres, les juifs,* even *les femmes* may obtain high
positions and much influence; it is a true republic. This lady introduced me to her colleague, a black physicist of more-than-
normal happenings, or *le paraphysique* as they call it, and the two
debated the matter during an entire day (not a Selenic day, of
course, since that would have amounted to a time equal to twenty-
eight days of our own). They could not agree, but in brief, as they
told me, either the railway tunnel at Beaulieu-sur-le-Pont has
achieved infinite connectivity or it is haunted. To be perfectly
sincere, I regretted leaving the Moon. But one has one's obliga-
tions. Just as my magic carpet here at Beaulieu is of the nature of a
railway tunnel, and just as I always find myself in *mes vacances* at
first situated on a railway platform, thus my return must also be ef-
fected by that so poetically termed road of iron; I placed myself
into the railway that connects two of the principal Selenic craters,
and behold!—I alight at the platform at Lyons, not a day older.

"Indeed, monsieur," (and here Madame Bertrand coughed delicately) "as we are both people of the world, I may mention that
certain other of the biological processes also suspend themselves, a
fact not altogether to my liking, since my dear Aloysius and myself
are entirely without family. Yet this suspension has its advantages;
if I had aged as I have lived, it would be a woman of seventy who
speaks to you now. In truth, how can one age in worlds that are, to
speak frankly, not quite real? Though perhaps if I had remained
permanently in one of these worlds, I too would have begun to age
along with the other inhabitants. That would be a pleasure on the
Moon, for my mathematical friend was aged two hundred when I
met her, and her acquaintance, the professor of *le paraphysique*,
two hundred and five."

Here Madame Bertrand, to whose recital I had been listening
with breathless attention, suddenly ceased speaking. Her lemon ice
stood untouched upon the table. So full was I of projects to make
the world acquainted with this amazing history that I did not at
first notice the change in Madame Bertrand's expression, and so I
burst forth:

"The National Institute—the Académie—no, the universities, and the newspapers also—"

But the charming lady, with a look of horror, had risen from the table, crying, *"Mon dieu!* My train! What will Garance think? What will she say? Monsieur, not a word to anyone!"

Imagine my consternation when Madame Bertrand here precipitously departed from the café and began to cross the station towards that ominous passageway. I could only expostulate, "But, madame, consider! Ceylon! Texas! Mars!"

"No, it is too late," said she. "Only at the former time in the train schedule. Monsieur, remember, please, not a word to anyone!"

Following her, I cried, "But if you do not return—" and she again favored me with her delightful smile, saying rapidly, "Do not distress yourself, monsieur. By now I have developed certain sensations—a *frisson* of the neck and shoulder blades—which warn me of the condition of the passageway. The later hour is always safe. But my train—!"

And so Madame Bertrand left me. Amazing woman! A traveler not only to the far regions of the earth but to those of the imagination, and yet perfectly respectable, gladly fulfilling the duties of family life, and punctually (except for this one time) meeting her sister-in-law, Mademoiselle Garance Bertrand, on the train platform at Lyons.

Is that the end of my story? No, for I was fated to meet Amélie Bertrand once again.

My business, which I have mentioned to you, took me back to Beaulieu-sur-le-Pont at the end of that same summer. I must confess that I hoped to encounter Madame Bertrand, for I had made it my intention to notify at least several of our great national institutions of the extraordinary powers possessed by the railway passage at Beaulieu, and yet I certainly could not do so without Madame Bertrand's consent. Again it was shortly before three in the afternoon; again the station platform was deserted. I saw a figure which I took to be that of Madame Bertrand seated upon the bench reserved for passengers and hastened to it with a glad cry—

But it was not Amélie Bertrand. Rather it was a thin and elderly female, entirely dressed in the dullest of black and completely without the charm I had expected to find in my fellow passenger.

The next moment I heard my name pronounced and was delighted to perceive, issuing from the ticket office, Madame Bertrand herself, wearing a light-colored summer dress.

But where was the gaiety, the charm, the pleasant atmosphere of June? Madame Bertrand's face was closed, her eyes watchful, her expression determined. I would immediately have opened to her my immense projects, but with a shake of her head the lady silenced me, indicating the figure I have already mentioned.

"My sister-in-law, Mademoiselle Garance," she said. I confess that I nervously expected that Aloysius Bertrand himself would now appear. But we were alone on the platform. Madame Bertrand continued: "Garance, this is the gentleman who was the unfortunate cause of my missing my train last June."

Mademoiselle Garance, as if to belie the reputation for loquacity I had heard applied to her earlier in the summer, said nothing but merely clutched to her meager bosom a small train case.

Madame Bertrand said to me, "I have explained to Garance the occasion of your illness last June and the manner in which the officials of the station detained me. I am glad to see you looking so well."

This was a clear hint that Mademoiselle Garance was to know nothing of her sister-in-law's history; thus I merely bowed and nodded. I wished to have the opportunity of conversing with Madame Bertrand more freely, but I could say nothing in the presence of her sister-in-law. Desperately I began: "You are taking the train today—"

"For the sake of nostalgia," said Madame Bertrand. "After today I shall never set foot in a railway carriage. Garance may if she likes, but I will not. Aeroplanes, motor cars, and ships will be good enough for me. Perhaps like the famous American, Madame Earhart, I shall learn to fly. This morning Aloysius told me the good news: a change in his business arrangements has enabled us to move to Lyons, which we are to do at the end of the month."

"And in the intervening weeks—?" said I.

Madame Bertrand replied composedly, "There will be none. They are tearing down the station."

What a blow! And there sat the old maid, Mademoiselle Garance, entirely unconscious of the impending loss to science! I stammered something—I know not what—but my good angel came to my rescue; with an infinitesimal movement of the fingers, she said:

"Oh, monsieur, my conscience pains me too much! Garance, would you believe that I told this gentleman the most preposterous stories? I actually told him—seriously, now—that the passageway of this train station was the gateway to another world! No, many worlds, and that I had been to all of them. Can you believe it of me?" She turned to me. "Oh, monsieur," she said, "you were a good listener. You only pretended to believe. Surely you cannot imagine that a respectable woman like myself would leave her husband by means of a railway passage which has achieved infinite connectivity?"

Here Madame Bertrand looked at me in a searching manner, but I was at a loss to understand her intention in so doing and said nothing.

She went on, with a little shake of the head. "I must confess it; I am addicted to storytelling. Whenever my dear Aloysius left home on his business trips, he would say to me, '*Occupe-toi, occupe-toi, Amélie!*' and, alas, I have occupied myself only too well. I thought my romance might divert your mind from your ill-health and so presumed to tell you an unlikely tale of extraordinary voyages. Can you forgive me?"

I said something polite, something I do not now recall. I was, you understand, still reeling from the blow. All that merely a fable! Yet with what detail, what plausible circumstance, Madame Bertrand had told her story. I could only feel relieved I had not actually written to the National Institute. I was about to press both ladies to take some refreshment with me when Madame Bertrand (suddenly putting her hand to her heart in a gesture that seemed to me excessive) cried, "Our train!" and turning to me, remarked, "Will you accompany us down the passage?"

Something made me hesitate; I know not what.

"Think, monsieur," said Madame Bertrand, with her hand still pressed to her heart, "where will it be this time? A London of the future, perhaps, enclosed against the weather and built entirely of glass? Or perhaps the majestic high plains of Colorado? Or will we find ourselves in one of the underground cities of the moons of

Jupiter, into whose awesome skies the mighty planet rises and sets with a visual diameter greater than that of the terrestrial Alps?"

She smiled with humor at Mademoiselle Garance, remarking, "Such are the stories I told this gentleman, dear Garance; they were a veritable novel," and I saw that she was gently teasing her sister-in-law, who naturally did not know what any of this was about.

Mademoiselle Garance ventured to say timidly that she "liked to read novels."

I bowed.

Suddenly I heard the sound of the train outside Beaulieu-sur-le-Pont. Madame Bertrand cried in an utterly prosaic voice, "Our train! Garance, we shall miss our train!" and again she asked, "Monsieur, will you accompany us?"

I bowed, but remained where I was. Accompanied by the thin, stooped figure of her sister-in-law, Madame Bertrand walked quickly down the passageway which divides the ticket room of the Beaulieu-sur-le-Pont station from the tiny café. I confess that when the two ladies reached the midpoint of the longitudinal axis of the passageway, I involuntarily closed my eyes, and when I looked again, the passage was empty.

What moved me then I do not know, but I found myself quickly traversing the passageway, seeing in my mind's eye Madame Bertrand boarding the Lyons train with her sister-in-law, Mademoiselle Garance. One could certainly hear the train; the sound of its engine filled the whole station. I believe I told myself that I wished to exchange one last polite word. I reached the other side of the station—

And there was no Lyons train there.

There were no ladies on the platform.

There is, indeed, no two-fifty-one train to Lyons whatsoever, not on the schedule of any line!

Imagine my sensations, my dear friend, upon learning that Madame Bertrand's story was true, all of it! It is true, all too true, all of it is true, and my Amélie is gone forever!

"My" Amélie I call her; yet she still belongs (in law) to Aloysius Bertrand, who will, no doubt, after the necessary statutory period of waiting is over, marry again, and thus become a respectable and unwitting bigamist.

That animal could never have understood her!

Even now (if I may be permitted that phrase) Amélie Bertrand may be drifting down one of the great Venerian rivers on a gondola, listening to the music of the *karakh;* even now she may perform acts of heroism on Airstrip One or chat with her mathematical friend on a balcony that overlooks the airy towers and flower-filled plazas of the Selenic capitol. I have no doubt that if you were to attempt to find the places Madame Bertrand mentioned by looking in the encyclopedia or a similar work of reference, you would not succeed. As she herself mentioned, they are "not quite real." There are strange discrepancies.

Alas, my friend, condole with me; by now all such concern is academic, for the train station at Beaulieu-sur-le-Pont is gone, replaced by a vast erection swarming with workmen, a giant *hangar* (I learned the name from one of them), or edifice for the housing of aeroplanes. I am told that large numbers of these machines will soon fly from *hangar* to *hangar* across the country.

But think: these aeroplanes, will they not in time be used for ordinary business travel, for scheduled visits to resorts and other places? In short, are they not even now the railways of the new age? Is it not possible that the same condition, whether of infinite connectivity or of hauntedness, may again obtain, perhaps in the same place where the journeys of my vanished angel have established a precedent or predisposition?

My friend, collude with me. The *hangar* at Beaulieu will soon be finished, or so I read in the newspapers. I shall go down into the country and establish myself near this *hangar;* I shall purchase a ticket for a ride in one of the new machines, and then we shall see. Perhaps I will enjoy only a pleasant ascension into the air and a similar descent. Perhaps I will instead feel that *frisson* of the neck and shoulder blades of which Madame Bertrand spoke; well, no matter: my children are grown, my wife has a generous income, the *frisson* will not dismay me. I shall walk down the corridor or passageway in or around the *hangar* at precisely nine minutes before three and into the space between the worlds; I shall again feel the strange retardation of time, I shall feel the heaviness of the body, I shall see the haziness at the other end of the tunnel, and then through the lashing wind, through the mistiness which envelops me, with the rushing and roaring of an invisible aeroplane in my ears, I shall proceed. Madame Bertrand was kind enough to delay her own holiday to conduct me back from Uganda; she was generous enough to offer to share the traversal of the passage with me a second time. Surely such kindness and generosity must have its effect! This third time I will proceed. Away from my profession, my daily newspaper, my chess games, my *digestif*—in short, away from all those habits which, it is understood, are given us to take the place of happiness. Away from the petty annoyances of life I shall proceed, away from a dull old age, away from the confusions and terrors of a Europe grown increasingly turbulent, to—

—*What?*

The above copy of a letter was found in a volume of the Encyclopédie (U–Z) in the Bibliothèque Nationale. It is believed from the evidence that the writer disappeared at a certain provincial town (called "Beaulieu-sur-le-Pont" in the manuscript) shortly after purchasing a ticket for a flight in an aeroplane at the flying field there, a pastime popular among holiday makers.

He has never been seen again.

The Soul of a Servant

LOUKA: You have the soul of a servant, Nicola.
NICOLA: Yes, that's the secret of success in service.

—G. B. Shaw,
Arms and the Man

Twice a day we clean and oil the big guns, once at noon and once at dusk, the noon always gray and overcast and the nights half-luminous with fog around the lights. No one knows how long ago the last shot was fired, so many years perhaps that to use them now would be to explode them with age and disuse, like a thought held too long in the mind. I like to walk the walls in the early evenings, perhaps catching a glimpse of the open sky in the west, still sea-green with one clear planet shining between the rifts of cloud. When I do that, I listen. Guards talk on the watch, or citizens come up for air, or a girl wrapped up against the cold. They don't talk freely to me, for I came to considerable position after a rather nondescript beginning here, and I am a foreigner. More than one would be glad to push me off the walls in the dark hours, if they thought no one would catch them, but I am too useful, as they know. So I enjoy a certain immunity.

As I said, I like to walk the walls of an evening, and I like to see the watchful rulers come up for air and look wisely towards the north, as if they expected the barbarian armies of the invasion to come sweeping down in the heart of a sudden blizzard. As far as I know, no one has ever seen them. I listen to them talk—repeating stories their great-grandfathers told them, discussing the latest gossip, and the occasional titter of respect when one of the lower classes is put in his place. We are quite a little city here. I am the one who keeps it all running. I give them all "good evening."

"Good evening, sir, good evening," say the masons, who have come to mend a section of the wall, bobbing their heads and taking off their fur caps. The soldiers turn away and talk ostentatiously of other things. A few years ago this could hurt me; now I speak to them all, so much the better; a girl's already rosy face blushes to the roots of her hair. But here is a young lady, Katerina Ivanovna, the niece of the governor, who thinks there is something daring in speaking to me. Only partly to annoy her uncle she puts her blonde head close to mine, the scandalously dark southern one, and says:

"Ah! You're on one of your promenades again."

"Good evening," say I.

She tucks her arm inside mine (we are almost of a height) and accompanies me around the walk. To the west the sun has set in a welter of cloud; to the north the mountains roll below us in a great sea, lower and lower, dying away on the icy plains, and to the east and south lies the vast sheet of Tengri Nor, the White Lake, full of salt and only four feet deep. We are the last outpost of a world I suspect is dying, as is the more civilized one farther south from which I was—shall we say—invited to leave? She knows what little incident forced me to do that; she thinks it broad-minded to forgive me. Besides it is only we southerners who remember any of the old ways, and they know that they need us.

"Soon it will be winter," she says, leaning close to me, "and we will have the blizzards. I so long for them."

"I hate them," I remark, shaking my head.

"Ah! I forgot," she says archly, "but you mustn't tease me. I love the stormy nights filled with noise and the glorious, serene mornings afterwards when the clouds lift and the sky is so intensely blue."

I think these people have nothing to do but cultivate their souls. At any rate she's very pretty, despite her soul, and healthy, and the only person who has spoken to me in a social way for several months; I put one hand against the wall she leans on, but in a flash she's in the arch of the door, shaking her head and letting the hood of her cloak fall down her back.

"We will miss you if you don't dine with us tonight!" she cries.

"God forbid," say I, "that I should cause such a calamity," and as I bow she smiles, showing her white teeth, and goes inside. It's freezing cold. The clouds in the west have sunk to the color of sulphur, and my hands are numb. Round the corner comes an old man, bobbing his head with eager respect:

"Please, sir, please, sir . . . "

"What the devil is it!" I say. "Has anything gone wrong?"

"Please, sir, please, sir, a favor, sir, I entreat the sir."

"Well?"

"Please, sir, please, I am poor, sir, let the sir be kind," and he shuffles from one foot to another, his fur hat in his hands.

"The sir must know it first," I say, glancing around impatiently.

"This poor old man has a son, sir," he whispers, his eyes watering.

"And you want him to be an officer?" I demand. The old man's shuffle begins again, a shifting from one foot to another and then a hop. "And you're too poor to pay?"

"Powerful sir," says the old man, "kind sir, I entreat him. I beg him. I beg the sir."

"All right," I say, waving him off, "all right. Yes. But don't tell anyone." He is bending double now, up and down, up and down like a spring; I say, "Yes, yes, but I want it back. Tell the officer in charge to come to me," and abruptly I turn inside, thinking angrily of the money I will have to ask from the governor because of all these old men and their sons, or their daughters' weddings, or their grandchildren. They come to me because the governor has made no provision for them and those who loan money for profit bleed them white. White to match the snow that falls ten months out of twelve;

let the governor's niece write that in her diary. I know she keeps a diary in which to record her exquisite thoughts!

There are almost two thousand of us in this town cut into the mountainside, and more than five hundred rooms—storerooms, halls, apartments. Mine is deep inside the mountain where the cold cannot come, near the great hall to take advantage of the heat. Those who built this place were marvelous engineers, but they never anticipated a mountainside heated entirely by wood-burning fireplaces. I have my rooms hung with imported rugs, brought slowly and expensively from the cities farther south, and I have a stove, a luxury for the upper classes. Moreover—and in this I am unique—I have a bath. I have also a slave (a gift from the governor-general whom we saw on a tour of inspection several years back), and the wags declare he is almost as black as I. Hot water, oils, coffee, embroidered carpets and pillows—I have my own cave! Here I retreat. I stand by the fire, thawing into some semblance of humanity, until I am mobile enough to take a bath, which I do.

"Your honor's clothes," says my slave with the faintest touch of contempt.

"You are a charming cool fellow," I say. "Drop them on the carpet," for if I die tomorrow I will have no animal skins in my place, not though everything I own—by the sufferance of the governor—has to be carried up three hundred miles of mountain roads by arctic mules. When the hot water grows cold I climb out and dress, unreasonably refreshed.

"Your honor asked to be reminded," says the black fellow wearily, "of an invitation to dinner."

"Absolutely," I say. "That is where I am if anyone wishes to find me. Good evening." And clapping to my nose a dried apple stuck with cinnamon (as the King of France was said to have done several millennia ago), the better to withstand the evening for, as I said, nobody bathes, I take up my cloak and my gloves in t'other hand, and out I go.

Our halls and stairs—the better ones—are lit by a few naked, hand-blown bulbs whose glass I should like to make cloudy instead of clear but the art is lost, alas, and the governor does not care for reviving ancient curiosities; high guests at dinner sit near the fire, both for the heat and the ruddy light. I find the governor's brother waiting for me, and with him his daughter, my friend the governor's niece, whose hair falls down her back like sunlight. One of our few amusements is a singer, who is at present discoursing musically on the impeccable strength of our defenses against the Enemy; the hall is warm, but full of sudden icy drafts. I have tried in vain for the past three years to persuade His Excellency that He could economize on fuel if only He would import metal and build stoves for all, but God forbid; every night they pile logs on the great fireplace (logs carried up three hundred miles of road on muleback) and most of the heat goes up the chimney. The governor's niece is wearing a blue-green stone on her bodice and her shoulders are bare. I take great care not to stare at her.

"How do you do, dear *thir*," says her father, who lisps, and he gives me a fishy hand to hold for an instant.

"Better than I could have ever hoped," say I, "since I have Your Excellency's splendid company and that of your extremely accomplished wife and beautifully educated daughter."

"*Thir*," lisps His Excellency. "They tell me that you wear fleece-lined boots. Is that true?"

"Papa!" whispers his shocked daughter. I pay no attention.

"Something of an exaggeration, Your Excellency," say I, gathering my cloak over one arm and seating myself on the bench. "But I do take the liberty of making a few amendments to the climate. Pray don't trouble yourself."

"You ought to go out more," says His Excellency, and his daughter turns scarlet (for which I love her). She begins hastily to talk to me about a manuscript I have lent her, and so we go on, the father supping his soup, the mother staring at me coldly and, when she condescends to talk at all, remarking with grim pleasure on the singer's lyrics, which grow more bloody as the meal progresses.

"You don't like it, do you?" whispers the governor's niece, Her Excellency Miss ——, for they are all Excellencies of some kind or other. I shake my head, picking at the blasted salt fish which is all we have been getting for the past six months and all we will get for another six, for I know, having kept the records on every ounce of it. "Well, you are odd," she says, with a toss of her head, "I must say."

"I hope," say I, venturing, "that you do not disesteem it."

"Ah! Esteem," she says. "Esteem is a noble emotion. I should say that esteem is the basis of every friendship."

"Then we are perhaps on the way to friendship," say I, "for you have not denied a certain esteem."

"Have I?" she says scornfully. "Why, I am not sure of anything of the sort," and she reminds me of my dislike for blizzards.

"What I like," I say, "dear Miss, is my glimpses of the clear heaven and the stars, for they remind me of happier times."

"Were those times," she says meltingly, "more happy than *these*?"

"Much, much happier," I say, "before my foolish rebelliousness ruined it all," and in revenge she goes off with the first young fellow who asks her to dance, for now the meal is over (they have taken away our salt fish, which the delicate Excellency Miss devoured like a workman) and, showing signs of life, her father says:

"We ought to have more hunting parties; what do you say, eh?"

"They are too expensive, Your Excellency," say I. "For every animal or bird the hunters bring in for us, a dozen common people eat the worse."

"Huh! *You* don't," says his wife bluntly, sitting in her furs like the Queen of Winter. Her husband drawls:

"When do we finish with this blasted fish?"

"I'm afraid I don't know, Your Excellency," I say. "It doesn't depend on me."

"Well, do something about it," he complains. "What are you, anyway?"

"I am only steward and manager, Your Excellency. It isn't up to me. As I—"

"This fellow won't do anything," he says to his wife, and then louder so that our neighbors at table hear him. "This fellow won't do anything!" They look incuriously at me, all of them, and I feel myself turn pale as I assume involuntarily what I once thought I had cured myself of forever; I mean a nervous grimace, a crawling, shrinking, servile smile which I struggle to control but cannot, and

I tremble while sitting at the table as if nothing has happened, idly playing with my wine glass, wine for the lords and bitter beer for the common people.

"I shall do my best—I assure you . . ." I say, catching my breath. "I wish only to serve . . . Your Excellency must understand . . . "

"The fellow doesn't know what he's for," remarks His Excellency loudly. "He doesn't know his business," and he and his wife make their way in state through the hall, stooping to chat with their equals, the great whales to the great whales. I knew once—or I was once—and why is it that the chances in life are each a little worse than the last? Her Excellency Miss, the governor's niece, having tired herself dancing, now comes back to me.

"Well!" she says in frank puzzlement. "Where are Mama and Papa? Didn't they invite you to go with them?"

"Alas, no," I say.

"Ah! Poor fellow!" she says archly. "You look pinched and chilled." This makes me start, and I look at her for a moment and then look away.

"Ah! That is rude," she says, with a definite note of disapproval in her voice, flushed and fanning herself. "I should never have expected that from a man of your sentiments."

"My sentiments," I say, taking a deep breath, "are not so fine as you pay me the compliment of thinking, dear Miss. I am afraid that you flatter me. But of course I am glad of a compliment from one of such discrimination."

She believes, I think, that people actually talk this way in the more civilized parts of the world. She rewards me with a dazzling smile.

"I hear," she says, "that this very evening you did another favor for some poor old man. That is kindness." I return her smile with a sort of shrug, to indicate that her praise is embarrassing me. "But it is," she says earnestly, "it is!" She reflects for a moment. "The poor," she says, "are so touching. They have such a purity of soul."

And so it goes.

Barbarians! Down the plains and up the mountains they ride like a black flood in many a governor-general's dreams. I myself have dreamed of them, wrenching open our doors, smashing the lights, firing my hangings and furniture while I stand in the doorway and roar with laughter, waking with an aftersense of unspeakable relief only to find my slave standing at my bedside, saying:

"There is someone to see your honor," or:

"Your honor is wanted at the gates."

At such times I have stood in front of a miniature I have, a painting of the town where my ruin first befell me, and I have stared at the flat white roofs and the sand and the blue sky until they made me weep. We know nothing of barbarians. We do not even know if they exist. But every noon and every dusk we clean and oil the big guns and every twilight I walk the walls of my cage, watching the young men with the polishing rags, and sure as death someday I will stoke and load one of those cannon and turn it on myself.

In the morning, my slave, whom I pity, gets up when it is cold to build up a banked fire. He makes my coffee, wakes me, and helps me dress. Sometimes I talk to him.

"What was your life like before you came to me?" I say.

"I had no life before I served your honor," is his courteous and conventional reply. I look at him for a moment, seeing for the first time how much he hates me. I say:

"Don't envy me, please!" rather lightly, and then I take the coffee and bread that is my morning meal and go out. He cleans my apartments, takes care of my clothes, and eats, I suppose, but I have never found out when or where.

Salt cod, flour, cordwood, I keep track of everything. I mend everything. . . . Towards noon it begins to snow. There are rumors that a hunting party sent out the day before has been seen in the distance with a herd of captured elephants. Very likely.

"May we go and see, sir? May we go and see, please, sir?"

"No."

"Oh, please, sir, please, sir!"

"No! Shut up and get to work." The snow muffles everything. In the evening I let myself into my rooms to find the governor's niece standing in front of my fire, her blue cloak thrown back, with its silver buckle gleaming in the firelight. She's holding a brass pitcher in her hand, a lovely piece of work inlaid with red and blue, and she looks like the picture of spring in a book.

"My dear friend," she says, "you mustn't be surprised. I've told you I despise false modesty, and after so many descriptions I simply wished to see your little nest for myself."

"Ah! Did you!" say I.

"The surroundings," she says archly, "tell the soul."

"I shudder to think of what they must tell of mine," say I, sinking into a chair.

"That you love loveliness," she says, "and comfort—although that is morbid of you!—and that your soul is too refined and subtle for our way of life." She sinks gracefully down by my chair in a cloud of skirts and takes both of my hands in hers. "I have something to tell you," she says, "but don't be gallant. I can't stand it when the emotions of the heart are overlaid with—well, it's like the red-and-blue border on your little jug; it is very pretty, but . . . "

"Madam," I say, "you should not be here; allow me . . . "

"But why not!"

"The slave . . . "

"*Votre esclave*," and she drops her eyes modestly. "I've been studying the old languages, you see."

"Madam," I say, "for heaven's sake, what do you think will happen if someone finds you here?"

"I do not care," she says seriously, and fixing her eyes on mine, she lets down the mass of her yellow hair.

"You can be frank with me," she says. "We are quite alone." Her face is tilted up to mine in the dancing firelight. "We are alone," she says again, tasting the words with pleasure. "We are free."

"But I wish to spare you!" I cry, hand on my heart. She is leaning against the chair, fingers to her lips, so pretty. "You do not know," I say eloquently. "You do not know what social penalties can be."

"My poor friend," she whispers.

"Yes, you are kind," I continue, "but I wish . . . to spare you . . . as much as I wish that . . . "

"Yes?" she whispers. "Yes?"

"As I wish that . . . but you . . . you have divined it . . . that your heart . . . that my heart . . . "

"Ah!" she says, tucking her feet under her.

"Forgive me if I stumble," I say desperately. "Forgive me if I misunderstand . . . if I dare . . . "

"It's not daring!" she cries, flaming up.

"But it is," I say, "and I have dared . . . "

"Why, what's the matter with you?" she says, for looking beyond her at one of the rugs that hangs on my wall, I am struck with a sudden memory, a Chinese girl I once knew who understood the art of dress if anyone alive ever did, and who used to get drunk with me, my sweet companion, laughing and swaying and chewing the fringes of red silk at the edge of her gown, like a baby . . . .

"There is no wall between us," says my charmer impatiently. "We are free now."

"Yes, we're free," I whisper, and because there's nothing left of all the prologue (which has all been said) I hold out my arms for this beautiful, healthy young bird of prey who wants to gulp down my heart and then go rooting for other frogs, that heart I would have gladly given her if only she had really wanted it. But if I am discreet and agreeable; perhaps there will be something in it for me after all, after all . . . .

There is a terrific thundering at the door.

"Oh, my God!" cries Her Excellency Miss. "Hide me! Hide me!"

"In my bath," I say, restored to my senses.

"I will *not* get into a bath!" she cries, revolted. "It's too disgusting!"

"Shut up!" I roar, "and do as you're told!" and as she tumbles into the next room, I take down a rapier from the wall (bought at the bazaars many years ago, in the sunlight, under the lemon trees) and open the door.

"Barbarians!" shouts the soldier at the door. He runs crazily away, pounding on the walls. I help Her Excellency Miss down the stairs, and once she is safely stowed away I run like mad to the court where I shiver and stamp (I have forgotten my outer clothes) with eight hundred others.

The hunting party has brought back their herd of animals. Waving, cheering, shouting, the hunters pass under the walls while thin band music drifts up from below. Around me carpenters and masons and cooks clap each other on the back, wring each other's hands: "Look at that! That's a good catch, sir!" "Look at that! Did you ever see the like, sir?" Grim and martial, triumphant and pleased, the hunting party escorts their prisoners into the inner court. The crowd watches breathless; then . . .

"Oh, look!" says someone. "They are *black*!"

Behind me someone whispers, and a low ripple of laughter runs through the crowd. The soldiers are grinning. In this snow-skinned, straw-headed commonalty, the captives stand out like blots from a coal pit, and someone has made a joke, another joke; those broad, white simple faces, those flat, blasted faces with noses like the edge of a thumb! At *me*! In my own despite, one shamed hand goes up to my traitorous black hair, lightly, tentatively, and I find myself pacing next to the head of the line, staring into yellow-skinned, broad-cheeked faces, staring into expressionless black eyes with my own black eyes, quite unable to stop myself, for I would very much like to find out—what? Behind me in the crowd I hear a familiar lisping drawl, "He'th looking for hith fa-ather," and I elbow my way through, taking the stairs two at a time. Then rushing down the hall next to me is my golden girl. "Really," she says, vexed, out of breath, "really, my friend, you're unaccountable!"

"Get away from me!" I gasp, turning her about by the shoulders. "Get out of here!"

"What?" she says, amazed. "What?"

"You disgust me," I manage to pronounce. "You are disgusting. Go away!" and she flees.

The old kitchen hall that we no longer use is full of soldiers and captives, officers issuing orders, cooks staring admiringly. I send my workmen for food and fire; the head of the hunting party objects.

"I have received no orders," he says stiffly, "and until I do . . . "

"You're receiving your orders from me," I say. "And don't forget it."

"What?" he says. "From you? You're a servant," with the easy, peevish pride of someone who has never been crossed; "you're a servant," lounging on his long legs.

"Don't speak to me!" he shouts suddenly, so I don't; I drive one fist into his stomach and the edge of my hand under his chin, snapping his head back; and by the time he recovers himself, I have a knife from one of my workmen.

"Go away, Captain," I say, "and don't trouble us!"

I like to see them eat. They look as if they hadn't eaten in days. They sit cross-legged round the fire, dipping their hands into the pot. I circle about them, approaching, retreating, feeling the

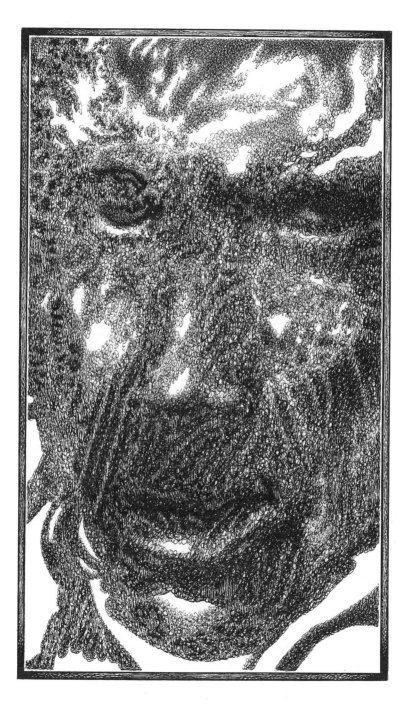

guards' eyes bore into my neck. But surely I can make an excuse. One of the women is too quick for me. As I approach, she thrusts something up at my face, and as I start back I fall, lying humiliated and ridiculous on the stone floor, struggling to rise while a dozen hands touch me curiously, like insects, on the back, the head, the limbs . . . .

Then there is an explicable little sound next to me, and looking up I see the bundle waving at me, all wrapped up, laced in hides, a small swarthy black-eyed baby.

"I see. Thank you," I say. The baby spits up, and laughter runs around the group, low and kind.

"Thank you," I say again. "Thank you. Thank you."

"Tank yoo"

"Tank yoo"

"Tank oo"

And from all over the room come echoes, halting, imperfect, *"Tan oo" "Aa oo,"* until the sound dies out in a rustling breeze in the corners.

Barbarians who wear stinking hides and eat unmentionable things.

Back in my apartments the governor's niece is waiting for me, sitting in my armchair with her feet propped up on a lacquered stool that was never meant for such a purpose.

"My friend," she says, "you are perfectly impossible. Impossible."

"Yes, yes, I know," I say, pouring myself a brandy.

"You don't know," she says. "I think you're mad—why, what's the matter?" For I've dropped my glass and stand horrified, rooted to the spot. I've just felt in my shirt for the knife I must return to one of my men, and it isn't there.

"You're ill!" she cries.

Of course not. When I fell—one of those curious hands . . .

"Why don't you say something?" she demands.

No. I gave it to them. I gave my knife to the barbarians without even knowing I was doing it, without even remembering it afterwards. Just like last time. I try and try, I deny myself, I watch myself, but in one moment—oh, just like the last time! *In one moment!*

"Come, it can't be as bad as that," she says.

They'll trace it to me. Of course.

"And despite your rudeness on the stairs, I will intercede with my uncle for you. Do you see?"

"Thank you, thank you," I say, falling onto a nearby bench, burying my face in my hands. "Thank you, thank you, thank you." She puts one hand on my shoulder, lightly, kindly.

"My friend," she says, "did not believe in my affection, I think, when I spoke to him before. That was lack of faith."

"I know, I know," I say, "yes, I know," trying to think, trying to pull myself together. When they find out that I . . .

"But it's all right," she says, "for my friend trusts me again."

"You are an angel."

"I will always keep my dear friend's safety close to my heart," she says with an enchanting smile. "Always, always."

"Yes, always, always," I say, losing my head, forgetting all caution, longing only for someone or something solid to hold on to, to keep me from falling into the abyss—*again, good God!*—so I clasp her by the waist as if she meant it, she with her white neck and her loose, long yellow hair.

"Why, what are you doing?" she exclaims sharply. "Let me go!" and she pushes me away violently.

"What? What?" I gasp, utterly at a loss.

"You are presuming!" she snaps. "You forget who you are."

"But . . . " I begin.

"Don't speak to me!" she cries. "I'm sorry I ever bothered with you!"

"But I thought . . . "

"*You* thought! You—who are you? *We* don't do such things!

"What are you doing?" she repeats, stepping forward.

"Do not distress yourself, dear Excellency, do not distress yourself about a man like me!"

"Let me out," and she steps backwards nervously, her little plump hands held out in front of her. "Let me out." She stumbles over the chair and falls, her high-heeled boots entangled in the hearth rug and her long skirts billowing. She screams, frightened:

"*Let me out!*"

Which I do—sometime later.

*   *   *

The chief of the prison, a solid citizen from cap to boots, comes to see me, saying, "You are vile. There is no word bad enough to describe you." He rocks back and forth, thrusting his hands virtuously into his pockets—his own pockets, mind. "We are going to make an example of you," he continues thoughtfully, "so that nobody else—warden, get me some beer—nobody else . . . What do you have to say for yourself?"

"Nothing."

"Nothing?"

"Nothing."

"Well, well," he says. "Well. You are the only prisoner who has ever had nothing to say for himself. I think that's shameful."

"Yes," I say, tickled.

"You had better think of something," he says. "We are going to make a public spectacle of you. You will be sorry." (The warden arrives with a mug.) "You will be very sorry. There is not only loss of life, to which an honorable man does not attach much weight, but which a criminal . . . "

"Ah, a criminal," I say softly.

" . . . which a criminal finds so dreadful, due to his heavy conscience . . . "

"His conscience . . . "

" . . . and the attendant public humilation, which is of all things the hardest to bear, especially to one of high station, though I daresay," (maliciously) "you have had time to get used to that, taking jobs away from honest men."

"May I have some beer?" say I, and as the chief of the prison stands frozen in appalled surprise, I take his tankard from his hand and rinse my mouth, spitting the vile stuff out on the ground.

"Help! Guards!" And off he goes.

Left alone, I would give even the hopes I had of eventually going back to my own country if only I could have what I had yesterday, the freedom of the town (such as it is) and my walks, and the evening sky that is better than a stone wall. And why is it that I never behave in any sane, any sensible, any reasonable way? With my advantages, with my money, with Her Excellency Miss as good as under my thumb . . .

Just like the last time. Down the corridor I can see someone coming, the guard, most likely. And another. And another. Thank heaven they have no imagination! They think everything can be done with their fists and do not know, poor fellows, *la savate.*

I wake in the middle of the night, smarting all over, having heard a noise in my sleep. A scrabbling, jingling, faint restless noise like a mouse with bells. There it is again. With a creak of the cot, I turn on my side.

"*Sssss! Ssssss!*" someone whispers.

Go away; I have heard you too often before in my sleep. I have dreamed that I walked the ramparts in thick fog that magnified my fancies, isolated like a god, that I saw faces on the shifting smoke, and "Come!" each one whispered. "Come! I'll save you . . . ."

The faint jingle begins again, like a handful of coins. Through the bars I see thrust, in the pale light from the corridor, a bundle of confetti that jingles and twinkles and shakes up and down.

It's the warden's keys.

Slipping on my shoes, I—no, I don't, I sit on the edge of the cot trying to clear my dizzy head.

"*Sssss!*"

Oh, go away, go away! Don't tempt me. A face is peering through the bars. As far as I can make out, it's the first-in-line of the barbarian prisoners.

"Get out!" I whisper sharply. They don't understand a word, of course. He jingles the keys at me, grinning.

"Listen," I whisper, hobbling to the bars, "why don't you go away? If you found your way here, you can find your way back again. Go away."

"Kank oo" comes from the darkness beyond the bars, a vast, many-throated breathing. "Kank oo," "Aa oo."

"*Go away!*" The keys clink and chime. I take them numbly and, finding the proper one, open the door, falling into the vast, shadowy barbarian horde, whose hands support me until my blood begins to flow in my veins again. Through the corridors (after thoughtfully locking the doors behind them), up endless stairs where my bruised feet painfully plod, in utter silence, surefooted in their skin boots—how the devil did they get the keys? The leader shows me the knife I gave him, its blade black.

"Good God!" I whisper in horror, and he grins from ear to ear.

This is the end.

I cannot possibly go with them. I will show them the way, and they must go on by themselves. I must make a stand here or nowhere, convince the governor's niece—somehow excuse, somehow implicate; things were going so well—but here we reach the gate to the southern road, from where come our supplies and down which my heart has gone so many times, so many times. I stop under the arch and point.

The leader takes my hand and I pull it away.

"Aaaa?" or he says something, something quick and low that I do not catch. I retreat into the shadow of the gate, for the weather has turned clear during the night and the vault of the stars casts a fair, faint shine.

"Go on," I say. "Go on," waving my arm helplessly. "You're free."

"Eeeee?"

"Go on, will you!" Patiently he takes my hand again, stroking it, and I jerk away. Behind me sleeps Her Excellency Miss, whose wounded pride may somehow be assuaged, I say may be, and who—if God is kind—will not demand for me the extremest penalty. And besides, they cannot get along without me, can they? The place would crumble into ruins; who would run the generator; they can't, can they?

With the horde on one side (a whiskered grandfather, a baby, an inky-browed girl) and on the other side the shadowy bulk of the southern gate, I turn to go back. I take a step forward, but before I can put my foot to the ground something knocks me into the snow: a terrifying swarm of black eyes like a swarm of ants, a heap of sinewy cords as alive as snakes; I try to shout, but something digs into my back and wakes a raw bruise; these unbearable, stinking savages. . . .

"Aaaa oo," says someone very politely, throwing a skin cloak over me, and six of these cheerful people lift me up and carry me off, the southern gate dipping behind me and the stars rocking crazily above, while the scene of my past career grows smaller and smaller behind me. And disappears.

But at last I have a future.

Gleepsite

I try to make my sales at night during the night shift in office buildings; it works better that way. Resistance is gone at night. The lobbies are deserted, the air filters on half power; here and there a woman stays up late amid piles of paper; things blow down the halls just out of the range of vision of the watch-ladies who turn their keys in the doors of unused rooms, who insert the keys hanging from chains around their necks in the apertures of empty clocks, or polish with their polishing rags the surfaces of desks, the bare tops of tables. You make some astonishing sales that way.

I came up my thirty floors and found on the thirty-first Kira and Lira, the only night staff: two fiftyish identical twins in the same gray cardigan sweaters, the same pink dresses, the same blue rinse

"Gleepsite" is a building material invented by architecture students at Cornell University. Gleepsite has no mass, infinite tensile strength, and its malleability, insulating properties, and so on are whatever you want them to be. In short, gleepsite is an imaginary material. This story is about another "imaginary material"—the human imagination itself. Can it do as much as the narrator thinks it can do? You must decide.—J.R.

on their gray sausage-curls. But Kira wore on her blouse (over the name tag) the emblem of the senior secretary, the Tree of Life pin with the cultured pearl, while Lira went without, so I addressed myself to the (minutes-) younger sister.

"We're closed," they said.

Nevertheless, knowing that they worked at night, knowing that they worked for a travel agency whose hints of imaginary faraway places (Honolulu, Hawaii—they don't exist) must eventually exacerbate the longings of even the most passive sister, I addressed myself to them again, standing in front of the semicircular partition over which they peered (alarmed but bland), keeping my gaze on the sans-serif script over the desk—or is it roses!—and avoiding very carefully any glance at the polarized vitryl panels beyond which rages hell's own stew of hot winds and sulfuric acid, it gets worse and worse. I don't like false marble floors, so I changed it.

Ladies.

"We're closed!" cried Miss Lira.

Here I usually make some little illusion so they will know who I am; I stopped Miss Kira from pressing the safety button, which always hangs on the wall, and made appear beyond the nearest vitryl panel a bat's face as big as a man's: protruding muzzle, pointed fangs, cocked ears, and rats' shiny eyes, here and gone. I snapped my fingers, and the wind tore it off.

No, no, no, no! cried the sisters.

May I call you Flora and Dora? I said. Flora and Dora in memory of that glorious time centuries past when ladies like yourselves danced on tables to the applause of admiring gentlemen, when ladies wore, like yourselves, scarlet petticoats, ruby stomachers, chokers and bibs of red velvet, pearls and maroon high-heeled boots, though they did not always keep their petticoats decorously about their ankles.

What you have just seen, ladies, is a small demonstration of the power of electrical brain stimulation—mine, in this case—and the field which transmitted it to you was generated by the booster I wear about my neck, metallic in this case, though they come in other colors, and tuned to the frequency of the apparatus which I wear in this ring. You will notice that it is inconspicuous and well designed. I am allowed to wear the booster only at work. In the year blank-blank, when the great neurosurgical genius, Blank, working with Blank and Blank, discovered in the human forebrain what has been so poetically termed the Circle of Illusion, it occurred to another great innovator, Blank, whom you know, to combine these two great discoveries, resulting in a Device that has proved to be of inestimable benefit to the human race. (We just call it the Device.) Why not, thought Blank, employ the common, everyday power of electricity for the stimulation, the energization, the concretization of the Center of Illusion, or (to put it bluntly) an aide-mémoire, crutch, companion, and record-keeping book for that universal human talent, daydreaming? Do you daydream, ladies? Then you know that daydreaming is harmless. Daydreaming is voluntary. Daydreaming is not night dreaming. Daydreaming is normal. It is not hallucination or delusion or deception but creation. It is an accepted form of mild escape. No more than in a daydream or reverie is it possible to confuse the real and the ideal; try it and see. The Device simply supplements the power of your own human brain. If Miss Kira—

"No, no!" cried Miss Lira, but Miss Kira had already taken my sample ring, the setting scrambled to erase the last customer's residual charge.

You have the choice of ten scenes. No two persons will see the same thing, of course, but the parameters remain fairly constant. Further choices on request. Sound, smell, taste, touch, and kinesthesia optional. We are strictly prohibited from employing illegal settings or the use of variable condensers with fluctuating parameters. Tampering with the machinery is punishable by law.

"But it's so hard!" said Miss Kira in surprise. "And it's not real at all!" That always reassures them. At first.

It takes considerable effort to operate the Circle of Illusion even with mechanical aid. Voltage beyond that required for threshold stimulation is banned by law; even when employed, it does not diminish the necessity for effort, but in fact increases it proportionately. No more than in life, ladies, can you get something for nothing.

Practice makes perfect.

Miss Kira, as I knew she would, had chosen a flowery meadow with a suggestion of honeymoon; Miss Lira chose a waterfall in a glade. Neither had put in a Man, although an idealized figure of a Man is standard equipment for our pastoral choices (misty, idealized, in the distance, some even see him with wings), and I don't imagine either sister would ever get much closer.

Miss Lira said they actually had a niece who was actually married to a man.

Miss Kira said a half niece.

Miss Lira said they had a cousin who worked in the children's nursery with real children and they had holidays coming *and if I use a variable condenser, what's it to you?*

Behind me, though I cannot imagine why, is a full-length mirror, and in this piece of inconstancy I see myself as I was when I left home tonight, or perhaps not, I don't remember: beautiful, chocolate-colored, naked, gold braided into my white hair. Behind me, bats' wings.

A mirror, ladies, produces a virtual image, and so does the Device.

Bats' faces.

Hermaphroditic.

It is no more addicting than thought.

Little snakes waving up from the counter, a forest of them. Unable to stand the sisters' eyes swimming behind their glasses, myopic Flora and Dora, I changed the office for them, gave them a rug, hung behind them on the wall original Rembrandts, made them younger, erased them, let the whole room slide, and provided for Dora a bedroom beyond the travel office, a bordello in white-and-gold baroque, embroidered canopy, goldfish pool, chihuahuas on the marble, and bats in the belfry.

I have two heads.

Flora's quite a whore.

The younger sister, not quite willing to touch the ring again, said they'd think about it, and Kira, in a quarrel that must have gone back years, began in a low, vapid whisper—

Why, they're not bats at all, I said, over at the nearest vitryl panel; *I was mistaken,* and Lira, Don't open that! We'll suffocate!

No one who is sane, of course, opens anything anymore into that hell outside, but this old, old, old place had real locks on the vitryl and real seams between, and a narrow balcony where someone had gone out perhaps fifty years ago (in a diving suit) to admire the up-drafts between the dead canyons where papers danced on the driving murk and shapes fluttered between the raw lights; one could see several streets over to other spires, other shafts, the hurricane tearing through the poisoned air. Nighttime makes a kind of inferno out of this, and every once in a while someone decides on a gaudy exit: the lungs eaten away, the room reeking of hydrosulfurous acid, torn paper settling on the discolored rug.

When you have traveled in the tubes as much as I have, when you have seen the playground in Antarctica time after time, when your features have melted enough between black and brown and white, man and woman, as plastic as the lazy twist of a thought, you get notions. You get ideas. I saw once in a much more elegant office building a piece of polished wood, so large, so lovely, a curve fully six feet long and so beautiful that if you could have made out of that wood an idea and out of that idea a bed, you could have slept on that bed. When you put your hand on the vitryl panels at night, the heat makes your hand sweat onto the surface; my hand's melted through many times, like oil on water. I stood before the window, twisting shapes for fun, seeing myself stand on the narrow balcony, bored with Kira and Lira, poor Kira, poor Lira, poor as-I-once-was, discussing whether they can afford it.

" . . . an outlet for creativity . . . "

" . . . she *said* it's only . . . "

What effort it takes, and what an athlete of illusion you become! Able to descend to the bottom of the sea (where we might as well be, come to think of it), to the manless moon, to the Southern Hemisphere where the men stay, dreaming about us; but no, they did away with themselves years ago, they were inefficient, and did themselves in (I mean all the men except themselves) in blank-blank. Only three percent of the population male, my word!

" . . . legal . . . "

" . . . never . . . "

"Don't!" cried Miss Kira.

They know what I'm going to do. Ever since I found out those weren't bats' faces. As Miss Kira and Miss Lira sign the contract (thumbsy-up, thumbsy-down), I wrench the lock off the vitryl and squeeze through, what a foul, screaming wind! shoving desperately at the panels, and stumble off the narrow railless balcony, feeling as I go my legs contract, my fingers grow, my sternum arch like the prow of a boat, little bat-man-woman with sketchy turned-out legs and grasping toes, and hollow bones and fingers down to my ankles, a thumb-and-forefinger grasper at the end of each wing, and that massive wraparound of the huge, hollow chest, all covered with blonde fur; in the middle of it all, sunk between the shoulders, is the human face. Miss Kira would faint. I would come up to Miss Lira's waist. Falling down the nasty night air until I shrug up hard, hard, hard, into a steep upward glide and ride down the currents of hell past the man-made cliff where Kira and Lira, weeping with pain, push the vitryl panel back into place. The walls inside are blackening, the fake marble floor is singed. It is comfy-cold, it is comfy-nice, I'm going to mate in midair, I'm going to give shuddering birth on the ledge of a cliff, I'm going to scream at the windows when I like. They found no corpse, no body.

Kira and Lira, mouths like O's, stare out as I climb past. They do a little dance.

> She was a Floradora baby
> With a chance to meet the best,
> But she had to go and marry Abie,
> The drummer with the fancy vest!

Tampering with the machinery is punishable by law, says Kira.
Oh, my dear, we'll tinker a bit, says Lira.
And so they will.

nobody's home

After she had finished her work at the North Pole, Jannina came down to the Red Sea refineries where she had family business, jumped to New Delhi for dinner, took a nap in a public hotel in Queensland, walked from the hotel to the station, bypassed the Leeward Islands (where she thought she might go, but all the stations were busy), and met Charley to watch the dawn over the Carolinas.

"Where've you *been*, dear C?"

"Tanzania. And you're married."

"No."

"I heard you were married," he said. "The Lees told the Smiths who told the Kerguelens who told the Utsumbés and we get around, we Utsumbés. A new wife, they said. I didn't know you were especially fond of women."

"I'm not. She's my husbands' wife. And we're not married yet, Charley. She's had hard luck: a first family started in '35, two husbands burned out by an overload while arranging transportation for a concert—of all things, pushing papers, you know!—and the second divorced her, I think, and she drifted away from the third (a big one), and there was some awful quarrel with the fourth, people chasing people around tables, I don't know."

"Poor woman."

In the manner of people joking and talking lightly they had drawn together, back to back, sitting on the ground and rubbing together their shoulders and the backs of their heads. Jannina said sorrowfully, "What lovely hair you have, Charley Utsumbé, like metal mesh."

"All we Utsumbés are exceedingly handsome." They linked arms. The sun, which anyone could chase around the world now, see it rise or set twenty times a day, fifty times a day—if you wanted to spend your life like that—rose dripping out of the cypress swamp. There was nobody around for miles. Mist drifted up from the pools and low places.

"My God," he said, "it's summer! I have to be at Tanga now."

"What?" said Jannina.

"One loses track," he said apologetically. "I'm sorry, love, but I have unavoidable business at home. Tax labor."

"But why summer, why did its being summer—"

"Train of thought! Too complicated." And already they were out of key, already the mild affair was over, there having come between them the one obligation that can't be put off to the time you like, or the place you like; off he'd go to plug himself into a road-mender or a doctor, though it's of some advantage to mend all roads of a continent at one time.

She sat cross-legged on the station platform, watching him enter the booth and set the dial. He stuck his head out the glass door.

"Come with me to Africa, lovely lady!"

She thumbed her nose at him. "You're only a passing fancy, Charley U!" He blew a kiss, enclosed himself in the booth, and disappeared. (The transmatter field is larger than the booth, for obvious reasons; the booth flicks on and off several million times a second and so does not get transported itself, but it protects the machinery from the weather and it keeps people from losing elbows or knees or slicing the ends off a package or a child. The booths at the cryogenics center at the North Pole have exchanged air so often with those of warmer regions that each has its own microclimate; leaves and seeds, plants and earth, are piled about them. Don't Step on the Grass!—say the notes pinned to the door—Wish to Trade Pawlownia Sapling for Subarctic Canadian Moss; Watch Your Goddamn Bare Six-Toed Feet!; Wish Amateur Cellist for Quartet, Six Months' Rehearsal Late Uhl with Reciter; I Lost a Squirrel Here Yesterday, Can You Find It Before It Dies? Eight Children Will be Heartbroken—Cecilia Ching, Buenos Aires.)

Jannina sighed and slipped on her glass woolly; nasty to get back into clothes, but home was cold. You never knew where you might go, so you carried them. Years ago (she thought) I came here with someone in the dead of winter, either an unmatched man or someone's starting spouse—only two of us, at any rate—and we waded through the freezing water and danced as hard as we could and then proved we could sing and drink beer in a swamp at the same time, Good Lord! And then went to the public resort on the Île de la Cité to watch professional plays, opera, games—you have to be good to get in there!—and got into some clothes because it was chilly after sundown in September—no, wait, it was Venezuela —and watched the lights come out and smoked like mad at a café table and tickled the robot waiter and pretended we were old, really old, perhaps a hundred and fifty. . . . Years ago!

But *was* it the same place? she thought, and dismissing the incident forever, she stepped into the booth, shut the door, and dialed home: the Himalayas. The trunk line was clear. The branch stop was clear. The family's transceiver (located in the anteroom behind two doors, to keep the task of heating the house within reasonable limits) had damn well better be clear, or somebody would be blown right into the vestibule. Momentum- and heat-compensators kept Jannina from arriving home at seventy degrees Fahrenheit internal temperature (seven degrees lost for every mile you teleport upward) or too many feet above herself (rise to the east, drop going west, to the north or south you are apt to be thrown right through the wall of the booth). Someday (thought Jannina) everybody will decide to let everybody live in decent climates. But not yet. Not this everybody.

She arrived home singing "The World's My Back Yard, Yes, the World Is My Oyster," a song that had been popular in her first youth, some seventy years before.

*   *   *

The Komarovs' house was hardened foam with an automatic inside line to the school near Naples. It was good to be brought up on your own feet. Jannina passed through; the seven-year-olds lay with their heads together and their bodies radiating in a six-personed asterisk. In this position (which was supposed to promote mystical thought) they played Barufaldi, guessing the identity of famous dead personages through anagrammatic sentences, the first letters of the words of which (unscrambled into aphorisms or proverbs) simultaneously spelled out a moral and a series of Gödel numbers (in a previously agreed-upon code) which—

"Oh, my darling, how felicitous is the advent of your appearance!" cried a boy (hard to take, the polysyllabic stage). "Embrace me, dearest maternal parent! Unite your valuable upper limbs about my eager person!"

"Vulgar!" said Jannina, laughing.

"Non sum filius tuus?" said the child.

"No, you're not my body-child; you're my godchild. Your mother bequeathed me to you when she died. What are you learning?"

"The eternal parental question," he said, frowning. "How to run a helicopter. How to prepare food from its actual revolting raw constituents. Can I go now?"

"*Can* you?" she said. "Nasty imp!"

"Good," he said. "I've made you feel guilty. Don't *do* that," and as she tried to embrace him, he ticklishly slid away. "The robin walks quietly up the branch of the tree," he said breathlessly, flopping back on the floor.

"That's not an aphorism." (Another Barufaldi player.)

"It is."

"It isn't."

"It is."

"It isn't."

"It is."

"It—"

The school vanished; the antechamber appeared. In the kitchen Chi Komarov was rubbing the naked back of his sixteen-year-old son. Parents always kissed each other; children always kissed each other. She touched foreheads with the two men and hung her woolly on the hook by the ham radio rig. Someone was always around. Jannina flipped the cover off her wrist chronometer: standard regional time, date, latitude-longitude, family computer hookup clear. "At my age I ought to remember these things," she said. She pressed the computer hookup: Ann at tax labor in the schools, bit-a-month plan, regular Ann; Lee with three months to go, five years off, heroic Lee; Phuong in Paris, still rehearsing; C.E. gone, won't say where, spontaneous C.E.; Ilse making some repairs in the basement, not a true basement, really, but the room farthest down the hillside. She went up the stairs and then came down and put her head round at the living-and-swimming room. Through the glass wall one could see the mountains. Old Al, who had joined them late in life, did a bit of gardening in the brief summers and generally stuck around the place. Jannina beamed. "Hullo, Old Al!" Big and shaggy, a rare delight, his white body hair. She sat on his lap. "Has she come?"

"The new one? No," he said.

"Shall we go swimming?"

He made an expressive face. "No, dear," he said. "I'd rather go to Naples and watch the children fly helicopters. I'd rather go to Nevada and fly them myself. I've been in the water all day, watching a very dull person restructure coral reefs and experiment with polyploid polyps."

"You mean *you* were doing it."

"One gets into the habit of working."

"But you didn't have to!"

"It was a private project. Most interesting things are."

She whispered in his ear.

With happily flushed faces, they went into Old Al's inner garden and locked the door.

Jannina, temporary family representative, threw the computer helmet over her head, and thus plugged in, she cleaned house, checked food supplies, did a little of the legal business entailed by a family of eighteen adults (two triplet marriages, a quad, and a group of eight). She felt very smug. She put herself through by radio to Himalayan HQ (above two thousand meters) and hooking computer to computer—a very odd feeling, like an urge to sneeze that never comes off—extended a formal invitation to one Leslie Smith ("Come stay, why don't you?"), notifying every free Komarov to hop it back and fast. Six hikers might come for the night—back-packers. More food. First thunderstorm of the year in Albany, New York (North America). Need an extra two rooms by Thursday. Hear the Palnatoki are moving. Can't use a room. Can't use a kitten. Need the geraniums back, Mrs. Adam, Chile. The best maker of hand-blown glass in the world has killed in a duel the second-best maker of hand-blown glass for joining the movement towards ceramics. A bitter struggle is foreseen in the global economy. Need a lighting designer. Need fifteen singers and electric pansensicon. Standby tax labor xxxxxpj through xxxyq to Cambaluc, great tectogenic—

With the guilty feeling that one always gets gossiping with a computer, for it's really not reciprocal, Jannina flipped off the helmet. She went to get Ilse. Climbing back through the white foam room, the purple foam room, the green foam room, everything littered with plots and projects of the clever Komarovs or the even cleverer Komarov children, stopping at the baby room for Ilse to nurse her baby. Jannina danced staidly around studious Ilse. They turned on the nursery robot and the television screen. Ilse drank beer in the swimming room, for her milk. She worried her way through the day's record of events—faults in the foundation, some people who came from Chichester and couldn't find C.E. so one of them burst into tears, a new experiment in genetics coming round the gossip circuit, an execrable set of equations from some imposter in Bucharest.

"A duel!" said Jannina.

They both agreed it was shocking. And what fun. A new fashion. You had to be a little mad to do it. Awful.

The light went on over the door to the tunnel that linked the house to the antechamber, and very quickly, one after another, as if the branch line had just come free, eight Komarovs came into the room. The light flashed again; one could see three people debouch one after the other, persons in boots, with coats, packs, and face masks over their woollies. They were covered with snow, either from the mountain terraces above the house or from some other place, Jannina didn't know. They stamped the snow off in the antechamber and hung their clothes outside; "Good heavens, you're not circumcised!" cried someone. There was as much hand-shaking and embracing all around as at a wedding party. Velet Komarov (the short, dark one) recognized Fung Pao-yu and swung her off her feet. People began to joke, tentatively stroking one another's arms. "Did you have a good hike? Are you a good hiker, Pao-yu?" said Velet. The light over the antechamber went on again, though nobody could see a thing since the glass was steamed over from the collision of hot with cold air. Old Al stopped, halfway into the kitchen. The baggage receipt chimed, recognized only by family ears—upstairs a bundle of somebody's things, orna-ments, probably, for the missing Komarovs were still young and the young are interested in clothing, were appearing in the baggage receptacle. "Ann or Phuong?" said Jannina. "Five to three, anybody? Match me!" but someone strange opened the door of the booth and peered out. Oh, a dizzying sensation. She was painted in a few places, which was awfully odd because really it was old-fashioned; and why do it for a family evening? It was a stocky young woman. It was an awful mistake (thought Jannina). Then the visitor made her second mistake. She said:

"I'm Leslie Smith." But it was more through clumsiness than be-ing rude. Chi Komarov (the tall, blond one) saw this instantly, and snatching off his old-fashioned spectacles, he ran to her side and patted her, saying teasingly:

"Now, haven't we met? Now, aren't you married to someone I know?"

"No, no," said Leslie Smith, flushing with pleasure.

He touched her neck. "Ah, you're a tightrope dancer!"

"Oh, no!" exclaimed Leslie Smith.

"*I'm* a tightrope dancer," said Chi. "Would you believe it?"

"But you're too—too *spiritual*," said Leslie Smith hesitantly.

"Spiritual, how do you like that, family, spiritual?" he cried, delighted (a little more delighted, thought Jannina, than the situa-tion really called for), and he began to stroke her neck.

"What a lovely neck you have," he said.

This steadied Leslie Smith. She said, "I like tall men," and al-lowed herself to look at the rest of the family. "Who are these peo-ple?" she said, though one was afraid she might really mean it.

Fung Pao-yu to the rescue: "Who are these people? Who are they, indeed! I doubt if they are anybody. One might say, 'I have met these people,' but has one? What existential meaning would such a statement convey? I myself, now, I have met them. I have been introduced to them. But they are like the Sahara; it is all wrapped in mystery; I doubt if they even have names," etc. etc. Then lanky Chi Komarov disputed possession of Leslie Smith with Fung Pao-yu, and Fung Pao-yu grabbed one arm and Chi the other; and she jumped up and down fiercely; so that by the time the lights dimmed and the food came, people were feeling better—or so Jannina judged. So embarrassing and delightful to be eating fifteen to a room! "We Komarovs are famous for eating whatever we can get whenever we can get it," said Velet proudly. Various Komarovs in various places, with the three hikers on cushions and Ilse at full length on the rug. Jannina pushed a button with her toe, and the fairy lights came on all over the ceiling. "The children did that," said Old Al. He had somehow settled at Leslie Smith's side and was feeding her so-chi from his own bowl. She smiled at him. "We once," said a hiking companion of Fung Pao-yu's, "arranged a dinner in an amphitheater where half of us played servants to the other half, with forfeits for those who didn't show. It was the result of a bet. Like the bad old days. Did you know there were once *five billion people* in this world?"

"The gulls," said Ilse, "are mating on the Isle of Skye." There were murmurs of appreciative interest. Chi began to develop an erection, and everyone laughed. Old Al wanted music and Velet didn't; what might have been a quarrel was ended by Ilse's furiously boxing their ears. She stalked off to the nursery.

"Leslie Smith and I are both old-fashioned," said Old Al, "because neither of us believes in gabbing. Chi—your theater?"

"We're turning people away." He leaned forward, earnestly, tapping his fingers on his crossed knees. "I swear, some of them are threatening to commit suicide."

"It's a choice," said Velet reasonably.

Leslie Smith had dropped her bowl. They retrieved it for her.

"Aiy, I remember—" said Pao-yu. "What I remember! We've been eating dried mush for three days, tax-issue. Did you know one of my dads killed himself?"

"No!" said Velet, surprised.

"Years ago," said Pao-yu. "He said he refused to live to see the time when chairs were reintroduced. He also wanted further genetic engineering, I believe, for even more intelligence. He did it out of spite, I'm sure. I think he wrestled a shark. Jannina, is this tax-issue food? Is it this year's style tax-issue sauce?"

"No, next year's," said Jannina snappishly. Really, some people! She slipped into Finnish, to show up Pao-yu's pronunciation. "Isn't that so?" she asked Leslie Smith.

Leslie Smith stared at her.

More charitably Jannina informed them all, in Finnish, that the Komarovs had withdrawn their membership in a food group, except for Ann, who had taken out an individual, because what the dickens, who had the time? And tax-issue won't kill you. As they finished, they dropped their dishes into the garbage field and Velet stripped a layer off the rug. In that went, too. Indulgently Old Al began a round:

"Red."

"Sun," said Pao-yu.

"The Red Sun Is," said one of the triplet Komarovs.

"The Red Sun Is—High," said Chi.

"The Red Sun Is High, The," Velet said.

"The Red Sun Is High, The Blue—" Jannina finished. They had come to Leslie Smith, who could either complete it or keep it going. She chose to declare for complete, not shyly (as before) but simply by pointing to Old Al.

"The red sun is high, the blue," he said. "Subtle! Another: Ching."

"Nü."

"Ching nü ch'i."

"Ching nü ch'i ch'u."

"Ssu."

"Wo."

"Ssu wo yü." It had got back to Leslie Smith again. She said, "I can't do that." Jannina got up and began to dance—I'm nice in my nasty way, she thought. The others wandered towards the pool and Ilse reappeared on the nursery monitor screen, saying, "I'm coming down." Somebody said, "What time is it in the Argentine?"

"Five A.M."

"I think I want to go."

"Go then."

"I go."

"Go well."

The red light over the antechamber door flashed and went out.

"Say, why'd you leave your other family?" said Ilse, settling near Old Al where the wall curved out. Ann, for whom it was evening, would be home soon; Chi, who had just got up a few hours back in western America, would stay somewhat longer; nobody ever knew Old Al's schedule, and Jannina herself had lost track of the time. She would stay up until she felt sleepy. She followed a rough twenty-eight-hour day, Phuong (what a nuisance that must be at rehearsals!) a twenty-two-hour one, Ilse six hours up, six hours dozing. Jannina nodded, heard the question, and shook herself awake.

"I didn't leave them. They left me."

There was a murmur of sympathy around the pool.

"They left me because I was stupid," said Leslie Smith. Her hands were clasped passively in her lap. She looked very genteel in her blue body paint, a stocky young woman with small breasts. One of the triplet Komarovs, flirting in the pool with the other two, choked. The nonaquatic members of the family crowded around Leslie Smith, touching her with little soft touches; they kissed her and exposed to her all their unguarded surfaces, their bellies, their soft skins. Old Al kissed her hands. She sat there, oddly unmoved. "But I *am* stupid," she said. "You'll find out." Jannina put her hands over her ears: "A masochist!" Leslie Smith looked at Jannina with a curious stolid look. Then she looked down and absently began to rub one blue-painted knee. "Luggage!" shouted Chi, clapping his hands together, and the triplets dashed for the stairs. "No, I'm going to bed," said Leslie Smith; "I'm tired," and quite simply, she got up and let Old Al lead her through the pink room, the blue room, the turtle-and-pet room (temporarily empty), the trash room, and all the other rooms, to the guest room with the view that looked out over the cold hillside to the terraced plantings below.

"The best maker of hand-blown glass in the world," said Chi, "has killed in a duel the second-best maker of hand-blown glass in the world."

"For joining the movement to ceramics," said Ilse, awed. Jannina felt a thrill: this was the tragic stuff under the surface of life, the fury that boiled up. A bitter struggle is foreseen in the global economy. Good old tax-issue stuff goes toddling along, year after year. She was, thought Jannina, extraordinarily grateful to be living now, to be in such an extraordinary world, to have so long to go before her death. So much to do!

Old Al came back into the living room. "She's in bed."

"Well, which of us—?" said the triplet-who-had-choked, looking mischievously round from one to the other. Chi was about to volunteer, out of his usual conscientiousness, thought Jannina, but then she found herself suddenly standing up, and then just as suddenly sitting down again. "I just don't have the nerve," she said. Velet Komarov walked on his hands towards the stairs, then somersaulted, and vanished, climbing. Old Al got off the hand-carved chest he had been sitting on and fetched a can of ale from it. He levered off the top and drank. Then he said, "She really is stupid, you know." Jannina's skin crawled.

"Oooh," said Pao-yu. Chi betook himself to the kitchen and returned with a paper folder. It was coated with frost. He shook it, then impatiently dropped it in the pool. The redheaded triplet swam over and took it. "Smith, Leslie," he said. "Adam Two, Leslie. Yee, Leslie. Schwarzen, Leslie."

"What on earth does the woman *do* with herself besides get married?" exclaimed Pao-yu.

"She drove a hovercraft," said Chi, "in some out-of-the-way places around the Pacific until the last underground stations were completed. Says when she was a child she wanted to drive a truck."

"Well, you can," said the redheaded triplet, "can't you? Go to Arizona or the Rockies and drive on the roads. The sixty-mile-an-hour road. The thirty-mile-an-hour road. Great artistic recreation."

"That's not work," said Old Al.

"Couldn't she take care of children?" said the redheaded triplet. Ilse sniffed.

"Stupidity's not much of a recommendation for that," Chi said. "Let's see—no children. No, of course not. Overfulfilled her tax work on quite a few routine matters here. Kim, Leslie. Went to Moscow and contracted a double with some fellow, didn't last.

Registered as a singleton, but that didn't last, either. She said she was lonely and they were exploiting her."

Old Al nodded.

"Came back and lived informally with a theater group. Left them. Went into psychotherapy. Volunteered for several experimental intelligence-enhancing programs, was turned down—hm! —sixty-five come the winter solstice, muscular coordination average, muscular development above average, no overt mental pathology, empathy average, prognosis: poor. No, wait a minute, it says, 'More of the same.' Well, that's the same thing.

"What I want to know," added Chi, raising his head, "is who met Miss Smith and decided we needed the lady in this Ice Palace of ours?"

Nobody answered. Jannina was about to say, "Ann, perhaps?" but as she felt the urge to do so—surely it wasn't right to turn somebody off like that, *just* for that!—Chi (who had been flipping through the dossier) came to the last page, with the tax-issue stamp absolutely unmistakable, woven right into the paper.

"The computer did," said Pao-yu, and she giggled idiotically.

"Well," said Jannina, jumping to her feet, "tear it up, my dear, or give it to me and I'll tear it up for you. I think Miss Leslie Smith deserves from us the same as we'd give to anybody else, and I—for one—intend to go *right up there*—"

"After Velet," said Old Al dryly.

"*With* Velet, if I must," said Jannina, raising her eyebrows, "and if you don't know what's due a guest, Old Daddy, I do, and I intend to provide it. Lucky I'm keeping house this month, or you'd probably feed the poor woman nothing but seaweed."

"You won't like her, Jannina," said Old Al.

"I'll find that out for myself," said Jannina with some asperity, "and I'd advise you to do the same. Let her garden with you, Daddy. Let her squirt the foam for the new rooms. And now"—she glared round at them—"I'm going to clean *this* room, so you'd better hop it, the lot of you," and dashing into the kitchen, she had the computer helmet on her head and the hoses going before they had even quite cleared the area of the pool. Then she took the helmet off and hung it on the wall. She flipped the cover off her wrist chronometer and satisfied herself as to the date. By the time she got back to the living room there was nobody there, only Leslie Smith's dossier lying on the carved chest. There was Leslie Smith; there was all of Leslie Smith. Jannina knocked on the wall cupboard and it revolved, presenting its openable side; she took out chewing gum. She started chewing and read about Leslie Smith.

Q: What have you seen in the last twenty years that you particularly liked?

A: I don't . . . the museum, I guess. At Oslo. I mean the . . . the mermaid and the children's museum, I don't care if it's a children's museum.

Q: Do you like children?

A: Oh, no.

(No disgrace in *that*, certainly, thought Jannina.)

Q: But you liked the children's museum.

A: Yes, sir. . . . Yes . . . I liked those little animals, the fake ones, in the—the—

Q: The crèche?

A: Yes. And I liked the old things from the past, the murals with the flowers on them, they looked so real.

(Dear God!)

Q: You said you were associated with a theater group in Tokyo. Did you like it?

A: No . . . yes. I don't know.

Q: Were they nice people?

A: Oh, yes. They were awfully nice. But they got mad at me, I suppose. . . . You see . . . well, I don't seem to get things quite right, I suppose. It's not so much the work, because I do that all right, but the other . . . the little things. It's always like that.

Q: What do you think is the matter?

A: You . . . I think you know.

Jannina flipped through the rest of it: normal, normal, normal. Miss Smith was as normal as could be. Miss Smith was stupid. Not even very stupid. It was too damned bad. They'd probably have enough of Leslie Smith in a week, the Komarovs; yes, we'll have enough of her (Jannina thought), never able to catch a joke or a tone of voice, always clumsy, however willing, but never happy, never at ease. You can get a job for her, but what else can you get for her? Jannina glanced down at the dossier, already bored.

Q: You say you would have liked to live in the old days. Why is that? Do you think it would have been more adventurous or would you like to have had lots of children?

A: I . . . you have no right . . . You're condescending.

Q: I'm sorry. I suppose you mean to say that then you would have been of above-average intelligence. You would, you know.

A: I know. I looked it up. Don't condescend to me.

Well, it *was* too damned bad! Jannina felt tears rise in her eyes. What had the poor woman done? It was just an accident, that was the horror of it, not even a tragedy, as if everyone's forehead had been stamped with the word "Choose" except for Leslie Smith's. She needs money, thought Jannina, thinking of the bad old days when people did things for money. Nobody could take to Leslie Smith. She wasn't insane enough to stand for being hurt or exploited. She wasn't clever enough to interest anybody. She certainly wasn't feeble-minded; they couldn't very well put her into a hospital for the feeble-minded or the brain-injured; in fact (Jannina was looking at the dossier again), they had tried to get her to work there and she had taken a good, fast swing at the supervisor. She had said the people there were "hideous" and "revolting." She had no particular mechanical aptitudes. She had no particular interests. There was not even anything for her to read or watch; how could there be? She seemed (back at the dossier) to spend most of her time either working or going on public tours of exotic lands, coral reefs, and places like that. She enjoyed aqualung diving, but didn't do it often because that got boring. And that was that. There was, all in all, very little one could do for Leslie Smith. You might even say that in her own person she represented all the defects of the bad old days. Just imagine a world made up of such creatures! Jannina yawned. She slung the folder away and padded into the kitchen. Pity Miss Smith wasn't good-looking, also a pity that she was too well balanced (the folder said) to think that cosmetic surgery would make that much difference. Good for you, Leslie, you've got some sense, anyhow. Jannina, half-asleep, met Ann in the kitchen, beautiful, slender Ann reclining on a cushion with her so-chi and melon. Dear old Ann. Jannina nuzzled her brown shoulder. Ann poked her.

"Look," said Ann, and she pulled from the purse she wore at her waist a tiny fragment of cloth, stained rusty brown.

"What's that?"

"The second-best maker of hand-blown glass—oh, you know about it—well, this is his blood. When the best maker of hand-blown glass in the world had stabbed to the heart the second-best maker of hand-blown glass in the world, and cut his throat, too, some small children steeped handkerchiefs in his blood and they're sending pieces all over the world."

"Good God!" cried Jannina.

"Don't worry, my dear," said lovely Ann; "it happens every decade or so. The children say they want to bring back cruelty, dirt, disease, glory, and hell. Then they forget about it. Every teacher knows that." She sounded amused. "I'm afraid I lost my temper today, though, and walloped your godchild. It's in the family, after all."

Jannina remembered when she herself had been much younger and Annie, barely a girl, had come to live with them. Ann had played at being a child and had put her head on Jannina's shoulder, saying, "Jannie, tell me a story." So Jannina now laid her head on Ann's breast and said, "Annie, tell me a story."

Ann said: "I told my children a story today, a creation myth. Every creation myth has to explain how death and suffering came into the world, so that's what this one is about. In the beginning, the first man and the first woman lived very contentedly on an island until one day they began to feel hungry. So they called to the turtle who holds up the world to send them something to eat. The turtle sent them a mango and they ate it and were satisfied, but the next day they were hungry again.

" 'Turtle,' they said, 'send us something to eat.' So the turtle sent them a coffee berry. They thought it was pretty small, but they ate it anyway and were satisfied. The third day they called on the turtle again, and this time the turtle sent them two things: a banana and a stone. The man and woman did not know which to choose, so they asked the turtle which thing it was they should eat. 'Choose,' said the turtle. So they chose the banana and ate that, but they used the stone for a game of catch. Then the turtle said, 'You should have chosen the stone. If you had chosen the stone, you would have lived forever, but now that you have chosen the banana, Death and Pain have entered the world, and it is not I who can stop them.' "

Jannina was crying. Lying in the arms of her old friend, she wept bitterly, with a burning sensation in her chest and the taste of death and ashes in her mouth. It was awful. It was horrible. She remembered the embryo shark she had seen when she was three, in the Auckland Cetacean Research Center, and how she had cried then. She didn't know what she was crying about. "Don't, don't!" she sobbed.

"Don't what?" said Ann affectionately. "Silly Jannina!"

"Don't, don't," cried Jannina, "don't, it's true, it's true!" and she went on in this way for several more minutes. Death had entered the world. Nobody could stop it. It was ghastly. She did not mind for herself but for others, for her godchild, for instance. He was going to die. He was going to suffer. Nothing could help him. Duel, suicide, or old age, it was all the same. "This life!" gasped Jannina. "This awful life!" The thought of death became entwined somehow with Leslie Smith, in bed upstairs, and Jannina began to cry afresh, but eventually the thought of Leslie Smith calmed her. It brought her back to herself. She wiped her eyes with her hand. She sat up. "Do you want a smoke?" said beautiful Ann, but Jannina shook her head. She began to laugh. Really, the whole thing was quite ridiculous.

"There's this Leslie Smith," she said, dry-eyed. "We'll have to find a tactful way to get rid of her. It's idiotic, in this day and age."

And she told lovely Annie all about it.

MY DEAR EMILY

San Francisco, 188-

I am so looking forward to seeing my dear Emily at last, now she is grown, a woman, although I'm sure I will hardly recognize her. She must not be proud (as if she could be!) but will remember her friends, I know, and have patience with her dear Will who cannot help but remember the girl she was and the sweet influence she had in her old home. I talk to your father about you every day, dear, and he longs to see you as I do. Think! a learned lady in our circle! But I know you have not changed. . . .

Emily came home from school in April with her bosom friend Charlotte. They had loved each other in school, but they didn't speak much on the train. While Emily read Mr. Emerson's poems, Charlotte examined the scenery through opera-glasses. She expressed her wish to see "savages."

"That's foolish," says Emily promptly.

"If we were carried off," says Charlotte, "I don't think you would notice it in time to disapprove."

"That's very foolish," says Emily, touching her round lace collar with one hand. She looks up from Mr. Emerson to stare Charlotte out of countenance, properly, morally, and matter-of-course young lady. It has always been her style.

"The New England look," Charlotte snaps resentfully. She makes her opera-glasses slap shut.

"I should like to be carried off," she proposes; "but then I don't have an engagement to look forward to. A delicate affair."

"You mustn't make fun," says Emily. Mr. Emerson drops into her lap. She stares unseeing at Charlotte's opera-glasses.

"Why do they close?" she asks helplessly.

"I beg your pardon?" blankly, from Charlotte.

"Nothing. You're much nicer than I am," says Emily.

"Look," urges Charlotte kindly, pressing the toy into her friend's hand.

"For savages?"

Charlotte nods, Emily pushes the spring that will open the little machine, and a moment later drops them into her lap where they fall on Mr. Emerson. There is a cut across one of her fingers and a blue pinch darkening the other.

"They hurt me," she says without expression, and as Charlotte takes the glasses up quickly, Emily looks with curious sad passivity at the blood from her little wound, which has bled an incongruous passionate drop on Mr. Emerson's clothbound poems. To her friend's surprise (and her own, too) she begins to cry, heavily, silently, and totally without reason.

He wakes up slowly, mistily, dizzily, with a vague memory of having fallen asleep on plush. He is intensely miserable, bound down to his bed with hoops of steel, and the memory adds nausea to his misery, solidifying ticklishly around his bare hands and the back of his neck as he drifts towards wakefulness. His stomach turns over with the dry brushy filthiness of it. With the caution of the chronically ill, he opens his eyelids, careful not to move, careful even to keep from focusing his gaze until—he thinks to himself— his bed stops holding him with the force of Hell and this intense miserable sickness goes down, settles . . . Darkness. No breath. A glimmer of light, a stone wall. He thinks: *I'm dead and buried, dead and buried, dead and—* With infinite care he attempts to breathe, sure that this time it will be easy; he'll be patient, discreet, sensible, he won't do it all at once—

He gags. Spasmodically he gulps, cries out, and gags again, springing convulsively to his knees and throwing himself over the low wall by his bed, laboring as if he were breathing sand. He starts to sweat. His heartbeat comes back, then pulse, then seeing, hearing, swallowing . . . High in the wall a window glimmers, a star is out, the sky is pale evening blue. Trembling with nausea, he rises to his feet, sways a little in the gloom, then puts out one arm and steadies himself against the stone wall. He sees the window, sees the door ahead of him. In his tearing eyes the star suddenly blazes and lengthens like a knife; his head is whirling, his heart painful as a man's; he throws his hands over his face, longing for life and strength to come back, the overwhelming flow of force that will crest at sunrise, leaving him raging at the world and ready to kill anyone, utterly proud and contemptuous, driven to sleep as the last resort of a balked assassin. But it's difficult to stand, difficult to breathe: *I wish I were dead and buried, dead and buried, dead and buried— But there!* he whispers to himself like a charm, *There, it's going, it's going away.* He smiles slyly round at his companionable, merciful stone walls. With an involuntarily silent, gliding gait he moves towards the door, opens the iron gate, and goes outside. Life is coming back. The trees are black against the sky, which yet holds some light; far away in the west lie the radiant memories of a vanished sun. An always vanished sun.

"Alive!" he cries, in triumph. It is—as usual—his first word of the day.

Dear Emily, sweet Emily, met Martin Guevara three days after she arrived home. She had been shown the plants in the garden and the house plants in stands and had praised them; she had been shown the sun-pictures and had praised *them*; she had fingered antimacassars, promised to knit, exclaimed at gaslights, and passed two evenings at home, doing nothing. Then in the hall that led to the pantry Sweet Will had taken her hand, and she had dropped her eyes because she was supposed to and that was her style. Charlotte (who slept in the same room as her friend) embraced her at bed-

time, wept over the hand-taking, and then Emily said to her dear,
dear friend (without thinking):

"Sweet William."

Charlotte laughed.

"It's not a joke!"

"It's so funny."

"I love Will dearly." She wondered if God would strike her dead
for a hypocrite. Charlotte was looking at her oddly, and smiling.

"You mustn't be full of levity," said Emily, peeved. It was then
that Sweet William came in and told them of tomorrow's garden-
party, which was to be composed of her father's congregation.
They were lucky, he said, to have acquaintances of such position
and character. Charlotte slipped out on purpose, and Will, seeing
they were alone, attempted to take Emily's hand again.

"Leave me alone!" Emily said angrily. He stared.

"I said leave me alone!"

And she gave him such a look of angry pride that, in fact, he did.

Emily sees Guevara across the parlor by the abominable cherry-
red sofa, talking animatedly and carelessly. In repose he is slight,
undistinguished, and plain, but no one will ever see him in repose;
Emily realizes this. His strategy is never to rest, to bewilder, he
would (she thinks) slap you if only to confuse you, and when he
can't he's always out of the way and attacking, making one look
ridiculous. She knows nobody and is bored; she starts for the door
to the garden.

At the door his hand closes over her wrist; he has somehow
gotten there ahead of her.

"The lady of the house," he says.

"I'm back from school."

"And you've learned—?"

"Let me go, please."

"Never." He drops her hand and stands in the doorway. She
says:

"I want to go outside."

"Never."

"I'll call my father."

"Do." She tries and can't talk; I wouldn't *bother*, she thinks to herself, loftily. She goes out into the garden with him. Under the trees his plainness vanishes like smoke.

"You want lemonade," he says.

"I'm not going to talk to you," she responds. "I'll talk to Will. Yes! I'll make him—"

"In trouble," says Mr. Guevara, returning silently with lemonade in a glass cup.

"No, thank you."

"She wants to get away," says Martin Guevara. "I know."

"If I had your trick of walking like a cat," she says, "I could get out of anything."

"I *can* get out of anything," says the gentleman, handing Emily her punch, "out of an engagement, a difficulty. I can even get *you* out of anything."

"I loathe you," whispers Emily suddenly. "You walk like a cat. You're ugly."

"Not out here," he remarks.

"Who has to be afraid of lights?" cries Emily energetically. He stands away from the paper lanterns strung between the trees, handsome, comfortable, and collected, watching Emily's cut-glass cup shake in her hand.

"I can't move," she says miserably.

"Try." She takes a step towards him. "See; you can."

"But I wanted to go *away!*" With sudden hysteria she flings the lemonade (cup and all) into his face, but he is no longer there.

"What are you doing at a church supper, you hypocrite!" she shouts tearfully at the vacancy.

Sweet William has to lead her in to bed.

"You thought better of it," remarks Martin, head framed in an evening window, sounds of footsteps outside, ladies' heels clicking in the streets.

"I don't know you," she says miserably, "I just don't." He takes her light shawl, a pattern in India cashmere.

"That will come," he says, smiling. He sits again, takes her hand, and squeezes the skin on the wrist.

"Let me go, please?" she says like a child.

"I don't know."

"You talk like the smart young gentlemen at Andover; they were all fools."

"Perhaps you overawed them." He leans forward and puts his hand around the back of her neck for a moment. "Come on, dear."

"What are you talking about!" Emily cries.

"San Francisco is a lovely city. I had ancestors here three hundred years ago."

"Don't think that because I came here—"

"She doesn't," he whispers, grasping her shoulder, "she doesn't know a thing."

"God damn you!"

He blinks and sits back. Emily is weeping. The confusion of the room—an overstuffed, overdraped hotel room—has gotten on her nerves. She snatches for her shawl, which is still in his grasp, but he holds it out of her reach, darting his handsome, unnaturally young face from side to side as she tries to reach round him. She falls across his lap and lies there, breathless with terror.

"You're cold," she whispers, horrified, "you're cold as a corpse." The shawl descends lightly over her head and shoulders. His frozen hands help her to her feet. He is delighted; he bares his teeth in a smile.

"I think," he says, tasting it, "that I'm going to visit your family."

"But you don't—" she stumbles—"you don't want to . . . with me. I know it."

"I can be a suitor like anyone else," he says.

That night Emily tells it all to Charlotte, who, afraid of the roué, stays up and reads a French novel as the light drains from the windows and the true black dark takes its place. It is almost dawn, and Charlotte has been dozing when Emily shakes her friend awake, kneeling by the bed with innocent blue eyes reflecting the dying night.

"I had a terrible dream," she complains.

"Hmmmm?"

"I dreamed," says Emily tiredly. "I had a nightmare. I dreamed I was walking by the beach and I decided to go swimming and then a . . . a thing, I don't know . . . it took me by the neck."

"Is that all?" says Charlotte peevishly.

"I'm sick," says Emily with childish satisfaction. She pushes Charlotte over in the bed and climbs in with her. "I won't have to see that man again if I'm sick."

"Pooh, why not?" mumbles Charlotte.

"Because I'll have to stay home."

"He'll visit you."

"William won't let him."

"Sick?" says Charlotte then, suddenly waking up. She moves away from her friend, for she has read more bad fiction than Emily and less moral poetry.

"Yes, I feel awful," says Emily simply, resting her head on her knees. She pulls away in tired irritation when her friend reaches for the collar of her nightdress. Charlotte looks and jumps out of bed.

"Oh," says Charlotte. "Oh—goodness—oh—" holding out her hands.

"What on earth's the matter with you?"

"He's—" whispers Charlotte in horror, "he's—"

In the dim light her hands are black with blood.

"You've come," he says. He is lying on his hotel sofa, reading a newspaper, his feet over one arm and a hand trailing on the rug.

"Yes," she answers, trembling with resolution.

"I never thought this place would have such a good use. But I never know when I'll manage to pick up money—"

With a blow of her hand, she makes a fountain of the newspaper; he lies on the sofa, mildly amused.

"Nobody knows I came," she says rapidly. "But I'm going to finish you off. I know how." She hunts feverishly in her bag.

"I wouldn't," he remarks quietly.

"Ah!" Hauling out her baby cross (silver), she confronts him with it like Joan of Arc. He is still amused, still mildly surprised.

"In your hands?" he says delicately. Her fingers are loosening, her face pitiful.

"My dear, the significance is in the feeling, the faith, not the symbol. You use that the way you would use a hypodermic needle. Now in your father's hands—"

"I dropped it," she says in a little voice. He picks it up and hands it to her.

"You can touch—" she says, her face screwing up for tears.

"I can."

"Oh, my God!" she cries in despair.

"My dear." He puts one arm around her, holding her against him, a very strong man for she pushes frantically to free herself. "How many times have I said that! But you'll learn. Do I sound like the silly boys at Andover?" Emily's eyes are fixed and her throat contracts; he forces her head between her knees. "The way you go on, you'd think I was bad luck."

"I—I—"

"And you without the plentiful lack of brains that characterizes your friend. She'll be somebody's short work, and I think I know whose."

Emily turns white again.

"I'll send her around to you afterwards. Good God! What do you think will happen to her?"

"She'll die," says Emily clearly. He grasps her by the shoulders.

"Ah!" he says with immense satisfaction. "And after that? Who lives forever after that? Did you know that?"

"Yes, people like you don't die," whispers Emily. "But you're not people—"

"No," he says intently, "no. We're not." He stands Emily on her feet. "We're a passion!" Smiling triumphantly, he puts his hands on each side of her head, flattening the pretty curls, digging his fingers into the hair, in a grip Emily can no more break than she could break a vise.

"We're passion," he whispers, amused. "Life is passion. Desire makes life."

"Ah, let me go," says Emily.

He smiles ecstatically at the sick girl.

"Desire," he says dreamily, "lives; *that* lives when nothing else does, and we're desire made purely, desire walking the earth. Can a dead man walk? Ah! If you want, want, want . . ."

He throws his arms around her, pressing her head to his chest and nearly suffocating her, ruining her elaborate coiffure and crushing the lace at her throat. Emily breathes in the deadness about him, the queer absence of odor, or heat, or presence; her mouth is pressed against the cloth of his fashionable suit, expensive stuff, a good dollar a yard, gotten by—what? But his hands are strong enough to get anything.

"You see," he says gently, "I enjoy someone with intelligence, even with morals; it adds a certain— And besides—" here he releases her and holds her face up to his— "we like souls that come to us; these visits to the bedrooms of unconscious citizens are rather like frequenting a public brothel."

"I abhor you," manages Emily. He laughs. He's delighted.

"Yes, yes, dear," he says, "but don't imagine we're callous parasites. Followers of the Marquis de Sade, perhaps—you see Frisco has evening hours for its bookstores!—but sensitive souls, really, and apt to long for a little conscious partnership." Emily shuts her eyes. "I said," he goes on, with a touch of hardness, "that I am a genuine seducer. I flatter myself that I'm not an animal."

"You're a monster," says Emily, with utter conviction. Keeping one hand on her shoulder, he steps back a pace.

"Go." She stands, unable to believe her luck, then makes what seems to her a rush for the door; it carries her into his arms.

"You see?" He's pleased; he's proved a point.

"I can't," she says, with wide eyes and wrinkled forehead . . .

"You will." He reaches for her and she faints.

Down in the dark where love and some other things make their hiding place, Emily drifts aimlessly, quite alone, quite cold, like a dead woman without a passion in her soul to make her come back to life.

She opens her eyes and finds herself looking at his face in the dark, as if the man carried his own light with him.

"I'll die," she says softly.

"Not for a while," he drawls, sleek and content.

"You've killed me."

"I've loved."

"Love!"

"Say 'taken' then, if you insist."

"I do! I do!" she cries bitterly.

"You decided to faint."

"Oh, the hell with you!" she shouts.

"Good girl!" And as she collapses, weeping hysterically, "Now, now, come here, dear . . ." nuzzling her abused little neck. He kisses it in the tenderest fashion with an exaggerated, mocking sigh; she twists away but is pulled closer, and as his lips open over the teeth of inhuman dead desire, his victim finds—to her surprise— that there is no pain. She braces herself and then, unexpectedly, shivers from head to foot.

"Stop it!" she whispers, horrified. "Stop it! Stop it!"

But a vampire who has found a soul-mate (even a temporary one) will be immoderate. There's no stopping them.

Charlotte's books have not prepared her for *this*.

"You're to stay in the house, my dear, because you're ill."

"I'm not," Emily says, pulling the sheet up to her chin.

"Of course you are." The Reverend beams at her, under the portrait of Emily's dead mother that hangs in Emily's bedroom. "You've had a severe chill."

"But I have to get out!" says Emily, sitting up. "Because I have an appointment, you see."

"Not now," says the Reverend.

"But I *can't* have a severe chill in the *summer!*"

"You look so like your mother," says the Reverend, musing. After he has gone away, Charlotte comes in.

"I have to stay in the damned bed," says Emily forcefully, wiggling her toes under the sheet. Charlotte, who has been carrying a tray with tea and a posy on it, drops it on the washstand.

"Why, Emily!"

"I have to stay in the damned bed the whole damned day," Emily adds.

"Dear, why do you use those words?"

"Because the whole world's damned!"

After the duties of his employment were completed at six o'clock on a Wednesday, William came to the house with a doctor and introduced him to the Reverend and Emily's bosom friend. The streetlamps would not be lit for an hour, but the sun was just down and the little party congregated in the garden under remains of

Japanese paper lanterns. No one ever worried that these might set themselves on fire. Lucy brought tea—they were one of the few civilized circles in Frisco—and over the tea, in the darkening garden, to the accompaniment of sugar-tongs and plopping cream (very musical) they talked.

"Do you think," says the Reverend, very worried, "that it might be consumption?"

"Perhaps the lungs are affected," says the doctor.

"She's always been such a robust girl." This is William, putting down the teapot, which has a knitted tube about the handle for insulation. Charlotte is stirring her tea with a spoon.

"It's very strange," says the doctor serenely, and he repeats "it's very strange" as shadows advance in the garden. "But young ladies, you know—especially at twenty—young ladies often take strange ideas into their heads; they do, they often do; they droop; they worry." His eyes are mild, his back sags, he hears the pleasant gurgle of more tea. A quiet consultation, good people, good solid people, a little illness, nothing serious—

"No," says Charlotte. Nobody hears her.

"I knew a young lady once—" ventures the doctor mildly.

"No," says Charlotte, more loudly. Everyone turns to her, and the maid, taking the opportunity, insinuates a plate of small-sized muffins in front of Charlotte.

"I can tell you all about it," mutters Charlotte, glancing up from under her eyebrows. "But you'll *laugh*."

"Now, dear—" says the Reverend.

"Now, miss—" says the doctor.

"As a friend—" says William.

Charlotte begins to sob.

"Oh," she says, "I'll—I'll tell you about it."

Emily meets Mr. Guevara at the Mansion House at seven, having recovered an appearance of health (through self-denial) and a good solid record of spending the evenings at home (through self-control). She stands at the hotel's wrought-iron gateway, her back rigid as a stick, drawing on white gloves. Martin materializes out of the blue evening shadows and takes her arm.

"I shall like living forever," says Emily, thoughtfully.

"God deliver me from Puritans," says Mr. Guevara.

"What?"

"You're a lady. You'll swallow me up."

"I'll do anything I please," remarks Emily severely, with a glint of teeth.

"Ah."

"I will." They walk through the gateway. "You don't care two pins for me."

"Unfortunately," says he, bowing.

"It's not unfortunate as long as *I* care for me," says Emily, smiling with great energy. "Damn them all."

"You proper girls would overturn the world." Along they walk in the evening, in a quiet, respectable rustle of clothes. Halfway to the restaurant she stops and says breathlessly:

"Let's go—somewhere else!"

"My dear, you'll ruin your health!"

"You know better. Three weeks ago I was sick as a dog and much you cared; I haven't slept for days and I'm fine."

"You look fine."

"Ah! You mean I'm beginning to look dead, like you." She tightens her hold on his arm, to bring him closer.

"Dead?" says he, slipping his arm around her.

"Fixed. Bright-eyed. Always at the same heat and not a moment's rest."

"It agrees with you."

"I adore you," she says.

When Emily gets home, there's a reckoning. The Reverend stands in the doorway and sad William, too, but not Charlotte, for she is on the parlor sofa, having had hysterics.

"Dear Emily," says the Reverend. "We don't know how to tell you this—"

"Why, Daddy, *what?*" exclaims Emily, making wide-eyes at him.

"Your little friend told us—"

"Has something happened to Charlotte?" cries Emily. "Oh, tell me, tell me, what happened to Charlotte?" And before they can stop her she has flown into the parlor and is kneeling beside her friend, wondering if she dares pinch her under cover of her shawl.

William, quick as a flash, kneels on one side of her and Daddy on the other.

"Dear Emily!" cries William with fervor.

"Oh, sweetheart!" says Charlotte, reaching down and putting her arms around her friend.

"You're well!" shouts Emily, sobbing over Charlotte's hand and thinking perhaps to bite her. But the Reverend's arms lift her up.

"My dear," says he, "you came home unaccompanied. You were not at the Society."

"But," says Emily, smiling dazzlingly, "two of the girls took all my hospital sewing to their house because we must finish it right away and I have not—"

"You have been lying to us," the Reverend says. *Now*, thinks Emily, *Sweet William will cover his face.* Charlotte sobs.

"She can't help it," says Charlotte brokenly. "It's the spell."

"Why, I think everyone's gone out of their minds," says Emily, frowning. Sweet William takes her from Daddy, leading her away from Charlotte.

"Weren't you with a gentleman tonight?" says Sweet Will firmly. Emily backs away.

"For shame!"

"She doesn't remember it," explains Charlotte; "it's part of his spell."

"I think you ought to get a doctor for *her*," observes Emily.

"You were with a gentleman named Guevara," says Will, showing less tenderness than Emily expects. "Weren't you? Well— weren't you?"

"Bad cess to you if I was!" snaps Emily, surprised at herself. The other three gasp. "I won't be questioned," she goes on, "and I won't be spied upon. And I think you'd better take some of Charlotte's books away from her; she's getting downright silly."

"You have too much color," says Will, catching her hands. "You're ill, but you don't sleep. You stay awake all night. You don't eat. But look at you!"

"I don't understand you. Do you want me to be ugly?" says Emily, trying to be pitiful. Will softens; she sees him do it.

"My dear Emily," he says. "My dear girl—we're afraid for you."

"Me?" says Emily, enjoying herself.

"We'd better put you to bed," says the Reverend kindly.

"You're so kind," whispers Emily, blinking as if she held back tears.

"That's a good girl," says Will, approving. "We know you don't understand. But we'll take care of you, Em."

"*Will* you?"

"Yes, dear. You've been near very grave danger, but luckily we found out in time, and we found out what to do; we'll make you well, we'll keep you safe, we'll—"

"Not with *that* you won't," says Emily suddenly, rooting herself to the spot, for what William takes out of his vest pocket (where he usually keeps his watch) is a broad-leaved, prickle-faced dock called wolfsbane; it must distress any vampire of sense to be so enslaved to pure superstition. But enslaved they are, nonetheless.

"Oh, no!" says Emily swiftly. "That's silly, perfectly silly!"

"Common sense must give way in such a crisis," remarks the Reverend gravely.

"You bastard!" shouts Emily, turning red, attempting to tear the charm out of her fiancé's hand and jump up and down on it. But the Reverend holds one arm and Charlotte the other and between them they pry her fingers apart and William puts his property gently into his vest pocket again.

"She's far gone," says the Reverend fearfully, at his angry daughter. Emily is scowling, Charlotte stroking her hair.

"Ssssh," says Will with great seriousness. "We must get her to bed," and between them they half carry Emily up the stairs and put her, dressed as she is, in the big double bed with the plush headboard that she has shared so far with Charlotte. Daddy and fiancé confer in the room across the long, low rambling hall, and Charlotte sits by her rebellious friend's bed and attempts to hold her hand.

"I won't permit it; you're a damned fool!" says Emily.

"Oh, Emmy!"

"Bosh."

"It's true!"

"Is it?" With extraordinary swiftness, Emily turns round in the bed and rises to her knees. "Do you know anything about it?"

"I know it's horrid, I—"

"Silly!" Playfully Emily puts her hands on Charlotte's shoulders. Her eyes are narrowed, her nostrils widened to breathe; she parts her lips a little and looks archly at her friend. "You don't know anything about it," she says insinuatingly.

"I'll call your father," says Charlotte quickly.

Emily throws an arm around her friend's neck.

"Not yet! Dear Charlotte!"

"We'll save you," says Charlotte doubtfully.

"Sweet Charrie; you're my friend, aren't you?"

Charlotte begins to sob again.

"Give me those awful things, those leaves."

"Why, Emily, I *couldn't!*"

"But he'll come for me and I have to protect myself, don't I?"

"I'll call your father," says Charlotte firmly.

"No, I'm *afraid.*" And Emily wrinkles her forehead sadly.

"Well—"

"Sometimes I—I—" falters Emily. "I can't move or run away and everything looks so—so strange and *horrible*—"

"Oh, here!" Covering her face with one hand, Charlotte holds out her precious dock leaves in the other.

"Dear, dear! Oh, sweet! Oh, thank you! Don't be afraid. He isn't after you."

"I hope not," says the bosom friend.

"Oh, no, he told me. It's me he's after."

"How awful," says Charlotte, sincerely.

"Yes," says Emily. "Look." And she pulls down the collar of her dress to show the ugly marks, white dots unnaturally healed up, like the pockmarks of a drug addict.

"Don't!" chokes Charlotte.

Emily smiles mournfully. "We really ought to put the lights out," she says.

"Out!"

"Yes, you can see him better that way. If the lights are on, he could sneak in without being seen; he doesn't mind lights, you know."

"I don't know, dear—"

"I do." (Emily is dropping the dock leaves into the washstand, under cover of her skirt.) "I'm afraid. Please."

"Well—"

"Oh, you must!" And leaping to her feet, she turns down the gas to a dim glow; Charlotte's face fades into the obscurity of the deepening shadows.

"So. The lights are out," says Emily quietly.

"I'll ask Will—" Charlotte begins. . . .

"No, dear."

"But, Emily—"

"He's coming, dear."

"You mean Will is coming."

"No, not Will."

"Emily, you're a—"

"I'm a sneak," says Emily, chuckling. "Ssssh!" And, while her friend sits paralyzed, one of the windows swings open in the night breeze, a lead-paned window that opens on a hinge, for the Reverend is fond of culture and old architecture. Charlotte lets out a little noise in her throat; and then—with the smash of a pistol shot—the gaslight shatters and the flame goes out. Gas hisses into the air, quietly, insinuatingly, as if explaining the same thing over and over. Charlotte screams with her whole heart. In the dark a hand clamps like a vise on Emily's wrist. A moment passes.

"Charlotte?" she whispers.

"Dead," says Guevara.

Emily has spent most of the day asleep in the rubble, with his coat rolled under her head where he threw it the moment before sunrise, the moment before he staggered to his place and plunged into sleep. She has watched the dawn come up behind the rusty barred gate, and then drifted into sleep herself with his face before her closed eyes—his face burning with a rigid, constricted, unwasting vitality. Now she wakes aching and bruised, with the sun of late afternoon in her face. Sitting against the stone wall, she sneezes twice and tries, ineffectually, to shake the dust from her silk skirt.

Oh, how—she thinks vaguely—*how messy.* She gets to her feet. *There's something I have to do.* The iron gate swings open at a touch. *Trees and gravestones tilted every which way. What did he say? Nothing would disturb it but a Historical Society.*

Having tidied herself as best she can, with his coat over her arm and the address of his tailor in her pocket, she trudges among the erupted stones, which tilt crazily to all sides as if in an earthquake.

Blood (Charlotte's, whom she does not think about) has spread thinly onto her hair and the hem of her dress, but her hair is done up with fine feeling, despite the absence of a mirror, and her dress is dark gray; the spot looks like a spot of dust. She folds the coat into a neat package and uses it to wipe the dust off her shoes, then lightens her step past the cemetery entrance, trying to look healthy and respectable. She aches all over from sleeping on the ground.

Once in town and having ascertained from a shop window that she will pass muster in a crowd, Emily trudges up hills and down hills to the tailor, the evidence over her arm. She stops at other windows, to look or to admire herself; thinks smugly of her improved coloring; shifts the parcel on her arm to show off her waist. In one window there is a display of religious objects—beads and crosses, books with fringed gilt bookmarks, a colored chromo of Madonna and Child. In this window Emily admires herself.

"It's Emily, dear!"

A Mrs. L—— appears in the window beside her, with Constantia, Mrs. L——'s twelve-year-old offspring.

"Why, dear, whatever happened to you?" says Mrs. L——, noticing no hat, no gloves, and no veil.

"Nothing; whatever happened to you?" says Emily cockily. Constantia's eyes grow wide with astonishment at the fine, free audacity of it.

"Why, you look as if you'd been—"

"Picnicking," says Emily, promptly. "One of the gentlemen spilled beer on his coat." And she's in the shop now and hanging over the counter, flushed, counting the coral and amber beads strung around the crucifix.

Mrs. L—— knocks doubtfully on the window-glass.

Emily waves and smiles.

Your father—form Mrs. L——'s lips in the glass.

Emily nods and waves cheerfully.

They do go away, finally.

"A fine gentleman," says the tailor earnestly, "a very fine man." He lisps a little.

"Oh, very fine," agrees Emily, sitting on a stool and kicking the rungs with her feet. "Monstrous fine."

"But very careless," says the tailor fretfully, pulling Martin's coat nearer the window so he can see it, for the shop is a hole-in-the-wall and dark. "He shouldn't send a lady to this part of the town."

"I was a lady once," says Emily.

"Mmmmm."

"It's fruit stains—something awful, don't you think?"

"I cannot have this ready by tonight," looking up.

"Well, you must, that's all," says Emily calmly. "You always have and he has a lot of confidence in you, you know. He'd be awfully angry if he found out."

"Found out?" sharply.

"That you can't have it ready by tonight."

The tailor ponders.

"I'll positively stay in the shop while you work," says Emily flatteringly.

"Why, Reverend, I saw her on King Street as dirty as a gypsy, with her hair loose and the wildest eyes and I *tried* to talk to her, but she dashed into a shop—"

The sun goes down in a broad belt of gold, goes down over the ocean, over the hills and the beaches, makes shadows lengthen in the street near the quays where a lisping tailor smooths and alters, working against the sun (and very uncomfortable he is, too), watched by a pair of unwinking eyes that glitter a little in the dusk inside the stuffy shop. (*I think I've changed*, meditates Emily.)

He finishes, finally, with relief, and sits with an *ouf!* handing her the coat, the new and beautiful coat that will be worn as soon as the eccentric gentleman comes out to take the evening air. The eccentric gentleman, says Emily incautiously, will do so in an hour by the Mansion House when the last traces of light have faded from the sky.

"Then, my dear miss," says the tailor unctuously, "I think a little matter of pay—"

"You don't think," says Emily softly, "or you wouldn't have gotten yourself into such a mess as to be this eccentric gentleman's tailor." And out she goes.

Now nobody can see the stains on Emily's skirt or in her hair;

streetlamps are being lit, there are no more carriages, and the number of people in the streets grows—San Francisco making the most of the short summer nights. It is perhaps fifteen minutes back to the fashionable part of the town where Emily's hatless, shawlless state will be looked on with disdain; here nobody notices. Emily dawdles through the streets, fingering her throat, yawning, looking at the sky, thinking: *I love, I love, I love—*

She has fasted for the day but she feels fine; she feels busy, busy inside as if the life within her is flowering and bestirring itself, populated as the streets. She remembers—

I love you. I hate you. You enchantment, you degrading necessity, you foul and filthy life, you promise of endless love and endless time . . . .

What words to say with Charlotte sleeping in the same room, no, the same bed, with her hands folded under her face! Innocent sweetheart, whose state must now be rather different.

Up the hills she goes, where the view becomes wider and wider, and the lights spread out like sparkles on a cake, out of the section that is too dangerous, too low, and too furtive to bother with a lady (or is it something in her eyes?), into the broader bystreets where shore-leave sailors try to make her acquaintance by falling into step and seizing her elbow; she snakes away with unbounded strength, darts into shadows, laughs in their faces: "I've got what I want!"

"Not like me!"

"Better!"

This is the Barbary Coast, only beginning to become a tourist attraction; there are barkers outside the restaurants advertising pretty waiter girls, dance halls, spangled posters twice the height of a man, crowds upon crowds of people, one or two guides with tickets in their hats, and Emily—who keeps to the shadows. She nearly chokes with laughter: *What a field of ripe wheat!* One of the barkers hoists her by the waist onto his platform.

"Do you see this little lady? Do you see this—"

"Let me go, God damn you!" she cries indignantly.

"This angry little lady—" pushing her chin with one sunburned hand to make her face the crowd. "This—" But here Emily hurts him, slashing his palm with her teeth, quite pleased with herself, but surprised, too, for the man was holding his hand cupped and the whole thing seemed to happen of itself. She escapes instantly into the crowd and continues up through the Coast, through the old Tenderloin, drunk with self-confidence, slipping like a shadow through the now genteel streets and arriving at the Mansion House gate having seen no family spies and convinced that none has seen her.

But nobody is there.

Ten by the clock, and no one is there, either; eleven by the clock and still no one. *Why didn't I leave this life when I had the chance!* Only one thing consoles Emily, that by some alchemy or nearness to the state she longs for, no one bothers or questions her and even the policemen pass her by as if in her little corner of the gate there is nothing but a shadow. Midnight and no one, half-past and she dozes; perhaps three hours later, perhaps four, she is startled awake by the sound of footsteps. She wakes: nothing. She sleeps again and in her dream hears them for the second time, then she wakes to find herself looking into the face of a lady who wears a veil.

"What!" Emily's startled whisper.

The lady gestures vaguely, as if trying to speak.

"What is it?"

"Don't—" and the lady speaks with feeling but, it seems, with difficulty also— "don't go home."

"Home?" echoes Emily, stupefied, and the stranger nods, saying: "In danger."

"Who?" Emily is horrified.

"He's in danger." Behind her veil her face seems almost to emit a faint light of its own.

"You're one of them," says Emily. "Aren't you?" and when the woman nods, adds desperately, "Then you must save him!"

The lady smiles pitifully; that much of her face can be seen as the light breeze plays with her net veil.

"But you must!" exclaims Emily. "You know how; I don't; you've got to!"

"I don't dare," very softly. Then the veiled woman turns to go, but Emily—quite hysterical now—seizes her hand, saying:

"Who are you? Who are you?"

The lady gestures vaguely and shakes her head.

"Who are you!" repeats Emily with more energy. "You tell me, do you hear?"

Somberly the lady raises her veil and stares at her friend with a tragic, dignified, pitiful gaze. In the darkness her face burns with unnatural and beautiful color.

It is Charlotte.

Dawn comes with a pellucid quickening, glassy and ghostly. Slowly, shapes emerge from darkness and the blue pours back into the world—twilight turned backwards and the natural order reversed. Destruction, which is simple, logical, and easy, finds a kind of mocking parody in the morning's creation. Light has no business coming back, but light does.

Emily reaches the cemetery just as the caldron in the east overflows, just as the birds (*idiots!* she thinks) begin a tentative cheeping and chirping. She sits at the gate for a minute to regain her strength, for the night's walking and worry have tried her severely. In front of her the stones lie on graves, almost completely hard and real, waiting for the rising of the sun to finish them off and make complete masterpieces of them. Emily rises and trudges up the hill, slower and slower as the ground ascends to its topmost swell, where three hundred years of peaceful Guevaras fertilize the grass and do their best to discredit the one wild shoot that lives on, the only disrespectful member of the family. Weeping a little to herself, Emily lags up the hill, raising her skirts to keep them off the weeds, and murderously hating in her heart the increasing light and the happier celebrating of the birds. She rounds the last hillock of ground and raises her eyes to the Guevaras' eternal mansion, expecting to see nobody again. There is the corner of the building, the low iron gate—

In front of it stands Martin Guevara between her father and Sweet Sweet Will, captived by both arms, his face pale and beautiful between two gold crosses that are just beginning to sparkle in the light of day.

"We are caught," says Guevara, seeing her, directing at her his fixed white smile.

"You let him go," says Emily—very reasonably.

"You're safe, my Emily!" cries Sweet Will.

"Let him go!" She runs to them, stops, looks at them, perplexed to the bottom of her soul.

"Let him go," she says. "Let him go, let him go!"

Between the two bits of jewelry, Emily's life and hope and only pleasure smiles painfully at her, the color drained out of his face, desperate eyes fixed on the east.

"You don't understand," says Emily, inventing. "He isn't dangerous now. If you let him go, he'll run inside and then you can come back anytime during the day and finish him off. I'm sick. You—"

The words die in her throat. All around them, from every tree and hedge, from boughs that have sheltered the graveyard for a hundred years, the birds begin their morning noise. A great hallelujah rises; after all, the birds have nothing to worry about. Numb, with legs like sticks, Emily sees sunlight touch the top of the stone mausoleum, sunlight slide down its face, sunlight reach the level of a standing man—

"I adore you," says Martin to her. With the slow bending over of a drowning man, he doubles up, like a man stuck with a knife in a dream; he doubles up, falls—

And Emily screams; what a scream! as if her soul were being haled out through her thoat; and she is running down the other side of the little hill to regions as yet untouched by the sun, crying inwardly: I need help! help! help!— She knows where she can get it. Three hundred feet down the hill in a valley, a wooded protected valley sunk below the touch of the rising sun, there she runs through the trees, past the fence that separates the old graveyard from the new, expensive cast-iron-and-polished granite—

There, just inside the door (for they were rich people and Charlotte's mother's sister lived in Frisco) lies Emily's good friend, her old friend, with her hat and cloak off and her blonde hair falling over the bier to her knees—Charlotte in a white wrap like a slip. Emily stops inside the door, confused; Charlotte beholds her intently.

"There's not much time," says Charlotte.

"Help him!" whispers Emily.

"I can't; he's already gone."

"Please—please—" but Charlotte only rises glidingly on her couch, lifting her beautiful bare shoulders out of the white silk, fixedly regarding her friend with that look that neither time nor age will do anything to dim.

"I won't," says Emily, frightened, "I don't think—" taking a few unwilling steps towards the coffin, "I don't think that now—"

"You only have a moment," says Charlotte. Emily is now standing by her friend, and slowly, as if through tired weakness, she slips to her knees.

"Quickly," says Charlotte, scarcely to be heard at all. Looping one arm around her friend's neck, she pulls her face up to hers.

"But not without him—" Emily is half-suffocated— "not without him! Not this way!" She tries to break the grip and cannot. Charlotte smiles and dips her head.

"Not without him," her voice dying away faintly. "Not without him . . . not without . . . without . . ."

Sunlight touches the door, a moment too late.

ThE nEW mEn

This is the story of Commissioner Ivan Mihailovich Glespov, who traveled from the Russian border to the experimental virology clinic near Lwów, and you may believe it or not, just as you wish. I got it from a friend, who got it from another friend, who got it from a French journalist in Prague, who had become curious about the Socialist government's latest cultural effort to restore the architectural monuments of Poland; and who swears that among the cultural embassies the two great uneasy friends have been slinging at each other lately (we have all seen the results on television), this one is different and he has chapter and verse to prove it. But the French are like that.

A few years ago, in the winter of 1985 or 1986, the local driver employed by Commissioner Glespov—who was traveling in a private car in the direction already mentioned—lost his way near dusk, and they found themselves in a Polish country road, bouncing over ruts frozen steel-hard, between fields that were as white—and as flat—and as dreary—as one can possibly imagine. Commissioner Glespov, who was watching the landscape out of a particular personal unease, noted only a few huts or farm buildings, at first gray in the white and then a darker gray against the graying dusk, but he saw—or thought he saw—a kind of château set in the middle of the fields; upon which he turned up the heating control (they were traveling in an '82 Chevrolet bought from the American embassy) to the highest position (he was still shivering), rapped on the glass partition, and said:

"What's that? Is that a museum?"

But he never found out, for at this point the car's engine died. They came to a stop. Commissioner Glespov (he had been in charge of the urban vehicular transport of a large city in the Ukraine) sat wrapped in his lap-robe while the driver went outside and tried to start the motor; but at length the driver disappeared down the road, with many apologies in rural Polish, while Glespov (who was already beginning to grow cold) rolled up the window and sat looking out onto fields fast indistinguishable from the gathering night. At length he began to think that his driver was not coming back—or at least not soon—and when he saw, or thought he saw, a light in the château, he gathered his lap-robe about him, stepped out of the car, and trudged across the fields.

The château was a kind of mansion. It was an overblown eighteenth-century Petit Trianon and rather ludicrous out in the middle of the fields, but half in ruin, of course, with part of the upper storeys missing, and fallen stonework all around it. It reminded Glespov strongly of a motion-picture set he had seen once on a visit to the Kazakh Regional Film Center when the company was engaged in filming a historical epic based on Pushkin's poems, and he stood and gaped at the building with his lap-robe trailing behind him, like an old man in a bathrobe who has just taken out all his teeth. But Glespov was decisive—there were years when he had had to be—and he was not interested in sensations but in a place to sleep; so he knocked and tried out his execrable Polish on the peasant who answered. The man let him in. Although Glespov saw at once that the place was uninhabited, it was out of the cold and he had no mind to start back across the fields immediately. I also believe he had a sneaking curiosity to see the country-house from the inside and form some idea of how the gentry had lived when they did live, for it occurred to him that the film set might not have been

entirely accurate. So he waved aside the peasant, who was talking to him earnestly in language he could not understand, sat down on what was left of the grand staircase, and was about to shout angrily that he was a sick man and must be left in peace (Glespov had been famous at one time for his rages) when he realized that there was a third person in the room. Someone—holding a candle—was standing in the shadowy end of the grand ballroom, just standing and looking at Commissioner Glespov, and not indicating by even a flicker of the candlelight whether or not he liked what he saw or what he was going to do about it.

Glespov's first reaction, as he afterwards confessed, was nothing at all. He expected the "old people," as he called the country people, to use candles in out-of-the-way places; Russians, better than anyone else, know the difficulty of changing rural thinking. It was only when the third person moved forward and Glespov got a good look at him that Glespov became frightened; not that he was a superstitious man or thought he was seeing ghosts, but for reasons quite different. Sixty years before he would have run out into the fields to rouse the villagers, cold or no cold; forty years before he might have run for the police; but contemporary Glespov had no wild thoughts about witnessing the presence of one of the old aristocracy, nor did he believe in actual counterrevolutionary plots. He did think for a minute of running for the alienist. It even occurred to him that he might be going mad himself, but he had never done so before and saw no reason why he should begin now; thus he merely sat and stared at his host; and I believe that some part of him exclaimed with satisfaction: "This is better than the Kazakh Film Center!"

And indeed it was. The gentleman whom Glespov saw advance into the room was a *gentleman* in a sense that no one is, or has been, in Europe for some time. He put his candle down on an immense oak table in the center of the room and stood behind it, against dusty, torn hangings that had been antiques three hundred years before; and the candlelight dimly and delicately picked out the lace at his cuffs, the gold embroidery on his coat, the glittering folds of the black cloak he held over one arm, all the trappings of nobility that no living man has worn in Europe—or anywhere else —for more than thirteen generations.

"Aha, so you're making a film?" said Glespov while the stranger, turning to the peasant who had stood obsequiously at the door all this while, said something very sharp; and the peasant vanished immediately. The door swung shut with a little click. The stranger brought his face down to the level of his candle—he appeared to be sitting on a bench next to the table—and the shadows flowed after themselves over his face, turning it sinister, flat, and then hollow, all in turn. Glespov saw a young man, pale, lean, expressionless, with hair falling untidily to his shoulders. The young man said:

"I am the Count Jan Wisniowiecki."

Glespov answered, a bit apologetically (and he was sorry the minute the words left his mouth):

"There are no classes in the People's Republic of Poland!"

"I don't follow such things," said the stranger, perfectly unruffled. "You must tell me about them yourself," and he rose, picked up the candle, and stepped across the long stone floor to what seemed to Glespov to be a fireplace, where he stooped and lit the kindling that was piled not very neatly in the center. The light of the little fire threw wobbly shadows all over the room, making it look more than ever like a cavern: the big table, the bench, a kind of wardrobe that appeared to have escaped utter ruin, and portraits on the walls, ranks of them, all kinds of them, but all infinitely dirty, infinitely uncared-for, the kind of thing that would happen to a museum if it were no longer a museum but a haunt for field mice, rabbits, the rain, scavengers, and all kinds of bad weather. Glespov shivered.

"Count—?" he said.

"Jan Wisniowiecki," said the other. "Descended from the great Jagiello." He spoke Russian but with some accent. "You'll be more comfortable now," he said. Glespov got to his feet with an effort. He intended to make some excuse about his driver and go, but before he could open his mouth the peasant who had let him in returned through the front door and locked it, plodding across the floor to hand the key to his master, but very reluctant to get too close to him. It occurred to Glespov that this madman had what he himself had never possessed, that is, the power to inspire absolute terror, and for a single moment he felt immensely envious; he even thought, "Yes, they had something in the old days," and he watched with awe as the servant came by him, for the man was literally shaking in his shoes. The Count jabbed the air with his thumb, and the servant fetched from the wardrobe a bottle and glass which he placed on the table.

"We shall have to put you up down here," said the Count. "If you were to go upstairs, you would be quite open to the weather; it is all a ruin up there," and he nodded as Glespov poured himself a drink—brandy, as Glespov saw on the bottle, reading with difficulty. He wiped his mouth, trembling, with the back of his hand, and poured himself another glass, saying, "Ah! that's something, my dear fellow!"

"Yes, that's something," said the Count, watching his guest drink with a quiet, intent, and altogether vigilant regard, a kind of still intensity that puzzled Glespov, who poured himself a third brandy, saying after he drank—he had a kind of superstitious belief in the medicinal value of alcohol—

"So you really live here, eh?" That made him nervous, to say it. He looked carefully at the Count. He clucked to himself and stared about the big room, remembering what his wife had recently read in *Gazeta Literaturnaya* about the new Freudian analysis of characters. He said, "Not that some of your things aren't—very beautiful —full of culture—" and remembering his summer villa on the Black Sea, furnished with what seemed to him the quintessence of modernity, he longed to be back on the terrace, overlooking the sparkling blue waves, playing bridge. He said, "Yes, very cultured, but still—!" and downed his brandy. It was better than nothing, though he longed for food. It was better, in fact, than any he had ever tasted (though perhaps not as strong as what he was used to), so he took another.

"Everything in this house is old," said the Count, with no particular expression on his young face; he shook his sleeve, taking out therefrom a lace handkerchief; and Glespov saw (through an increasing brandy fog) that all his clothes were old, old and incredibly dirty, incredibly dusty, like clothes left too long in an attic until the dust is a gauze film over everything and underneath can be glimpsed—but only dimly and inaccurately—the original beauty, as if embalmed, like half-razed letters on an old monument. Glespov blinked. He said, "You come here sometimes, eh?" He thought

of the neurotic character as defined by his wife from the article in
Gaz. Lit. and about the fixation to the past which corresponds, in a
social sense, to an attempt to escape the dialectic of the historical
process; he thought, "nostalgia—yes, yes," and shivered a little, for
he had always had the deepest respect for the historical process,
even when his daughter had been disciplined for deviationist remarks in high school. He said blurrily, "Well, you're young," and
nodded a few times as the Count—now by his side in some unaccountable manner—helped him up and over to a cot on the far side
of the great fireplace, holding his elbow with unwavering courtesy,
remarking his stumbling and his yawns and shivers without the
slightest comment. Glespov found himself shouting suddenly,
"You're young! You're young!" and trying to pull off his expensive,
conservative shoes, recalling the urban transit authority and scenes
from the opera of Lermontov's life, but all mixed up—no doubt because of the brandy—with memories of his daughter's terrible disgrace and the motion-picture studio in Kharkhov, where he had
chatted for half an hour with a young actress and had permitted
himself the rare indulgence of imagining what it might be like to
have an affair with a really pretty woman—though he had always
been very fond of his wife, who was a physician and had wide interests. Then he fell asleep and maintains that he remembers nothing else until morning.

However, from certain documents and various bits of evidence,
it did become clear that mixed up with all this material was something else, and that in the middle of the night Ivan Mihailovich
Glespov had a rather extraordinary dream. He dreamed (though he
later denied it) that he heard a voice calling his name softly and
opened his eyes to find his host bending over him in the light from
the dying fire. He said that the young man's gray eyes were as clear
as a child's and his face as fresh and pale; he sat next to Glespov,
smiling gravely, and said:

"Ivan Mihailovich, you must tell me about the People's Republic
of Poland."

But Glespov could not say a word. Then it seemed to him that
the young man held him with his eyes until, in his mind, there appeared a vision of the room as it had once been in life, and that
against the living presence of long-dead splendor, the beautiful

women, the glasses, the elegant company, even the furniture, he—
Commissioner Glespov—was ashamed and could find nothing at
all to say. At length, said Glespov, he managed to whisper, "But it's
gone! it's all gone!" and the Count—who seemed extraordinarily
handsome at this point, though it puzzled Glespov to be able to see
him in the dark, as the fire had quite clearly gone out—murmured
gently, "Aren't you too afraid of death, Comrade?" which remark
(said Glespov) chilled him to the heart, for such thoughts had been
much in his mind lately. He was not a well man. He tried to cry
out, but as one does in dreams, could not; he tried to get out of bed
and could not do that either; then it occurred to him that he was
asleep, upon which he tried to open his eyes, fleeted through a long
succession of dreams in which he woke, fell asleep, got up, found
himself asleep again, and finally woke up.

The fire was very low and smoking. The uncurtained high window, half boarded-up, showed through occasional openings the
deep blue of the beginning of dawn. It was very cold. Sick, dizzy,
shivering in the dusty blankets he had drawn round his overcoat,
the Commissioner managed to sit up. He was afraid he had grown
much worse during the night. He got out of bed, clacking his false
teeth half in nervousness and half absentmindedly: gray-haired,
stooped, weak, and wrinkled, the very prototype of an old man.
He envied his host's youth. He wandered a few steps over the cold
stone floor when a bundle of rags caught his eye under one of the
windows. He had already started towards it when it began to
move; he did not realize for a second what it was but stopped with
a premonition of unpleasantness (he thought it might be an animal
come through some break in the walls from outside in the fields),
and then something pale turned up and outward from the bundle of
rags. It was the face of the Count.

Never, says Glespov, had he gone through anything like that.
Never, although he had served in the Battle of Moscow and had
gone through his share of liberating the concentration camps, never
had he seen insanity like that. The man was crouching below the
window on all fours like an animal, his face was white as paper and
disfigured with a long smear of blood, and for his expression—
Glespov, who had been in the War, would not speak of it; it was
mere insane rage, it was diseased, it was unhuman. Glespov, who

could hardly stand for illness, was in a better way than the Count, who could not stand at all; yet he dragged himself across the floor, tearing his clothes on the stone and inspiring Glespov with an irrational horror above the terrified weakness he already felt, *a horror (so he said) of seeing the madman's private parts,* for it seemed to him that a body so racked, so driven, so abused, must long ago have been turned into a thing, a puppet, a piece of wood; and that such a puppet should still carry the intestines, the skin, the organs, of a human being, seemed to him thoroughly unbearable. The Count had risen to his feet, swaying, and stumbled upon Glespov with fists clenched above his head; the Commissioner, terrified, could not move; the dry, distorted, shocking white face hissed out *"You! Poisoner!"* and at that moment the Count's body, dead as a log of wood, fell on top of Commissioner Glespov, burying him (he said) in an avalanche like the contents of an ancient wardrobe, dusty, choking, smothering, and horrible. He fainted. When he woke, sunlight was streaming through the windows and the Count was gone.

Commissioner Glespov, a sick man, past sixty, gathered his laprobe around his coat and staggered out of that Polish country mansion—cold or no cold—into the arms of his driver, who had been trying to force the door since sunrise.

And that is why, according to a French journalist stationed in Prague, the Soviet government has been so insistent lately about restoring the architectural monuments of Poland. If you put your ear to the Polish earth, says he, you can all but hear them: like a team of beavers, tapping walls, crating statuary, opening crypts, and excavating foundations; they are admired by the country people for their vitality, their cheerfulness, their square haircuts, and their gold teeth, and the Polish government is absolutely furious.

Glespov died several months later, quite comfortably, at the virology clinic near Lwów despite the advanced treatments for leukemia given him at that truly admirable institution.

But you can believe the story or not, just as you wish.

My Boat

Milty, have I got a story for you!

No, sit down. Enjoy the cream cheese and bagel. I guarantee this one will make a first-class TV movie; I'm working on it already. Small cast, cheap production— it's a natural. See, we start with this crazy chick, maybe about seventeen, but she's a waif, she's withdrawn from the world, see? She's had some kind of terrible shock. And she's fixed up this old apartment in a slum, really weird, like a fantasy world—long blonde hair, maybe goes around barefoot in tie-dyed dresses she makes out of old sheets, and there's this account executive who meets her in Central Park and falls in love with her on account of she's like a dryad or a nature spirit—

All right. So it stinks. I'll pay for my lunch. We'll pretend you're not my agent, okay? And you don't have to tell me it's been done; I know it's been done. The truth is—

Milty, I have to talk to someone. No, it's a lousy idea, I know, and I'm not working on it and I haven't been working on it, but what are you going to do Memorial Day weekend if you're alone and everybody's out of town?

I have to talk to someone.

Yes, I'll get off the Yiddische shtick. Hell, I don't think about it; I just fall into it sometimes when I get upset, you know how it is. You do it yourself. But I want to tell you a story and it's not a story for a script. It's something that happened to me in high school in 1952, and *I just want to tell someone.* I don't care if no station from here to Indonesia can use it; you just tell me whether I'm nuts or not, that's all.

Okay.

It was 1952, like I said. I was a senior in a high school out on the Island, a public high school but very fancy, a big drama program. They were just beginning to integrate, you know, the early fifties, very liberal neighborhood; everybody's patting everybody else on the back because they let five black kids into our school. Five out of eight hundred! You'd think they expected God to come down from Flatbush and give everybody a big fat golden halo.

Anyway, our drama class got integrated, too—one little black girl aged fifteen named Cissie Jackson, some kind of genius. All I remember the first day of the spring term, she was the only black I'd ever seen with a natural, only we didn't know what the hell it was, then; it made her look as weird as if she'd just come out of a hospital or something.

Which, by the way, she just had. You know Malcolm X saw his father killed by white men when he was four and that made him a militant for life? Well, Cissie's father had been shot down in front of her eyes when she was a little kid—we learned that later on— only it didn't make her militant; it just made her so scared of everybody and everything that she'd withdraw into herself and wouldn't speak to anybody for weeks on end. Sometimes she'd withdraw right out of this world and then they'd send her to the loony bin; believe me, it was all over school in two days. And she looked it; she'd sit up there in the school theater—oh, Milty, the Island high schools had *money,* you better believe it!—and try to disappear into the last seat like some little scared rabbit. She was only four-eleven anyhow, and maybe eighty-five pounds sopping wet. So maybe that's why she didn't become a militant. Hell, that had nothing to do with it. She was scared of *everybody.* It wasn't just the white-black thing, either; I once saw her in a corner with one of the other black students: real uptight, respectable boy, you know, suit and white shirt and tie and carrying a new briefcase, too, and he was talking to her about something as if his life depended on it. He was actually crying and pleading with her. And all she did was shrink back into the corner as if she'd like to disappear and shake her head No No No. She always talked in a whisper unless she was onstage and sometimes then, too. The first week she forgot her cues four times—just stood there, glazed over, ready to fall through the floor—and a couple of times she just wandered off the set as if the play was over, right in the middle of a scene.

So Al Coppolino and I went to the principal. I'd always thought Alan was pretty much a fruitcake himself—remember, Milty, this is 1952—because he used to read all that crazy stuff, The Cult of Cthulhu, Dagon Calls, The Horror Men of Leng—yeah, I remember that H. P. Lovecraft flick you got ten percent on for Hollywood *and* TV *and* reruns—but what did we know? Those days you went to parties, you got excited from dancing cheek to cheek, girls wore ankle socks and petticoats to stick their skirts out, and if you wore a sport shirt to school that was okay because Central High was liberal, but it better not have a pattern on it. Even so, I knew Al was a bright kid and I let him do most of the talking; I just nodded a lot. I was a big nothing in those days.

Al said, "Sir, Jim and I are all for integration and we think it's great that this is a really liberal place, but—uh—"

The principal got that look. Uh-oh.

"But?" he said, cold as ice.

"Well, sir," said Al, "it's Cissie Jackson. We think she's—um—sick. I mean wouldn't it be better if . . . I mean everybody says she's just come out of the hospital and it's a strain for all of us and it must be a lot worse strain for her and maybe it's just a little soon for her to—"

"Sir," I said, "what Coppolino means is, we don't mind integrating blacks with whites, but this isn't racial integration, sir; this is integrating normal people with a filbert. I mean—"

He said, "Gentlemen, it might interest you to know that Miss Cecilia Jackson has higher scores on her IQ tests than the two of you put together. And I am told by the drama department that she has also more talent than the two of you put together. And considering the grades both of you have managed to achieve in the fall term, I'm not at all surprised."

Al said under his breath, "Yeah, and fifty times as many problems."

Well, the principal went on and told us about how we should welcome this chance to work with her because she was so brilliant she was positively a genius, and that as soon as we stopped spreading idiotic rumors, the better chance Miss Jackson would have to adjust to Central, and if he heard anything about our bothering her again or spreading stories about her, both of us were going to get it but good, and maybe we would even be expelled.

And then his voice lost the ice, and he told us about some white cop shooting her pa for no reason at all when she was five, right in front of her, and her pa bleeding into the gutter and dying in little Cissie's lap, and how poor her mother was, and a couple of other awful things that had happened to her, and if *that* wasn't enough to drive anybody crazy—though he said "cause problems," you know—anyhow, by the time he'd finished, I felt like a rat and Coppolino went outside the principal's office, put his face down against the tiles—they always had tiles up as high as you could reach, so they could wash off the graffiti, though we didn't use the word "graffiti" in those days—and he blubbered like a baby.

So we started a Help Cecilia Jackson campaign.

And by God, Milty, could that girl *act!* She wasn't reliable, that was the trouble; one week she'd be in there, working like a dog, voice exercises, gym, fencing, reading Stanislavsky in the cafeteria, gorgeous performances, the next week: nothing. Oh, she was there in the flesh, all right, all eighty-five pounds of her, but she would walk through everything as if her mind was someplace else: technically perfect, emotionally nowhere. I heard later those were also the times when she'd refuse to answer questions in history or geography classes, just fade out and not talk. But when she was concentrating, she could walk onto that stage and take it over as if she owned it. I never saw such a natural. At fifteen! And tiny. I mean not a particularly good voice—though I guess just getting older would've helped that—and a figure that, frankly, Milt, it was the old W.C. Fields joke, two aspirins on an ironing board. And tiny, no real good looks, but my God, you know and I know that doesn't matter if you've got the presence. And she had it to burn. She played the Queen of Sheba once, in a one-act play we put on before a live audience—all right, our parents and the other kids, who else?—and she *was* the role. And another time I saw her do things from Shakespeare. And once, of all things, a lioness in a mime class. She had it all. Real, absolute, pure concentration. And she was smart, too; by then she and Al had become pretty good friends; I once heard her explain to him (that was in the green room the afternoon of the Queen of Sheba thing when she was taking off her makeup with cold cream) just how she'd figured out each bit of business for the character. Then she stuck her whole arm out at me, pointing straight at me as if her arm was a machine gun, and said:

"For you, Mister Jim, let me tell you: the main thing is *belief*!"

It was a funny thing, Milt. She got better and better friends with Al, and when they let me tag along, I felt privileged. He loaned her some of those crazy books of his and I overheard things about her life, bits and pieces. That girl had a mother who was so uptight and so God-fearing and so respectable it was a wonder Cissie could even breathe without asking permission. Her mother wouldn't even let her straighten her hair—not ideological reasons, you understand, not then, but because—get this—*Cissie was too young*. I think her mamma must've been crazier than she was. Course I was a damn stupid kid (who wasn't?) and I really thought all blacks were real loose; they went around snapping their fingers and hanging from chandeliers, you know, all that stuff, dancing and singing. But here was this genius from a family where they wouldn't let her out at night; she wasn't allowed to go to parties or dance or play cards; she couldn't wear makeup or even jewelry. Believe me, I think if anything drove her batty it was being socked over the head so often with a Bible. I guess her imagination just had to find some way out. Her mother, by the way, would've dragged her out of Central High by the hair if she'd found out about the drama classes; we all had to swear to keep that strictly on the q.t. The theater was more sinful and wicked than dancing, I guess.

You know, I think it shocked me. It really did. Al's family was sort-of-nothing-really Catholic and mine was sort-of-nothing Jewish. I'd never met anybody with a mamma like that. I mean she would've beaten Cissie up if Cissie had ever come home with a gold circle pin on that white blouse she wore day in and day out; you remember the kind all the girls wore. And of course there were no horsehair petticoats for Miss Jackson; Miss Jackson wore pleated skirts that were much too short, even for her, and straight skirts that looked faded and all bunched up. For a while I had some vague idea that the short skirts meant she was daring, you know, sexy, but it wasn't that; they were from a much younger cousin, let down. She just couldn't afford her own clothes. I think it was the mamma and the Bible business that finally made me stop seeing Cissie as the Integration Prize Nut we had to be nice to because of the principal or the scared little rabbit who still, by the way, whispered everyplace but in drama class. I just saw Cecilia Jackson plain, I guess, not that it lasted for more than a few minutes, but I knew she was something special. So one day in the hall, going from one class to another, I met her and Al and I said, "Cissie, your name is going to be up there in lights someday. I think you're the best actress I ever met and I just want to say it's a privilege knowing you." And then I swept her a big corny bow, like Errol Flynn.

She looked at Al and Al looked at her, sort of sly. Then she let down her head over her books and giggled. She was so tiny you sometimes wondered how she could drag those books around all day; they hunched her over so.

Al said, "Aw, come on. Let's tell him."

So they told me their big secret. Cissie had a girl cousin named Gloriette, and Gloriette and Cissie together owned an honest-to-God slip for a boat in the marina out in Silverhampton. Each of them paid half the slip fee—which was about two bucks a month then, Milt—you have to remember that a marina then just meant a long wooden dock you could tie your rowboat up to.

"Gloriette's away," said Cissie, in that whisper. "She had to go visit auntie, in Carolina. And mamma's goin' to follow her next week on Sunday."

"So we're going to go out in the boat!" Al finished it for her. "You wanna come?"

"Sunday?"

"Sure, mamma will go to the bus station after church," said Cissie. "That's about one o'clock. Aunt Evelyn comes to take care of me at nine. So we have eight hours."

"And it takes two hours to get there," said Al. "First you take the subway; then you take a bus—"

"Unless we use your car, Jim!" said Cissie, laughing so hard she dropped her books.

"Well, thanks very much!" I said. She scooped them up again and smiled at me. "No, Jim," she said. "We want you to come, anyway. Al never saw the boat yet. Gloriette and me, we call it *My Boat*." Fifteen years old and she knew how to smile at you so's to twist your heart like a pretzel. Or maybe I just thought: what a wicked secret to have! A big sin, I guess, according to her family.

I said, "Sure, I'll drive you. May I ask what kind of boat it is, Miss Jackson?"

"Don't be so *damn'* silly," she said daringly. "I'm Cissie or Cecilia. Silly Jim."

"And as for *My Boat*," she added, "it's a big yacht. Enormous."

I was going to laugh at that, but then I saw she meant it. No, she was just playing. She was smiling wickedly at me again. She said we should meet at the bus stop near her house, and then she went down the tiled hall next to skinny little Al Coppolino, in her old baggy green skirt and her always-the-same white blouse. No beautiful, big white sloppy bobby socks for Miss Jackson; she just wore old loafers coming apart at the seams. She looked different, though: her head was up, her step springy, and she hadn't been whispering.

And then it occurred to me it was the first time I had ever seen her smile or laugh—offstage. Mind you, she cried easily enough, like the time in class she realized from something the teacher had said that Anton Chekhov—you know, the great Russian playwright—was dead. I heard her telling Alan later that she didn't believe it. There were lots of little crazy things like that.

Well, I picked her up Sunday in what was probably the oldest car in the world, even then—not a museum piece, Milty; it'd still be a mess—frankly I was lucky to get it started at all—and when I got to the bus station near Cissie's house in Brooklyn, there she was in her faded, hand-me-down, pleated skirt and that same blouse. I guess little elves named Cecilia Jackson came out of the woodwork every night and washed and ironed it. Funny, she and Al really did make a pair—you know, he was like the Woody Allen of Central High and I think he went in for his crazy books—sure, Milt, *very* crazy in 1952—because otherwise what could a little Italian punk do who was five foot three and so brilliant no other kid could understand half the time what he was talking about? I don't know why I was friends with him; I think it made me feel big, you know, generous and good, like being friends with Cissie. They were almost the same size, waiting there by the bus stop, and I think their heads were in the same place. I know it now. I guess he was just a couple of decades ahead of himself, like his books. And maybe if the civil rights movement had started a few years earlier—

Anyway, we drove out to Silverhampton and it was a nice drive, lots of country, though all flat—in those days there were still truck farms on the Island—and found the marina, which was nothing more than a big old quay, but sound enough; and I parked the car and Al took out a shopping bag Cissie'd been carrying. "Lunch," he said.

My Boat was there, all right, halfway down the dock. Somehow I hadn't expected it would exist, even. It was an old leaky wooden rowboat with only one oar, and there were three inches of bilge in the bottom. On the bow somebody had painted the name "My Boat" shakily in orange paint. *My Boat* was tied to the mooring by a rope about as sturdy as a piece of string. Still, it didn't look like it would sink right away; after all, it'd been sitting there for months, getting rained on, maybe even snowed on, and it was still floating. So I stepped down into it, wishing I'd had the sense to take off my shoes, and started bailing with a tin can I'd brought from the car. Alan and Cissie were taking things out of the bag in the middle of the boat. I guess they were setting out lunch. It was pretty clear that *My Boat* spent most of its time sitting at the dock while Cissie and Gloriette ate lunch and maybe pretended they were on the *Queen Mary*, because neither Alan nor Cissie seemed to notice the missing oar. It was a nice day but in-and-outish; you know, clouds one minute, sun the next, but little fluffy clouds, no sign of rain. I bailed a lot of the gunk out and then moved up into the bow, and as the sun came out I saw that I'd been wrong about the orange paint. It was yellow.

Then I looked closer: it wasn't paint but something set into the side of *My Boat* like the names on people's office doors; I guess I must've not looked too closely the first time. It was a nice, flowing script, a real professional job. Brass, I guess. Not a plate, Milt, kind of—what do they call it, parquet? Intaglio? Each letter was put in separately. Must've been Alan; he had a talent for stuff like that, used to make weird illustrations for his crazy books. I turned around to find Al and Cissie taking a big piece of cheesecloth out of the shopping bag and draping it over high poles that were built into the sides of the boat. They were making a kind of awning. I said:

"Hey, I bet you took that from the theater shop!"

She just smiled.

Al said, "Would you get us some fresh water, Jim?"

"Sure," I said. "Where, up the dock?"

"No, from the bucket. Back in the stern. Cissie says it's marked."

Oh, sure, I thought, sure. Out in the middle of the Pacific we set out our bucket and pray for rain. There was a pail there all right, and somebody had laboriously stenciled "Fresh Water" on it in green paint, sort of smudgy, but that pail was never going to hold anything ever again. It was bone-dry, empty, and so badly rusted that when you held it up to the light, you could see through the bottom in a couple of places. I said, "Cissie, it's empty."

She said, "Look again, Jim."

I said, "But look, Cissie—" and turned the bucket upside-down. Cold water drenched me from my knees to the soles of my shoes.

"See?" she said. "Never empty." I thought: Hell, I didn't look, that's all. Maybe it rained yesterday. Still, a full pail of water is heavy and I had lifted that thing with one finger. I set it down—if it had been full before, it certainly wasn't now—and looked again.

It was full, right to the brim. I dipped my hand into the stuff and drank a little of it: cold and clear as spring water and it smelled—I don't know—of ferns warmed by the sun, of raspberries, of field flowers, of grass. I thought: my God, I'm becoming a filbert myself! And then I turned around and saw that Alan and Cissie had replaced the cheesecloth on the poles with a striped blue-and-white awning, the kind you see in movies about Cleopatra, you know? The stuff they put over her barge to keep the sun off. And Cissie had taken out of her shopping bag something patterned orange-and-green-and-blue and had wrapped it around her old clothes. She had on gold-colored earrings, big hoop things, and a black turban over that funny hair. And she must've put her loafers somewhere because she was barefoot. Then I saw that she had one shoulder bare, too, and I sat down on one of the marble benches of *My Boat* under the awning because I was probably having hallucinations. I mean she hadn't had *time*—and where were her old clothes? I thought to myself that they must've lifted a whole bagful of stuff from the theater shop, like that big old wicked-looking knife she had stuck into her amber-studded leather belt, the hilt all covered with gold and stones: red ones, green ones, and blue ones with little crosses of light winking in them that you couldn't really follow with your eyes. I didn't know what the blue ones were then, but I know now. You don't make star sapphires in a theater shop. Or a ten-inch crescent-shaped steel blade so sharp the sun dazzles you coming off its edge.

I said, "Cissie, you look like the Queen of Sheba."

She smiled. She said to me, "Jim, iss not Shee-bah as in thee Bible, but Saba. Sah-bah. You mus' remember when we meet her."

I thought to myself: Yeah, this is where little old girl genius Cissie Jackson comes to freak out every Sunday. Lost weekend. I figured this was the perfect time to get away, make some excuse, you know, and call her mamma or her auntie, or maybe just the nearest hospital. I mean just for her own sake; Cissie wouldn't hurt anybody because she wasn't mean, not ever. And anyhow she was too little to hurt anyone. I stood up.

Her eyes were level with mine. And she was standing below me.

Al said, "Be careful, Jim. Look again. Always look again." I went back to the stern. There was the bucket that said "Fresh Water," but as I looked the sun came out and I saw I'd been mistaken; it wasn't old rusty galvanized iron with splotchy, green-painted letters.

It was silver, pure silver. It was sitting in a sort of marble well built into the stern, and the letters were jade inlay. It was still full. It would always be full. I looked back at Cissie standing under the blue-and-white-striped silk awning with her star sapphires and emeralds and rubies in her dagger and her funny talk—I know it now, Milt, it was West Indian, but I didn't then—and I knew as sure as if I'd seen it that if I looked at the letters "My Boat" in the sun, they wouldn't be brass but pure gold. And the wood would be ebony. I wasn't even surprised. Although everything had changed, you understand, I'd never seen it change; it was either that I hadn't looked carefully the first time, or I'd made a mistake, or I hadn't noticed something, or I'd just forgotten. Like what I thought had been an old crate in the middle of *My Boat*, which was really the roof of a cabin with little portholes in it, and looking in I saw three bunk beds below, a closet, and a beautiful little galley with a refrigerator and a stove, and off to one side in the sink, where I couldn't really see it clearly, a bottle with a napkin around its neck, sticking up from an ice bucket full of crushed ice, just like an old Fred Astaire–Ginger Rogers movie. And the whole inside of the cabin was paneled in teakwood.

Cissie said, "No, Jim. Is not teak. Is cedar, from Lebanon. You see now why I cannot take seriously in this school this nonsense about places and where they are and what happen in them. Crude oil in Lebanon! It is cedar they have. And ivory. I have been there many, many time. I have talk' with the wise Solomon. I have been at court of Queen of Saba and have made eternal treaty with the Knossos women, the people of the double ax which is waxing and waning moon together. I have visit Akhnaton and Nofretari, and have seen great kings at Benin and at Dar. I even go to Atlantis, where the Royal Couple teach me many things. The priest and priestess, they show me how to make *My Boat* go anywhere I like, even under the sea. Oh, we have·manhy improvin' chats upon roof of Pahlahss at dusk!"

It was real. It was all real. She was not fifteen, Milt. She sat in the bow at the controls of *My Boat*, and there were as many dials and toggles and buttons and switches and gauges on that thing as on a B-57. And she was at least ten years older. Al Coppolino, too, he looked like a picture I'd seen in a history book of Sir Francis Drake, and he had long hair and a little pointy beard. He was dressed like Drake, except for the ruff, with rubies in his ears and rings all over his fingers, and he, too, was no seventeen-year-old. He had a faint scar running from his left temple at the hairline down past his eye to his cheekbone. I could also see that under her turban Cissie's hair was braided in some very fancy way. I've seen it since. Oh, long before everybody was doing "corn rows." I saw it at the Metropolitan Museum, in silver face-mask sculptures from the city of Benin, in Africa. Old, Milt, centuries old.

Al said, "I know of other places, Princess. I can show them to you. Oh, let us go to Ooth-Nargai and Celephais the Fair, and Kadath in the Cold Waste—it's a fearful place, Jim, but we need not be afraid—and then we will go to the city of Ulthar, where is the very fortunate and lovely law that no man or woman may kill or annoy a cat."

"The Atlanteans," said Cissie in a deep sweet voice, "they pro-mise' that next time they show me not jus' how to go undersea. They say if you think hard, if you fix much, if you believe, then can make My Boat go straight up. Into the stars, Jim!"

Al Coppolino was chanting names under his breath: Cathuria, Sona-Nyl, Thalarion, Zar, Baharna, Nir, Oriab. All out of those books of his.

Cissie said, "Before you come with us, you must do one last thing, Jim. Untie the rope."

So I climbed down My Boat's ladder onto the quay and undid the braided gold rope that was fastened to the slip. Gold and silk inter-twined, Milt; it rippled through my hand as if it were alive; I know the hard, slippery feel of silk. I was thinking of Atlantis and Celephais and going up into the stars, and all of it was mixed up in my head with the senior prom and college, because I had been lucky enough to be accepted by The-College-Of-My-Choice, and what a future I'd have as a lawyer, a corporation lawyer, after be-ing a big gridiron star, of course. Those were my plans in the old days. Dead certainties every one, right? Versus a thirty-five-foot yacht that would've made John D. Rockefeller turn green with envy and places in the world where nobody'd ever been and nobody'd ever go again. Cissie and Al stood on deck above me, the both of them looking like something out of a movie—beautiful and dangerous and very strange—and suddenly I knew I didn't want to go. Part of it was the absolute certainty that if I ever offended Cissie in any way—I don't mean just a quarrel or disagreement or something you'd get the sulks about, but a real bone-deep kind of offense—I'd suddenly find myself in a leaky rowboat with only one oar in the middle of the Pacific Ocean. Or maybe just tied up at the

dock at Silverhampton; Cissie wasn't mean. At least I hoped so. I just—I guess I didn't feel *good* enough to go. And there was something about their faces, too, as if over both of them, but especially over Cissie's, like clouds, like veils, there swam other faces, other expressions, other souls, other pasts and futures, and other kinds of knowledge, all of them shifting like a heat mirage over an asphalt road on a hot day.

I didn't want that knowledge, Milt. I didn't want to go that deep. It was the kind of thing most seventeen-year-olds don't learn for years: Beauty. Despair. Mortality. Compassion. Pain.

And I was still looking up at them, watching the breeze fill out Al Coppolino's plum-colored velvet cloak and shine on his silver-and-black doublet, when a big, heavy, hard, fat hand clamped down on my shoulder and a big, fat, nasty, heavy Southern voice said:

"Hey, boy, you got no permit for this slip! What's that rowboat doin' out there? And what's yo' name?"

So I turned and found myself looking into the face of the great-granddaddy of all Southern red-neck sheriffs: face like a bulldog with jowls to match, and sunburnt red, and fat as a pig, and mountain-mean. I said, "Sir?"—every high-school kid could say that in his sleep in those days—and then we turned towards the bay, me saying, "What boat, sir?" and the cop saying just, "What the—"

Because there was nothing there. *My Boat* was gone. There was only a blue shimmering stretch of bay. They weren't out farther and they weren't around the other side of the dock—the cop and I both ran around—and by the time I had presence of mind enough to look up at the sky—

Nothing. A seagull. A cloud. A plane out of Idlewild. Besides, hadn't Cissie said she didn't yet know how to go straight up into the stars?

No, nobody ever saw *My Boat* again. Or Miss Cecilia Jackson, complete nut and girl genius, either. Her mamma came to school and I was called into the principal's office. I told them a cooked-up story, the one I'd been going to tell the cop: that they'd said they were just going to row around the dock and come back, and I'd left to see if the car was okay in the parking lot, and when I came back, they were gone. For some crazy reason I *still* thought Cissie's mamma would look like Aunt Jemima, but she was a thin little woman, very like her daughter, and as nervous and uptight as I ever saw: a tiny lady in a much-pressed, but very clean, gray business suit, like a teacher's, you know, worn-out shoes, a blouse with a white frill at the neck, a straw hat with a white band, and proper white gloves. I think Cissie knew what I expected her mamma to be and what a damned fool I was, even considering your run-of-the-mill, seventeen-year-old white liberal racist, and that's why she didn't take me along.

The cop? He followed me to my car, and by the time I got there—I was sweating and crazy scared—

He was gone, too. Vanished.

I think Cissie created him. Just for a joke.

So Cissie never came back. And I couldn't convince Mrs. Jackson that Alan Coppolino, boy rapist, hadn't carried her daughter off to some lonely place and murdered her. I tried and tried, but Mrs. Jackson would never believe me.

It turned out there was no Cousin Gloriette.

Alan? Oh, he came back. But it took him a while. A long, long while. I saw him yesterday, Milt, on the Brooklyn subway. A skinny, short guy with ears that stuck out, still wearing the sport shirt and pants he'd started out in, that Sunday more than twenty years ago, and with the real 1950s haircut nobody would wear today. Quite a few people were staring at him, in fact.

The thing is, Milt, *he was still seventeen.*

No, I know it wasn't some other kid. Because he was waving at me and smiling fit to beat the band. And when I got out with him at his old stop, he started asking after everybody in Central High just as if it had been a week later, or maybe only a day. Though when I asked him where the hell he'd been for twenty years, he wouldn't tell me. He only said he'd forgotten something. So we went up five flights to his old apartment, the way we used to after school for a couple of hours before his mom and dad came home from work. He had the old key in his pocket. And it was just the same, Milt: the gas refrigerator, the exposed pipes under the sink, the summer slip-covers nobody uses anymore, the winter drapes put away, the valance over the window muffled in a sheet, the bare parquet floors, and the old linoleum in the kitchen. Every time I'd ask him a question, he'd only smile. He knew me, though, because he called me by name a couple of times. I said, "How'd you recognize me?" and he said, "Recognize? You haven't changed." Haven't changed, my God. Then I said, "Look, Alan, what did you come back for?" and with a grin just like Cissie's, he said, "*The Necronomicon* by the mad Arab, Abdul Alhazred, what else?" but I saw the book he took with him and it was a different one. He was careful to get just the right one, looked through every shelf in the bookcase in his bedroom. There were still college banners all over the walls of his room. I know the book now, by the way; it was the one you wanted to make into a quick script last year for the guy who does the Poe movies, only I *told* you it was all special effects and animation: exotic islands, strange worlds, and the monsters' costumes alone—sure, H. P. Lovecraft. *The Dream-Quest of Unknown Kadath*. He didn't say a word after that. Just walked down the five flights with me behind him and then along the old block to the nearest subway station, but of course by the time I reached the bottom of the subway steps, he wasn't there.

His apartment? You'll never find it. When I raced back up, even the house was gone. More than that, Milt, the street is gone; the address doesn't exist anymore; it's all part of the new expressway now.

Which is why I called you. My God, I had to tell somebody! By now those two psychiatric cases are voyaging around between the stars to Ulthar and Ooth-Nargai and Dylath-Leen—

But they're not psychiatric cases. *It really happened.*

So if they're not psychiatric cases, what does that make you and me? Blind men?

I'll tell you something else, Milt: meeting Al reminded me of what Cissie once said before the whole thing with *My Boat* but after we'd become friends enough for me to ask her what had brought her out of the hospital. I didn't ask it like that and she didn't answer it like that, but what it boiled down to was that sooner or later, at every place she visited, she'd meet a bleeding man with wounds in his hands and feet who would tell her, "Cissie, go back, you're needed; Cissie, go back, you're needed." I was fool enough to ask her if he was a white man or a black man. She just glared at me and walked away. Now wounds in the hands and feet, you don't have to look far to tell what that means to a Christian

Bible-raised girl. What I wonder is: will she meet Him again, out there among the stars? If things get bad enough for black power or women's liberation, or even for people who write crazy books, I don't know what, will *My Boat* materialize over Times Square or Harlem or East New York with an Ethiopian warrior-queen in it and Sir Francis Drake Coppolino, and God-only-knows-what kind of weapons from the lost science of Atlantis? I tell you, I wouldn't be surprised. I really wouldn't. I only hope He—or Cissie's idea of Him—decides that things are still okay, and they can go on visiting all those places in Al Coppolino's book. I tell you, I hope that book is a *long* book.

Still, if I could do it again . . .

Milt, it is not a story. *It happened.* For instance, tell me one thing, how did she know the name Nofretari? That's the Egyptian Queen Nerfertiti, that's how we all learned it, but how could she know the real name decades, literally decades, before anybody else? And Saba? That's real, too. And Benin? We didn't have any courses in African History in Central High, not in 1952! And what about the double-headed ax of the Cretans at Knossos? Sure, we read about Crete in high school, but nothing in our history books ever told us about the matriarchy or the labrys, that's the name of the ax. Milt, I tell you, there is even a women's lib bookstore in Manhattan *called—*

Have it your own way.

Oh, sure. She wasn't black; she was green. It'd make a great TV show. Green, blue, and rainbow-colored. I'm sorry, Milty, I know you're my agent and you've done a lot of work for me and I haven't sold much lately. I've been reading. No, nothing you'd like: existentialism, history, Marxism, some Eastern stuff—

Sorry, Milt, but we writers do read every once in a while. It's this little vice we have. I've been trying to dig deep, like Al Coppolino, though maybe in a different way.

Okay, so you want to have this Martian, who wants to invade Earth, so he turns himself into a beautiful tanned girl with long, straight blonde hair, right? And becomes a high-school student in a rich school in Westchester. And this beautiful blonde girl Martian has to get into all the local organizations like the women's consciousness-raising groups and the encounter therapy stuff and the cheerleaders and the kids who push dope, so he—she, rather—can learn about the Earth mentality. Yeah. And of course she has to seduce the principal and the coach and all the big men on campus, so we can make it into a series, even a sitcom maybe; each week this Martian falls in love with an Earth man or she tries to do something to destroy Earth or blow up something, using Central High for a base. Can I use it? Sure I can! It's beautiful. It's right in my line. I can work in everything I just told you. Cissie was right not to take me along; I've got spaghetti where my backbone should be.

Nothing. I didn't say anything. Sure. It's a great idea. Even if we only get a pilot out of it.

No, Milt, honestly, I really think it has this fantastic spark. A real touch of genius. It'll sell like crazy. Yeah, I can manage an idea sheet by Monday. Sure. "The Beautiful Menace from Mars"? Uh-huh. Absolutely. It's got sex, it's got danger, comedy, everything; we could branch out into the lives of the teachers, the principal, the other kids' parents. Bring in contemporary problems like drug abuse. Sure. Another Peyton Place. I'll even move to the West Coast again. You are a genius.

Oh, my God.

Nothing. Keep on talking. It's just—see that little skinny kid in the next booth down? The one with the stuck-out ears and the old-fashioned haircut? You don't? Well, I think you're just not looking properly, Milt. Actually I don't think I was, either; he must be one of the Met extras, you know, they come out sometimes during the intermission: all that Elizabethan stuff, the plum-colored cloak, the calf-high boots, the silver-and-black. As a matter of fact, I just remembered—the Met moved uptown a couple of years ago, so he couldn't be dressed like that, could he?

You still can't see him? I'm not surprised. The light's very bad in here. Listen, he's an old friend—I mean he's the son of an old friend—I better go over and say hello, I won't be a minute.

Milt, this young man is important! I mean he's connected with somebody very important. Who? One of the biggest and best producers in the world, that's who! He—uh—they—wanted me to—you might call it do a script for them, yeah. I didn't want to at the time, but—

No, no, you stay right here. I'll just sort of lean over and say hello. You keep on talking about the Beautiful Menace from Mars; I can listen from there; I'll just tell him they can have me if they want me.

Your ten percent? Of course you'll get your ten percent. You're my agent, aren't you? Why, if it wasn't for you, I just possibly might not have— Sure, you'll get your ten percent. Spend it on anything you like: ivory, apes, peacocks, spices, and Lebanese cedarwood!

All you have to do is collect it.

But keep on talking, Milty, won't you? Somehow I want to go over to the next booth with the sound of your voice in my ears. Those beautiful ideas. So original. So creative. So true. Just what the public wants. Of course there's a difference in the way people perceive things, and you and I, I think we perceive them differently, you know? Which is why you are a respected, successful agent and I—well, let's skip it. It wouldn't be complimentary to either of us.

Huh? Oh, nothing. I didn't say anything. I'm listening. Over my shoulder. Just keep on talking while I say hello and my deepest and most abject apologies, Sir Alan Coppolino. Heard the name before, Milt? No? I'm not surprised.

You just keep on talking . . . .

USEFUL PHRASES
FOR THE TOURIST

THE LOCRINE: peninsula and surrounding regions.
High Lokrinnen.
X 437894 = II
Reasonably Earth-like (see companion audio tapes and transliterations)

For physiology, ecology, religion, and customs, Wu and Fabricant, Prague, 2355, Vol. 2 *The Locrine, Useful Knowledge for the Tourist*, q.v.

AT THE HOTEL:
That is my companion. It is not intended as a tip.
I will call the manager.
This cannot be my room because I cannot breathe ammonia.
I will be most comfortable between temperatures of 290 and 303 degrees Kelvin.
Waitress, this meal is still alive.

AT THE PARTY:
Is that you?
Is that all of you? How much (many) of you is (are) there?

I am happy to meet your clone.

Interstellar amity demands that we make some physical display at this point, but I beg to be excused.

Are you toxic?

Are you edible? I am not edible.

We humans do not regenerate.

My companion is not edible.

That is my ear.

I am toxic.

Is that how you copulate?

Is this intended to be erotic?

Thank you very much.

Please explain.

Do you turn colors?

Are you pregnant?

I shall leave the room.

Can't we just be friends?

Take me to the Earth Consulate immediately.

Although I am very flattered by your kind offer, I cannot accompany you to the mating pits, as I am viviparous.

IN THE HOSPITAL:

No!

My eating orifice is not at that end of my body.

I would rather do it myself.

Please do not let the atmosphere in (out) as I will be most uncomfortable.

I do not eat lead.

Placing the thermometer there will yield little or no useful information.

SIGHTSEEING:

You are not my guide. My guide was bipedal.

We Earth people do not do that.

Oh, what a jolly fine natatorium (mating perch, arranged spectacle, involuntary phenomenon)!

At what hour does the lovelorn princess fling herself into the flaming volcano? May we participate?

That is not demonstrable.

That is hardly likely.
That is ridiculous.
I have seen much better examples of that.
Please direct me to the nearest sentient mammal.
Take me to the Earth Consulate without delay.

AT THE THEATER:
Is that amusing?
I am sorry; I did not mean to be offensive.
I did not intend to sit on you. I did not realize that you were in this
    seat.
Could you deform yourself a little lower?
My eyes are sensitive only to light of the wavelengths 3000–7000 Å.
Am I imagining this?
Am I supposed to imagine this?
Should I be perturbed by the water on the floor?
Where is the exit?
Help!
This is great art.
My religious convictions prevent me from joining in the perfor-
    mance.
I do not feel well.
I feel very sick.
I do not eat living food.
Is this supposed to be erotic?
May I take this home with me?
Is this part of the performance?
Stop touching me.
Sir or madam, that is mine. (extrinsic)
Sir or madam, that is mine. (intrinsic)
I wish to visit the waste-reclamation units.
Have you finished?
May I begin?
You are in my way.
Under no circumstances.
If you do not stop that, I will call the attendant. That is forbidden
    by my religion.
Sir or madam, this is a private unit.
Sir and madam, this is a private unit.

COMPLIMENTS:
You are more than before.
Your hair is false.
If you uncover your feet, I will faint.
There is no room.
You will undoubtedly be here tomorrow.

INSULTS:
You are just the same.
There are more of you than previously.
Your fingers are showing.
How clean you are!
You are clean, but animated.

GENERAL:
Take me to the Earth Consulate.
Direct me to the Earth Consulate.
The Earth Consulate will hear of this.
This is no way to treat a visitor.
Please direct me to my hotel.
At what time does the moon rise? Is there a moon?
Is it a full moon? Take me to the Earth Consulate immediately.
May I have the second volume of Wu and Fabricant, entitled *Physiology, Ecology, Religion, and Customs of the Locrine?* Price is no object.
Something has just gone amiss with my vehicle.
I am dying.

corruption

I

 Look—four black chess pieces, each rising fifty storeys out of a sea of grass, each windowless under the perpetually moving grey sky, each grey-slick with unceasing rain.

Four hundred feet down, the towers' foundations grip one another before they sink into the rock, the one spine of the one continent on Outpost. Travelers enter below the poisonous pea-soup swamp through an elaborate system of locks, germicidal sprays, protective uniforms, the exchange of atmospheres. There are cyanogens in the grass and water, airborne and waterborne microorganisms that are lethal. No one inside the towers ever sees daylight, or goes outside to repair any piece of equipment, or watches water falling from the sky. No one witnesses the seasons' only drama: an increase of five minutes in the eleven-hour day up to the summer solstice, a decrease of five minutes during the rest of the sixty-week year. Television remotes rust, the towers' metal plating becomes corroded. Outpost on Outpost.

It won't last long.
It'll last long enough.
And Alpha is pretending to be one of them.

II

Look—Alpha in a room inside Outpost. The walls are bright
yellow, the desk bright green, the curtains bright blue. Everything's
hard and slick. The window takes its scene from a television
remote: moving clouds, grey rain, expanse of grass—these are five
seconds in the past. The lag: time it takes to make a master tape for
every window in the section. Some greyness has got into the inside
air. On the desk, Alpha's possessions: razor, fake nameplate,
deodorizer, clothes (plastic, bright orange). He is more intelligent
than anyone here. He will run the place in ten years. The man in the
room on the chair (bright green, hard and slick) takes writing
materials from the top drawer of the desk. Not thinking, he writes:

> servant
> spy
> bondman
> ruler
> bondservant
> slave
> madman

Crumples the sheet of plastic, melts it on a grill set in the corner of
the desk. If you were blind, you would certainly feel this: the flare
of heat, the acrid smell. Though you could not tell the desk from
the wall. Alpha will be all right because he (like his people)
understands very quickly what is expected of him in personal in-
teractions. He'll use others as mirrors. He thinks of technical matters and watches the false window: a stately caravan of clouds, un-
changing grey rain, the ocean of grass. Not an outside wall.

(A sensation of cumulative blindness. It'll never catch up.)

III

Look—a large room. This is where they eat. The men's clothing is
bright yellow, bright blue, bright orange, everything to lift the

spirits. The walls are wood color. Unless you are an authority (they eat upstairs) you take your tray, go through the line, and select your food by color, all very brilliant to the eye; then, when you're finished, you take it back to a hole in the wall where it goes to be steam-sterilized, burned, washed. The food on Outpost is not good; it comes from off-planet: boiled, irradiated, freeze-dried, doctored, sealed. Alpha sits, enjoying the muted hum of talk that tells you the size of the room (he is not blind, but has—had—a blind friend) and making mashed food and baked food into shapes, for some enjoyment. He remembers the different-colored walls that indicate the different floors in Outpost: brown for gregariousness, yellow for brainwork, green for handwork, blue for authority, grey for planning, white for transport. Red for something else? One of his mirrors comes up to talk, a great glowing flare of blue, sits down opposite. Smiles. They shake hands. The pleasant shock of touching skin, of seeing a human face: long and thin, furrowed, flaking, old. The handclasp disinfected by an aggressive squeeze.

"New here?"

"Very."

"Wish you were upstairs?"

"Food's the same," says Alpha.

The conversation dies. Alpha doesn't trouble to keep it up. Everyone knows that Outpost is a good place, a very important place to be. The large false window across the room shows what has happened.

"Like it here?"

Alpha takes his first risk. Playing at arrogance, he tells the truth: "No."

It is the right, the blazingly right, the daring, ambitious, dangerous, good thing to do. Perhaps no one on Outpost credits the truth. That makes it simpler for him. Across the room the outside scene forms and re-forms: clouds, rain, a field of alien wheat.

The other says, "You'll soon stop watching that."

IV

Eating's petty. Who cares about it? Alpha sleeps in a bed that clings and wrinkles under him, nonabsorbent, too hot or too cold. When he bathes he can never get wet all over. Alpha the technician loves his work, loves planning, loves designs, lives for his work. (You can't see that; it's just a man sitting alone in a room.) Though there are lovely things on Outpost: curtains of glass beads like waterfalls, flashing and revolving lights, slides of mountains and seas projected with the immaterial, radiant solidity of dreams. There are patterns so intricate under a hard surface that you almost think you can feel them, there are kaleidoscopes, there are drugs for which people save up their privileges (to sunlamps, mineral water, leisure, even sex).

No paper.

No wood.

No plush.

No straw.

No fur.

No crystals.

No stone. (Heavy, veins, translucency, unevenness.)

No velvet skin, no body heat, no touch. For weeks he dreams of lions' manes, Persian kittens who claw. Feels his own skin, the wedges of soap and hair left in his razor, the articulation of his toes, his toe- and fingernails, the way his kneecaps slide. His hands dislike touching anything else. His own tears, reassuring him at night, his own semen. Crazy plans for saving his cast-off flakes of skin, his shit. But where? He keeps careful records of Outpost's descent into winter: 1.43 seconds a day, though there's no visible sun; the day dims vaguely into night.

He opaques his false windows. Many do, here. He has at least fifteen years to go because seniority will put him in a position to do damage, even if he doesn't rise. He must never talk to his own people, who are far away. In fifteen years they'll come for him.

Don't touch.

V

Look—a red room. Red is for sex. Alpha's hired some sex. There are no women on Outpost (luxury!), but Alpha doesn't prefer one way or the other. He avoids memories of his own people. In a small room with a padded floor and mirrors on the ceiling; he could've rented 3-D pictures. There are pillows on the floor: silky, shaggy, coarse. In the wall a revolving platform presents a young man dressed in a black mask, genitals jouncing as he walks into the room. Yellow head hair, white skin, dark body hair. Alpha is affected by the presentation of an entire uncovered human body in this dead place, the movement of the chest and belly in breathing, the muscles down the legs in walking, the slight stir of the fingers. Too beautiful. The sex gets down on hands and knees. Alpha, kneeling also, prepares to pull him down, embrace him, wrestle with him body to body, straddle him. First he runs the palms of his hands down the back of the shimmering mirage: again, again, again, again.

Is made aware by the sudden turning of the masked head—lily on a stalk—that this is not the right thing.

"Hurry up, can't you?"

The mask—twisted about—looks at him.

The sex holds its sex up out of the way with one hand, for its own comfort. Shoulder braced against the padded wall. Rather tired. He gets into position, spreads the cheeks, pushes in, grasps the other man by the thighs, his erection going half into his hands. Starving all over. He withdraws and stealthily twists body to body, slaps the other, pushes his face into the floor, twists his wrists, pretends to hit him, smuggles an embrace, uses his elbows on the back beneath him, groans, almost bursts between the passive, real thighs, comes over a pillow. The other man sits up, fingering his bruises. He says: "You should've told me. You owe extra." And pointing to the spoilt pillow:

"You'll have to replace that."

VI

Look—happy Alpha is walking along a green catwalk, asking questions of machines which link towers to towers to outside to below: eyes, ears, power, remote manipulators, light, air, water. Happier Alpha. Another green man is with him, checking that he checks properly. There are standard questions. Alpha's mirror says, startled, "Stop that!"

"Get away." Alpha is asking his own questions, just for fun.

"What is the purpose of life?"

Irrelevant. Cancel. Ready.
"Am I happy?"
Irrelevant. Cancel. Ready.
"It falleth as the gentle rain from Heaven."
It Query. What Query.
"Cancel rain distillation."
Interdict.
"Cancel air decontamination."
Interdict.
"Kill us."
Interdict.
There's a bit of a brawl on the catwalk. Laughing, catches the other green man a terrific openhanded slap across the face. Trips him up and kicks him repeatedly. In his own country such training is a matter for embarrassment. Alpha twists the man's right arm back and up—dislocating it—vehemently bangs the man's face against the patterned green fake tessellated floor. A gush of red. Gets up and reports himself to the bank of keys, smiling, sitting before it like a pianist. Asks the incidence of such events—common. He erases his request, which action should not be possible, but he can. Adds:
"I enjoy it. Should I enjoy it?"
It Query. What Query.
"Guess."
Irrelevant. Cancel. Ready.
The red man begins to stir. Alpha types:
"I'm afraid you people know what you're doing."
He adds:
"Correction. You know what you're doing."
Irrelevant. Cancel. Ready.
He adds:
"Correction. I'm just afraid."
Irrelevant. Cancel. Ready.

VII

Alpha is now a blue man. He does nothing but work. In front of his full-length concave mirror, a whim he's been able to have made for him after only eighteen months' advancement, is an upside-down

Alpha, radiant in blue, extending a hand from the virtual image that hangs in front of the glass. His coverall is the blue of winter twilights, dreams, unopened rooms, endless possibility. He owns a bath now but prefers the common man's asceticism: a nozzle with driving fog that uses only a few pints of water at a time. One does not feel it as water. He has begun to learn isometrics because there's so little room on Outpost. Soon he will wear a protective suit inside a sealed land vehicle shot like a bullet into Outpost's poisonous sea of grass. Such vehicles have television remotes, not windows. It will be the summer solstice: wild wheat, rain, perpetually moving clouds. He will see—briefly—the four blank chess pieces covered with rain before the land turtle bores down into the swamp to reenter Outpost from below.

He'll dream about it for weeks.

Then he'll forget it.

VIII

Look—Alpha among his peers, sitting around the table. Blue. Blue. Blue. Robes the color of gas flames. He is the only computer expert there and works harder than anybody else. They know this. The table is covered with a veneer made of pressed sawdust; there's also an aluminum pitcher of cold water on the tabletop. Temperature is the luxury, not metal.

A Blue says, "We are committed to standards of excellence." The plastic drapes absorb the sound; the blue ceiling kills it. It goes round the table: *We are committed to excellence. Standards of excellence must be our goal. We must press forward ever to our goal of excellence. Excellence is the goal to which we are committed. We are totally committed to attaining total excellence. Excellence and pure excellence are what we must attain. Our standards of excellence must never falter, come what may. Excellence first, last, and always. The very reason for our presence here is the maintaining of excellence. It is excellence for which we have been sent here and we must labor to attain it.*

Alpha says, "We are committed to excellence." He always echoes too closely. He's often been demoted but doesn't seem to mind, so he's not looked on as a threat. He would like to take his shoes off, though the grittiness of the blue rug would be unpleasant. The excellence talk is about a remote manipulator which is beginning to rust badly and which must be repaired from within.

"Impossible," says Alpha. A great assault on him. But he always keeps his word. He never says, *Our standards require that we make certain sacrifices*— "It'll cost."

"Standards—"

"What we are talking about," says Alpha unforgivably, "is not a roof-scanner or a television recontrol lag; it's the most vulnerable point in the air filtration system. It's out, we're out. You can plot that as beautifully as you like on the machines, but what good's a machine analogue when the feedback's broken down? Changing the numbers doesn't change the rust. Do you want spores in your lungs?"

"Your job—" says one Blue.

"It can't be done."

More fuss.

"All right," he says, "all right. We can cannibalize the mole equipment, send out two men in decontamination suits. But those rigs aren't built for light stuff: fluff and gases."

"Standards—" says two Blue.

"The suits will have to go, after. Acid. Burning. Not reliable."

"And the personnel?" (six Blue)

"Same."

"No need to bruit it about," says eight Blue.

Alpha says, leaning forward intently, fingertips together, "I'll need extra programming time on the interhookup. I'll need a staff of four. I'll need free materials requisitions quickly, no red tape, no signatures. I'll need a machine liaison with the sub-subbasement people. I'll need two moles—no, three—and I'll want the suits and I'll want the men." He's doodling on the pad in front of him. Nothing interesting. Just dates. Numbers of years.

"For the work?"

"For the preliminary models," says Alpha.

He adds, characteristically, "Don't *worry*." Smiling. How lucky they are to have an eccentric who knows how to work. He concentrates on looking bored while they discuss what is called internal public relations: i.e. how to kill four men without anybody knowing. Suddenly he says, "I'll need a private holograph projector."

"For—?"

"For myself. I told you it would cost." The touch of arrogance has done it again, relieved him as the meeting breaks up, that frightening time when work and silence aren't enough. He studies his shadows, aware of his own observational lag, always a little slow, a little too literal. He points to the pad in front of him:

"That's the roof scanner in its analogic form, in numbers. That's the incipient filtration break. That's the plot down from the roof face, in numbers. That's the computer linkup, by analogy." He wishes them all Outside. He crumples what he's written and incinerates it in the convenient (tiny) oven of bubbled glass set in the corner of the table. A rug that would grate on your bare feet. There for anyone to read (though they don't know how), for any inner-room Eye to scan, for the table itself to sense by pressure (if there's anything built into it or under it), there in ForTrol, LogLan, AlGol, InterLing, six other computer languages:

COME HOME
COME HOME
COME HOME
COME HOME
TAKE ME HOME

IX

What bothers Alpha mildly at times: he can't really remember the faces or names of the people who are going to rescue him. Maybe it doesn't matter. He wonders which of his possessions to take with him: The vacuum shaver? The holograph projector? The fog shower? The concave mirror? His small library of slides made from abstract designs refracted through the lenses of a teleidoscope? His back vibrator? The computer printout plans which tell where everything in Outpost is?

He decides finally that he will, of course, take them all. He feels a lot better.

X

Look—here's Alpha walking down the narrow aisles of the library. It's filled with blueprints and instructions about Outpost. The floors and shelves are painted yellow (for brainwork), and it's the only place one can be alone. He reads much more about Outpost than he has to. He used to like the blueprints better than the scanners, but now he prefers the scanners; they're easier. He looks up, and there at the end of the narrow aisle is a young man, a nobody in orange. Alpha's heard of such assignations, such approaches, doesn't believe them.

"You have business?"

Orange shakes its head. (Alpha might be tempted; he might betray things; he might talk.)

It stands there, a face on top of clothes.

(He might wake up. He might feel. He might be touched.)

"Please—!" says the face, wet on the cheeks, a hoarse croak trying to be seductive but not knowing how.

Alpha says mildly, "I will report you. Go away," and goes back to his scanning. Not that he would; nobody ever does. Would he even be believed? He doesn't know.

It's all nonsense.

He forgets it.

XI

Alpha dreamed. It was all right. He was going to be rescued. Two young people from home, Quadrus and Sola, walked through the door from the red room. He knew them instantly. Quadrus is the spatial expert; he knows architecture, human behavior in human-built habitations, how not to get lost anywhere, ever, what the arrangements of halls and rooms indicates, how life-support machinery betrays its presence, what levels mean in buildings and how to read them, what signs mean and only pretend to mean, what the difference of the width of a wall can lead to when it is no wider than your thumbnail.

Sola is the bomb expert. Blind from birth, she wears all over her white clothes little round dots of metal which are both visual receivers and radar scanners. Sola lacks the nerves leading to the visual centers of her brain; thus it isn't possible merely to cue her prosthetics into normal sight. Sola's "map" of the world (which is largely supersonic and in the near infrared) is tactile; she "sees" through hundreds of thousands of sharp metal points pressed in a continuous tactile whispering on the skin of her trunk. To her every surface in Alpha's room, like every interior in Outpost (save a few that are warmer than the rest), is the same color.

He wakes up. There they are. They're real. Their skins are dark and flaking as if they'd been made out of leather. Quadrus, with his white chin-stubble, is dressed as he used to be twenty years ago when he went on geology hikes, just wandered off for weeks at a time in his khaki shorts, khaki shirts, high boots (for snakes), all hung about with cooking things, compass, and geologists' tools. He still wears his thick rimless spectacles, and the peculiar ancient crumpled cap with its visor. Sola, grown fat, smiles and shows discolored teeth, her hair like grey straw. A small egg-shaped machine in her left hand reads colors for her. They must have come through the roof, bringing spores and disease with them; poisonous grass stems ride on Quadrus's hair, on the edge of Sola's robe. They have developed immunizations, antitoxins. Alpha has spent the past two years wiring through the computer a destruct system attached to Outpost's fissionables; it was to have a quarter-hour delay. That was the plan.

He thinks: *There's no delay.*

A voice—trembling as in Alpha's dreams but more rusty, more weak, Quadrus's voice—says, "Don't you want to come home?"

It would hurt their feelings to answer. It wouldn't be polite.

He averts his eyes.

Weeping as easily as ever, a joke to others but a great practical inconvenience to him ("I have to wipe my glasses!"), Quadrus drops on the bed that stupid canvas bag just like the one he used to take on hikes. Maybe the same one. Alpha watches not him but Sola, knowing what she can do with what else she carries. He remembers that Sola and he were lovers somewhere, sometime; the memory has no content, only the knowledge that it was so. He can't remember when or where. He can't remember that other world at all.

A voice—somebody's, not his—cries, "I want to stay!"

A voice—somebody's, not his—cries, "I like it here!"

He draws back his hand—

Oh, they are filthy! They have no form, no feeling for the right thing. Ugly, ugly people. They are spies and intruders, come twenty years too late to take from him everything he cares for, to rob him—

—pushes the—

To kiss?—to drug?—Quadrus moves, and Sola (lumbering as she is) likewise—and for a moment he sees them as beautiful and scarred, like old trees, what he has always needed: like him, helpless, human, and free.

Then fat Sola knocks his arm away, and as he slams the heel of his left hand up against her nose, which kills her, driving splinters of bone into that brain she has never been able to use for real seeing (pity), he pushes the alarm button with his insulted right arm. He has lied to himself. There's a very short delay. The system is keyed to the window replication: five seconds. He knows they have ruined Outpost anyway. He holds Sola's gun on Quadrus and says very rapidly twenty-four words before Outpost blows sky-high from the tube-arrival system set four hundred feet down in the rock to the remote manipulator on the roof, the one that was beginning to weaken badly but which will never (fortunately or unfortunately) be fixed now.

Outpost on Outpost no longer exists.

They'll find others.

(Alpha's people will colonize, after the crater has turned to steaming mud, after the swamp currents disperse and dilute the radioactive wastes, after the grasses begin to reinvade.

(Arriving in their twos and threes, their tribes and families, immune to spores and microscopic life, casually careful about poisons, they will have a lovely idea: three heroes caught in flight. A bronze statue. A legend. A fairy tale for children. Not bad in its way, as Outpost is not bad once the other Outpost is gone: the clouds change endlessly, the soft rain sweeps across the wheat, the grasses bloom and seed and fall, all in the same season.)

What Alpha said, before the final destruction:

"You don't understand, it's because they don't feed you properly.

"They give you so little and it's all for the eyes.

"*They starve you. . . .* "

Tⱨere is another shore, you know, upon the other side

Fanny Kemble, the dead actress, looked very much like the *Inglese* who came to the American Bar every night in Rome to mingle with the tourists. Meeting her was a little like falling asleep; you never saw her come in. The proprietor would lift his head and there she would be, listening to the English people, with her head·cocked to one side and a dreamy smile on her face. It was always clear that she had been there for twenty or thirty minutes. She never stayed long with one group but would listen and nod and play with her fair hair, always in the same dress, winter or summer. Perhaps she had left her coat with the hatcheck girl, who was also English. One night the proprietor had asked her her name.

"Jane," she had answered, backing off a little and smiling. She had a trick of attending sideways to what people said. "You make your home here in Rome, Signorina Jane?" he had inquired politely in Italian but she had only continued to smile, curling a lock of hair between her fingers. He then said, in English, "Do you like Rome?" She nodded quickly.

"Oh, yes," she said, "I've been to Keats's tomb—and the museums—and the palaces—"

"And the churches?" he urged; "the beautiful churches of Rome? Your stay, signorina, would not be complete without a visit to some of our famous churches. To Saint Peter's. And if you are an inhabitant, how much worse—" but, looking aside at one of his waiters, he turned back to find that Signorina Jane was across the room by the telephone, talking to an American couple.

When Jane left the American Bar—and she usually left two hours or so after midnight, just before closing time—she did not at first go anywhere in particular. She would walk down one street or down another, she would tag the steps of stray travelers for a few minutes and then abandon them, she would pause at the edges of squares as if she were too timid to cross them alone, and often—very often—she would simply stand indecisively with her hands clasped behind her back. Parts of the city remained populated all night, and it was to these that Jane seemed drawn after her initial puzzlement or confusion. She wandered through them, quickening her steps when she came to a crowd, and pushing through knots of people with eagerness and pleasure. Her face grew flushed and pretty. Near the Via Colombia there was a coffee shop that catered to students and stayed open all night; very late one summer night—or, properly speaking, very early one summer morning when the sky was still black as pitch—Jane pushed open the iron gate of the coffee shop and sat down at a table by herself.

"Snow White, where have you been all my life!" (Jane was pale as pale could be. She said nothing, only lifted her head with a vague smile, not understanding.)

"Snow White, what are you doing here!"

("She must live in a cellar," said someone behind a hand; a girl exclaimed, "Look at your dress!")

"What?" said Jane, becoming evasive at once as she always did when people spoke directly to her, half-trying to slide away and turning her face so that she could look at the speaker over her shoulder.

"*Sua veste,*" said the girl, louder. "Your dress. It's very pretty."

"Oh, I see."

"Listen, she's English," said the girl in Italian. "Giovanni, come look. She looks like Madame Récamier. She's incredible."

"Well, she isn't lying on a sofa," said he, laughing.

"I'm going over. Come on."

They petted her and examined the material of her sleeves—which appeared to make her nervous—and then another couple came over and sat at the table which had been crowded enough with one.

"*Com'è simpatica!*"

"What lovely eyes she's got!"

"Signorina—"

Jane told her name. She said in her soft voice, "Signorina means 'miss,' doesn't it?"

Giovanni nodded, propping his chin on his fists, beaming at her. "Yes, that means 'miss.'"

"In England," said the other man, "to call somebody 'miss' is an insult."

"That shows you what the English are like," said the first girl, positively.

"I beg your pardon," said Jane.

"That shows—" began the girl awkwardly in English; then she went off into Italian. They laughed until their chairs clattered on the floor.

"What did you say?" said Jane. Giovanni took her hands and began to explain.

"Coffee?" said the other girl. "Coffee for everyone."

"No, no, I don't want any," said Jane, "I have to go. *Non, grazie,*" struggling vainly to get up, pale and out of breath. Tears came to her eyes.

"What have you done to her? Look what you've done to her!" cried Giovanni's girl.

"I didn't do a thing," said he.

"Yes, you did."

"I did not!"

"What time is it?" said someone.

"It's four. Let's watch the sun come up."

"No, let's not."

"Yes, let's. It's a holiday."

Then Jane said, "Goodbye." She stood up, cold and abstracted.

"What?"

"What's the matter?"

"Let us walk you home," pleaded Giovanni. "Please. It's late."

The table broke out in a babel of explanations, questions, con-
tradictions. The waitress brought the coffee. Jane started to the
door, and Giovanni leapt after her and caught her arm.

"Please, miss—" he said. "No, I'm sorry—I forgot—Jane?"
Against the darkness of the open door which looked absolute from
inside the shop but which seemed to swim, to dissolve, as they
reached the street into a blue bath, the Englishwoman who looked
like Julie Récamier (the same high waist and full sleeves and the
same pointed satin shoes) said laconically, "It's too late." She
added, "I don't want it."

"Never again?" said Giovanni, looking next to her as he never
did with his friends—dark, sensitive, "foreign."

"No," said Jane, and she walked into the street.

"Go after her!" cried Giovanni's girl from inside the shop. "Go
on, stupid!" but Giovanni did not move. "And why didn't you
follow her?" said the girl crossly, coming up behind him; "I suppose
she runs too fast."

"She's gone," said Giovanni, and it was true; the street was
empty.

"Oh, *wait* till I tell Sylvia! Just wait! And don't talk to me about
going to see the sunrise because I don't want to. Not tonight." They
linked arms and started back into the coffee shop. "She was absolutely unique. Unbelievable." The girl was yawning and swinging
her free arm.

"Maybe," said Giovanni, "she will be back."

Jane never ate in company. She carried the drinks people gave
her until she accidentally spilled them or they were taken away
from her, she stirred tea or coffee but never touched it, and she
crumbled pastries in her fingers. With peanuts and chocolate she
made ornamental rows on the tops of tables. When Giovanni met
her the next night in a bookstore off the Via Venezia he could not
believe his good luck. The sun had set an hour before, and
Signorina Jane stood like a tall night-blooming flower, reading an
English book, a translation of the *Inferno*, the *Purgatorio*, the
Paradiso.

"Do you like Dante, Jane?" said Giovanni quietly.

"Oh, very much," she said. "I used to read him in school."

"Where did you go to school?" said Giovanni.

"In Derbyshire."

"Do you want me to buy you the book?"

"No, I don't read now," said Jane, and she put the book back on the shelf.

"I am still in school," said he. "I will get a master's degree in literature. Jane, do you want me to take you somewhere?"

"All right," she said. She followed him out onto the pavement.

"Do you live in Rome?" he asked.

"Yes, I do."

"Where?"

"At a hotel."

"Will you let me take you home tonight?"

"No."

"*What is the matter?*"

"Why, nothing's the matter," said Jane, surprised. "I don't want you to take me home, that's all."

"Do you have," said Giovanni, "a cold, correct English mamma who doesn't approve of Italians?"

"I live by myself," said Jane. "Look, the light's changing," and she took him by the arm and pulled him across the street. She was looking into a store window at a mannequin wearing the latest ball gown *alla moda*. "Now that's what I should like," she said thoughtfully. "But it doesn't last, you know."

"We were very hurt last night," said Giovanni, a little exasperated.

"Hurt?" said Jane, stopping in her tracks.

"Yes, hurt," he repeated emphatically. He took her arm. "Signorina—I forget, you don't like that—well—Jane—Jane, don't run away from me." She moved closer to his side, her mouth a little open and her brow wrinkled. "Listen, can I take you to a circus? Would you like that?"

"Oh, *yes!*" She threw her arms around him, looking up into his face. "Yes, *please!*" Then she blushed and stepped away.

"I haven't been, you see," she added in an explanatory tone of voice, "because I haven't got any money so I can only go to what's free."

"Then," said Giovanni, "you are a poor, lost girl in Rome and I think I should take you everywhere."

"I don't think you'd like that," said Jane in a subdued voice.

"Well, I'll see," said he in good spirits. "Now, to begin, I'll buy you something."

"That lasts," said Jane quickly.

"Yes," said Giovanni, "it will last a lifetime."

"A lifetime!" said Jane scornfully. "That's nothing."

"How long have you decided to live?"

"Oh, I'm eighteen."

In a little store at the corner of the Via Venezia and the Via Canale, Giovanni bought his new girl a ring made of silver and a polished granite pebble, because that kind of thing was cheap but pretty.

"It's granite!" said Jane in dismay, recognizing it. "Oh, I don't want that."

"What's the matter?" said Giovanni.

"I want the pink thing," said Jane, pointing and leaning over the counter. "The one over there."

"But that's only quartz," said Giovanni, joking. "It won't last forever. Only a lifetime, perhaps."

"It goes with my dress," said Jane, stretching out her hand, and "Oh, look," she said as the shopkeeper put it in her palm. When it was in its box and paid for she carried it carefully and tenderly, like an egg.

They walked for a while, and as they reached the approach to one of Rome's smaller bridges, "Jane," said Giovanni, "will you meet me in the afternoon tomorrow?"

"I can't," she said.

"Please. I will be dining with my mother and sister."

"When will you take me to the circus?"

"Never," he said, laughing, "never, unless you see me tomorrow."

"I'll come at night."

"Ah, that's too late." She took her pink ring out of the box and turned it this way and that. In the dark it caught a sparkle from the streetlight.

"If I don't meet you, I'll meet you here," she said. "I'm very busy, you know."

"If you are busy at eighteen," he said, "how much busier you will be at thirty!"

Jane said nothing.

"We are at the Palazzo Vecchione at four," Giovanni said, "and you and I will go that night to the circus and we will even ride through here on our way."

But Jane was putting on her ring and said nothing.

"Now, Jane," said Giovanni, exasperated, "it's not polite not to look at me when I'm talking to you."

"Oh!" She looked up, so startled that he felt tender for her, this inexperienced foreign girl, alone at eighteen. He took her by the shoulders and kissed her, but it was an unsatisfactory, evasive sort of kiss, and when he tried to repeat it she slipped away. She was repeating the name of the restaurant he had told her and smiling and waving.

"Now, Jane!" he said indignantly, "you are not saying goodbye to a train!"

"Goodbye, dear!" she cried, ever farther and farther away, "Goodbye!" and she walked rapidly over the bridge, still waving, until she disappeared into the darkness.

"Those crazy English," quoted Giovanni. Then he thought of her standing in the bookstore, rose-colored dress, rose-colored mouth, rose-colored heart. They would see her in the daylight, at least, where she couldn't slip away like that.

Maybe, he thought, his sister would be able to get to the bottom of it.

Jane did not appear the next day at the Palazzo Vecchione, but that evening when Giovanni drove over the bridge they had visited—there she was, standing at the farther end. He stopped the cab and opened the door for her to get in.

"Where were you?" he said.

"I didn't come," said Jane artlessly.

"But you *said* you would come!"

"Don't be angry with me, dear," said she, distressed. "Please don't. You see"—she was twisting her hands together in her lap—"I have a kind of illness—"

Giovanni took her hands, saying, "Jane, *mia*, don't do that; it's ugly."

"I have a disease," she went on, "that doesn't allow me to go out in the sunlight. I have to stay inside all day. I lie down with a cloth over my eyes."

"My God, where's your ring!"

"It wouldn't—" Jane said. "It wouldn't stay on my finger. I've sent it out to be fixed."

"Is that the truth?"

"I promise," she said. Then she laughed. "I didn't sell it," she said.

"I wouldn't put it past you," said Giovanni dryly.

"No! Never!" She added drolly, "Do you think I'm crazy, handsome *Italiano*?"

"Well!" he exclaimed, "am I handsome?"

"Oh, yes," said she, glancing at him sidewise. "Very."

At the circus Giovanni bought popcorn, which Jane crumbled and dropped on the floor under her seat. She was excited about everything. She climbed on the seat in front of them and screamed, "Make the tiger walk around!" at the tiger-and-lion-tamer. She even threw popcorn into the ring.

"I can't bloody well aim," she said, red-faced. "I'm bloody well out of practice."

"You might hit somebody on the head," said Giovanni.

"You'd mind that, wouldn't you?" said she, contemptuously. "Men are cowards. I suppose I'd dent his skull, wouldn't I? Fat chance!"

"I don't understand you," said Giovanni, laughing.

"If I *wanted* to dent anybody's skull," said Jane heatedly, standing up with her arms akimbo, "I jolly well would do it, but I jolly well wouldn't use"—she exploded—"*popcorn!*"

"Help, help," said Giovanni, covering his head with his hands.

Afterwards they went backstage to see one of Giovanni's friends who had become a clown.

"I despaired of ever becoming a Doctor of Laws," said the clown, "and I had no money, so now I have become—signorina?"

"A doctor of mortality," said Jane, but with no air of having said a good thing. She was staring at his white, painted face and holding on to Giovanni's hand.

"You make me think that we're all going to die," she said. "I don't know why. Because your face is only paint, I suppose, and if you died tomorrow someone else could wear it."

"But I won't die tomorrow," said the clown, grinning. "I have no plans in that direction."

"You might all the same," said Jane.

"Then," said Giovanni's friend, wiping off his false face with a towel, "I would die eternally grateful that at least I am not a Doctor of Laws. Giovanni, you have strange tastes, but I like you. Would you care to join me for a drink?"

"Not tonight," said Giovanni. "I think I'll find a riverbank and sit on it and hear Jane talk about death."

"I don't know anything about that," said Jane off-handedly as they walked off, skirting a tangle of ropes. She added suddenly, "Do you know, I studied singing."

"No, really?" said Giovanni, delighted. *"Canta. Canta."*

"What?"

"Sing for me."

So Jane sang, and what she sang was this:

"What matters it how far we go?" his scaly friend replied,
"There is another shore, you know, upon the other side.
The further off from England the nearer is to France—
Then turn not pale, beloved snail, but come and join the dance.
   Will you, won't you, will you, won't you, will you join the
      dance?
   Will you, won't you, will you, won't you, won't you join the
      dance?"

"You have a very good voice," said Giovanni, "do you know that? A really good voice."

"The less I use it the better it gets," said Jane. She twined her arm in his. "Oh, my dear," she said, "I'm so old and it galls me."

"You're profound," he said, dazzled. "You're amazing. You're truly profound and beautiful."

"Take me home," she said, and then: "No, don't."

"Why not?"

"No, that's all." She rubbed her cheek against his shoulder. "Because I'm profound," she said. "And the reason I know I'm profound is that you told me so." She looked up at him like a pretty serpent.

"If you don't wear my ring tomorrow," he said, "I shall go to London and throw myself into the Thames."

"I was to London once," said Jane, yawning.

"Yes?"

"To see a doctor."

"And what did he tell you?"

"That I was going to die."

"What!"

"Of course. Nobody lives forever. What time is it?"

"It's past midnight, Cinderella," said Giovanni, stopping in the shadow of a doorway.

"How far past?" said she, languidly.

"Too far. You'll turn into a squash."

"That's what *you* think." She wound her arms around his neck. "I wonder what I'll do," she said.

"*Madonna mia!*" said Giovanni. "What's this?"

"Oh! Nothing. I'll never do anything."

"And why not?" demanded Giovanni.

"Because," she said. "Because." She leaned closer. "Do you know London slang?" she said. "I'll teach you. Damned mortician's nark!"

"What's the matter?" said Giovanni.

"What time is it?"

"But—"

"*What time is it?*"

"It's almost three."

"Oh." She sighed, leaning against his arm. "Take me home."

"Take you—"

"Take me home, my dear."

"Where do you live, you crazy English?"

"At the Rand," she said, "where I share an apartment with my maiden grandmother."

In the lobby of the Rand Hotel they kissed goodnight. Giovanni walked out; on the street he could see Jane through a window, seated on a divan and curiously turning the pages of an American magazine. He did not see her get up fifteen minutes later, wave offhandedly to the night clerk (who waved back at the young lady who must—he thought—be a casual American), and walk out.

The next day Giovanni telephoned the Rand, got his connection, and recalled with a shock that he did not know Jane's last name. He had made no arrangements to meet her. He went to the bookstore on the Via Venezia, to the coffee shop (not yet open), to the bridge, but it hardly looked the same place in the daytime. He called his sister and asked if anyone had left a message for him, he instructed the switchboard operator at the Rand to give a note to a young English girl named Jane. He had visions of the operator's giving his note to a Jane of straw-colored braids who was eleven years old. He sat on a bench with his head in his hands. At eight o'clock he had dinner at his home; at ten he went to the coffee shop.

Jane was sitting at a table by the door, wearing her pink dress.

"Where were *you*?" she said severely, pretending to look at him through imaginary binoculars. She glided to her feet and they slipped outside. Halfway down the street, in a doorway guarded by an iron grate, they suddenly embraced, kissing desperately, panting, half-smothered. Giovanni leaned against the grate, wiping his forehead.

"*Dio!*" he said expressively.

"You're so good," said Jane, "so sweet, so good to me." He was not surprised to see that she had begun to cry hysterically. "You don't know," she said. "You don't know."

"I know everything," he said, half-choked.

"Ass!" She shook her head. "What shall we do tonight?"

"Ah, Jane!" said Giovanni, reaching for her again. She stood beyond him, regarding him seriously while he tried to recover himself.

"I want to go to the American Bar," she said. She advanced a step and put out her hands. "Oh, dear, oh, dear," she said.

"Not again! Not here!" He turned and rested his forehead against the iron grating. "I'll take you anywhere," he said pleadingly, "but, *cara*, stay away from me in public, please."

"My goodness, you're sensitive."

"I am mad as the wind and the water," said he.

Jane swept into the American Bar like a freakish gale; Giovanni could almost see the glasses blowing off the bar into her wake. She said hello to everyone, she talked incessantly while hanging on his arm, about a fish her father had caught that was so big—no, so big—no, *so* big—about her childhood, about an albino squirrel, about Giovanni, about newspapers, about the Russian language. She let a man persuade her to play billiards and she hiked her skirt up so as to put one foot on a chair.

"Damn it, Jane!" whispered Giovanni. "Don't let all these people see your knees!"

"Why, what's wrong with them?" she whispered back. She was smoking for the first time and puffing like a fiery furnace.

"They're *my* knees!"

"You can look at them like everybody else," said Jane wickedly.

They left the American Bar before midnight and went to an old hotel, all gilt and plush and plaster, where the furniture vomited dust and no one had cleaned the ceilings for fifty years. Jane stood against the heavy crimson curtains of their room, looking a little lost and a little sad.

"Will you love me forever, do you think?" she said in the most ordinary conversational tone imaginable.

"My God!" exclaimed Giovanni. "Look at you—long-waisted—long legs—like Diana!"

"No, of course you won't," mused Jane. "Of course not; you'll die someday; it's a pity."

"My dear—my darling—please—"

"But till then," said Jane, sighing. "Ah, till then—" She had insisted on leaving the curtains open, even though their room looked across a court to the other side of the hotel; Giovanni was trying to get to her without being seen through the windows.

"For God's sake," he said piteously, "do you want to kill me?"

"No," Jane smiled. "Wait," and with an extraordinarily graceful gesture she wrapped herself in the hangings. Leaning across the window like a kind of Roman sprite or sylph, she turned out the lights.

But the uncurtained windows bothered him and about an hour later he stole out of bed and drew the hangings, his instinct for privacy satisfied at last. Later, in his sleep, he heard Jane talking to herself and he woke to find her sitting on the bed with her shoes in her hand and her dress open down the back.

"*Dove va?*" he said sleepily.

"Ssssh." She patted his head.

"*Cara*, where are you going?"

"Home, love."

"But it's early," he complained. "It's dark out."

"Yes, yes," she whispered hurriedly, slipping on her shoes. There was a vague light in the air, filtering under the curtains. "I know, love. But I can't be too careful. I've slept like the dead. For hours. Fasten my dress, won't you?" He fumbled with it. "Oh, hurry!" She pulled away from him and did it herself. It seemed to him in his stupor that her fingers merely flashed over the buttons without touching them. He sank back into the bed. "It's dark," he muttered resentfully; "go and see," and when he heard her steps, mixed with his dreams, cross the room, he fell back into sleep. There was a moment's silence; then he heard a gasp—Jane had touched the curtains. She flung them back and in an instant the room was light. It was almost day. Roman sparrows racketed on the cobbles below and a man in the courtyard—a milkman or a cook—raised his arm to her in a friendly greeting.

"Damn you, damn you, damn you!" she shouted. Her face was suffused with blood. She pounced on her lover, shaking him.

"*Cara*—" he stumbled to his feet. "*Cara, cara,* what is it?"

"Look!" she shrieked, sobbing, "Look! Look!" and she hauled the naked man to the window. Then Jane stepped back and smashed her fist through the window; glass shattered and fell; she thrust her other hand through; she sawed both wrists on the edges.

"Don't!" cried Giovanni. "Don't! My God! You'll hurt yourself—" and he grasped both her hands, both white as lilies and both unmarked.

"You ass," she hissed slowly. "You bloody ass! I can't hurt myself; *don't you understand?*"

"No, I don't understand," said he, trembling, "I don't understand. I love you." Sunlight touched the tops of the buildings across the court and Jane fell silent, watching it with fascinated attention. She turned slowly and quietly in his arms; her hands dropped and she smiled vaguely, as if deaf. Sunlight touched the stone carvings over the window, flooded through the smashed glass, and dropped a slanted shadow across the sill.

"Oh, my dear," Jane said, "it's all gone," and Giovanni tightened his arms around her.

He was holding dust; it slid through his hands, hung for a moment sparkling in the sunlight, and fell lightly to the floor.

*　　*　　*

In his attempts to trace her steps through Rome, Giovanni spoke to the proprietor of the American Bar and the next day visited Rome's English Cemetery where lie so many of the illustrious and consumptive dead. But when the twilight fell, no beautiful, mad *Inglese* glided sepulchrally from behind the stones or rose like a fog out of the ground. Only—near the gates where the light shone in from the street—he found a block of granite, half-lost in weeds. It said:

SACRED TO THE MEMORY OF

JANE HODD

BORN OCTOBER 17,1803, OAKS, DERBYSHIRE
DIED MAY 30, 1821, ROME, OF CONSUMPTION

THE JOURNEY THAT WAS TO HAVE SAVED HER PROVED HER DEATH. FAR FROM HOME AND FRIENDS SHE LIES, NEVER HAVING TASTED THE FULLNESS OF LIFE. MAY GOD IN HIS INFINITE MERCY RECEIVE HER AND GIVE HER PEACE.

A Game of Vlet

In Ourdh, near the sea, on a summer's night so hot and still that the marble blocks of the Governor's mansion sweated as if the earth itself were respiring through the stone—which is exactly what certain wise men maintain to be the case—the Governor's palace guard caught an assassin trying to enter the Governor's palace through a secret passage too many unfortunates have thought they alone knew. This one, his arm caught and twisted by the Captain, beads of sweat starting out on his pale black-bearded face, was a thin young man in aristocratic robes, followed by the oddest company one could possibly meet—even in Ourdh—a cook, a servant girl, a couple of waterfront beggars, a battered hulk of a man who looked like a professional bodyguard fallen on evil days, and five peasants. These persons remained timidly silent while the Captain tightened his grip on the young man's arm; the young man made an inarticulate sound between his teeth but did not cry out; the Captain shook him, causing him to fall to his knees; then the Captain said, "Who are you, scum!" and the young man answered, "I am Rav." His followers all nodded in concert, like mechanical mice.

"He is," said one of the guards, "he's a magician. I seen him at the banquet a year ago," and the Captain let go, allowing the young man to get to his feet. Perhaps they were a little afraid of magicians, or perhaps they felt a rudimentary shame at harming someone known to the Governor—though the magician had been out of favor for the last eleven zodiacal signs of the year—but this seems unlikely. Humanity, of course, they did not have. The Captain motioned his men back and stepped back himself, silent in the main hall of the Governor's villa, waiting to hear what the young nobleman had to say. What he said was most surprising. He said (with difficulty):

"I am a champion player of Vlet."

It was then that the Lady appeared. She appeared quite silently, unseen by anybody, between two of the Governor's imported marble pillars, which were tapered towards the base and set in wreaths of carved and tinted anemones and lilies. She stood a little behind one of the nearby torches, which had been set into a bracket decorated with a group of stylized young women known to aristocratic Ourdh as The Female Virtues: Modesty, Chastity, Fecundity, and Tolerance, a common motif in art, and from this vantage point she watched the scene before her. She heard Rav declare his intention of having come only to play a game of Vlet with the Governor, which was not believed, to say the least; she saw the servant girl blurt out a flurry of deaf-and-dumb signs; she heard the guards laugh until they cried, hush each other for fear of waking the Governor, laugh themselves sick again, and finally decide to begin by flaying the peasants to relieve the tedium of the night watch.

It was then that she stepped forward.

"You woke up Sweetie," she said.

That she was not a Lady in truth and in verity might have been seen from certain small signs in a better light—the heaviness of her sandals, for instance, or the less-than-perfect fit of her elaborate jeweled coiffure, or the streaking and blurring of the gold paint on her face (as if she had applied cosmetics in haste or desperation)—but she wore the semitransparent, elaborately gold-embroidered black robe Ourdh calls "the gown of the night" (which is to be sharply distinguished from "the gown of the evening"), and as she came forward this fell open, revealing that she wore nothing at all underneath. Her sandals were not noticed. She closed the robe again. The Captain, who had hesitated between anticipations of a bribe and a dressing down from the Governor, hesitated no longer. He put out his hand for money. Several guards might have wondered why the Governor had chosen such an ordinary-looking young woman, but just at that moment—as she came into the light, which was (after all) pretty bad—the Lady yawned daintily like a cat, stretched from top to bottom, smiled a little to herself, and gave each of the five guards in turn a glance of such deep understanding, such utter promise, and such extraordinary good humor that one actually blushed. Skill pays for all.

"Poor Sweetie," she said.

"Madam—" began the Captain, a little unnerved.

"I said to Sweetie," went on the Lady, unperturbed, "that his little villa was just the quietest place in the city and so cutey-darling that I could stay here forever. And then *you* came in."

"Madam—" said the Captain.

"Sweetie doesn't like noise," said the Lady, and she sat down on the Governor's gilded audience bench, crossing her knees so that her robe fell away, leaving one leg bare to the thigh. She began to swing this bare leg in and out of the shadows so confusingly that none could have sworn later whether it was beautiful or merely passable; moreover, something sparkled regularly at her knee with such hypnotic precision that a junior guard's head began to bob a little, like a pendulum, and he had to be elbowed in the ribs by a comrade. She gave the man a sharp, somehow disappointed look. Then she appeared to notice Rav.

"Who's that?" she said carelessly.

"An assassin," said the Captain.

"No, no," said the Lady, drawling impatiently, "the cute one, the one with the little beard. Who's *he*?"

"I said—" began the Captain with asperity.

"Rav, madam," interrupted the young man, holding his sore arm carefully and wincing a little (for he had bowed to her automatically), "an unhappy wretch formerly patronized by the Governor, his 'magician,' as he was pleased to call me, but no Mage, madam, no Grandmaster, only a player with trifles, a composer of little tricks; however, I have found out something, if only that, and I came here tonight to offer it to His Excellentness. I am, my Lady, as you may be yourself, an addict of that wonderful game called Vlet, and I came here tonight to offer to the Governor the most extraordinary board and pieces for the game that have ever been made. That is all; but these gentlemen misinterpreted me and declare that I have come to assassinate His Excellentness, the which" (he took a shuddering breath) "is the furthest from my thoughts. I abhor the shedding of blood, as any of my intimates can tell you. I came only to play a game of Vlet."

"Oooooh!" said the Lady. "Vlet! I adore Vlet!"

"I have been away," continued Rav, "for nearly a year, making this most uncommon board and pieces, as I know the Governor's passion for the game. This is no ordinary set, madam, but a virgin board and virgin pieces which no human hands have ever touched. You may have heard—as all of us have, my Lady—of the virgin speculum or mirror made by certain powerful Mages, and which can be used once—but only once—to look anywhere in the world. Such a mirror must be made of previously unworked ore, fitted in the dark so that no ray of light ever falls upon it, polished in the dark by blind polishers so that no human sight ever contaminates it, and under these conditions, and these conditions only, can the first person who looks into the mirror look anywhere and see anything he wishes. A Vlet board and pieces, similarly made from unworked stone, and without the touch of human hands, is similarly magical, and the first game played on such a board, with such pieces, can control anything in the world, just as the user of the virgin speculum can look anywhere in the world. This gentleman with me" (he indicated the exbodyguard) "is a virtuoso contortionist, taught the art under the urgings of the lash. He has performed all the carvings of the pieces with his feet so that we may truly say no human hands have touched them. That gentleman over there" (he motioned towards the cook) "lost a hand in an accident in the Governor's kitchens, and these" (he waved at the peasants) "have had their right hands removed for evading the taxes. The beggars have been similarly deformed by their parents for the practice of their abominable and degrading trade, and the young lady is totally deaf from repeated boxings on the ears given her by her mistress. It is she who crushed the ore for us so that no human ears might hear the sounds of the working. This Vlet board has never been touched by human hands and neither have the pieces. They are entirely virgin. You may notice, as I take them from my sleeve, that they are wrapped in oiled silk, to prevent my touch from contaminating them. I wished only to present this board and pieces to the Governor, in the hope that the gift might restore me to his favor. I have been out of it, as you know. I am an indifferent player of Vlet but a powerful and sound student, and I have worked out a classical game in the last year in which the Governor could—without the least risk to himself—defeat all his enemies and become emperor of the world. He will play (as one player must) in his own person; I declare that I am his enemies *in toto*, and then we play the game, in which, of course, he defeats me. It is that simple."

"Assassin!" growled the Captain of the Guard. "Liar!" But the Lady, who had been gliding slowly towards the magician as he talked, with a perfectly practical and unnoticeable magic of her own, here slipped the board and pieces right out of his hands and said, with a toss of her head:

"You will play against *me*."

The young man turned pale.

"Oh, I know you, I know you," said the Lady, slowly unwrapping the oiled silk from the set of Vlet. "You're the one who kept pestering poor Sweetie about justice and taxes and cutting off people's heads and all sorts of things that were none of your business. Don't interrupt. You're a liar, and you undoubtedly came here to kill Sweetie, but you're terribly inept and very cute, and so" (here she caught her breath and smiled at him) "sit down and play with me." And she touched the first piece.

Now it is often said that in Vlet experienced players lose sight of everything but the game itself, and so passionate is their absorption in this intellectual haze that they forget to eat or drink, and sometimes even to breathe in the intensity of their concentration (this is why Grandmasters are always provided with chamber pots during an especially arduous game), but never before had such a thing actually happened to the Lady. As she touched the first piece—it was a black one—all the sounds in the hall died away, and everyone there, the guards, the pitiful band this misguided magician had brought with him, and the great hall itself, the pillars, the fitted blocks of the floor, the frescoes, the torches, everything faded and dissolved into mist. Only she herself existed, she and the board of Vlet, the pieces of Vlet, which stood before her in unnatural distinctness, as if she were looking down from a mountain at the camps of two opposing armies. One army was red and one was black, and on the other side of the great smoky plain sat the magician, himself the size of a mountain or a god, his lean pale face working and his black beard standing out like ink. He held in one hand a piece of Red. He looked over the board as if he looked into an abyss, and he smiled pitifully at her, not with fear, but with some intense, fearful hope that was very close to it.

"You are playing for your life," she said, "for I declare myself to be the Government of Ourdh."

"I play," said he, "as myself and for the Revolution. As I planned."

And he moved his first piece.

Outside, in the night, five hundred farmers moved against the city gates.

She moved all her Common Persons at once, which was a popular way to open the game. They move one square at a time.

So did he.

In back of her Common Persons she put her Strongbox, which is a very strong offensive piece but weak on the defense; she moved her Archpriest—the sliding piece—in front of her Governor, who is the ultimate object of the game, and brought her Elephant to the side, keeping it in reserve. She went to move a set of Common Persons and discovered with a shock that she seemed to have no Common Persons at all and her opponent nothing else; then she saw that all her black Common Persons had fled to the other side of the board and that they had all turned red. In those days it was possible—depending on the direction from which your piece came—either to take an enemy's piece out of the game—"kill it," they said—or to convert it to your own use. One signaled this by standing the piece on its head. The Lady had occasionally lost a game to her own converted Vlet pieces, but never in her life before had she seen ones that literally changed color, or ones that slipped

away by themselves when you were not looking, or pieces that made noise, for something across the board was making the oddest noise she had ever heard, a shrill keening sound, a sort of tinny whistling like insects buzzing or all the little Common Persons singing together. Then the Lady gasped and gripped the edge of the Vlet board until her knuckles turned white, for that was exactly what was happening; across the board her enemy's little red pieces of Vlet, Common Persons all, were moving their miniature knees up and down and singing heartily, and what they were singing was:

> "The Pee-pul!
> The Pee-pul!"

"An ancient verse," said Rav, mountainous across the board. "Make your move," and she saw her own hand, huge as a giant's, move down into that valley, where transparent buildings and streets seemed to spring up all over the board. She moved her Strongbox closer to the Governor, playing for time.

Lights on late in the Councilors' House; much talk; someone has gone for the Assassins. . . .

He moved another set of Common Persons.

A baker looked out at his house door in Bread Street. In the Street of Conspicuous Display torches flicker and are gone around the buildings. "Is it tonight?" "Tonight!" Someone is scared; someone wants to go home; "Look here, my wife—"

Her Tax-Collector was caught and

stabbed in the back in an alley while the rising simmer of the city, crowds spilling, not quite so aimlessly, into the main boulevards

Rav horrified

"We've got to play a clean game! Out in the open! No—"

While she moved the Archpriest

Governor's barricades going up around the Treasury, men called out, they say the priests are behind

And in horror watched him shake his fist at her and stand sullenly grimacing in the square where she had put him; then, before she could stop him, he had hopped two more squares, knocked flat a couple of commoners whose blood and intestines flowed tinily out onto the board, jeered at her, hopped two more, and killed a third man before she could get her fingers on him.

"He killed a man! With his own hands!"
"Who?"
"The Archpriest!"
"Get him!"

So she picked up the squirming, congested Archpriest, younger son of a younger son, stupid, spiteful, ambitious (she knew him personally), and thrust him across the board, deep into enemy territory.

Trying to flee the city by water, looks up from under a bale of hides, miserably stinking—

Where the Commons could pothook him to their hearts' content

Sees those faces, bearded and unwashed, a flash of pride among the awful fear, cowers—

"We don't do things that way," said Rav, his voice rolling godlike across the valley, across the towers and terraces, across the parties held on whitewashed roofs where ladies ate cherries and pelted gentlemen with flowers, where aristocratic persons played at darts, embroidered, smoked hemp, and behaved as nobles should. One couple was even playing—so tiny as to be almost invisible—a miniature game of Vlet.

"We play a clean game," said Rav.

Which is so difficult (she thought) that only a Grandmaster of Grandmasters attempts it more than once a year. Pieces must be converted but not killed.

The crowd on Market Street is turned back by the troops.

Her Elephant, which she immobilized

Men killed, children crushed, a dreadful silence, in which someone screams, while the troops, not knowing why

and set her Nobles to killing one another, which an inept player can actually do in Vlet

stand immobilized, the Captains gone; some secret fear or failure of will breathes through the city, and again the crowds surge forward, but cannot bring themselves to

She threw away piece after piece

not even to touch, perhaps thinking: these are our natural masters? or: where are we going? What are we doing?

Give him the opportunity for a Fool's Kill, which he did not take

The Viceroy to the Governor walks untouched through superstitious awe, through the silent crowd; he mounts the steps of the Temple—

Exposed every piece
begins to address the crowd

While Rav smiled pitifully, and far away, out in the city suburbs, in the hovels of peasant freeholds that surrounded the real city, out in the real night she could hear a rumble, a rising voice, thunder; she finds herself surrounding

Arrest that man

the Red Governor, who wasn't a Governor but a Leader, a little piece with Rav's features and with the same pitiful, nervous, gallant smile.

"Check," said the Lady, "and Mate." She did not want to do it. A guard in the room laughed. Out in the city all was quiet. Then, quite beside herself, the strange Lady in the black *gown of the night*, seeing a Red Assassin with her own features scream furiously from the other side of the board and dart violently across it, took the board in both hands and threw the game high into the air. Around her everything whirled: board, pieces, the magician, who was one moment huge, the next moment tiny, the onlookers, the guards, the very stone blocks of the hall seemed to spin. The torches blazed hugely. The pieces, released from the board, were fighting in midair. Then the Lady fell to her knees, rearranging the game, surrounding the last remnant of Black, snatching the Red Leader out of his trap, muttering desperately to herself as Rav cried, "What are you doing? What are you doing?" and around them the palace shook, the walls fell, the very earth shuddered on its foundations.

"Check," said the Lady, "and Mate." A rock came sailing lazily past them, shattering the glass of the Governor's foreign window, brought at enormous expense over sea and marsh in a chest full of sawdust, the only piece of transparent glass in the city. "Trust a mob to find a window!" said the Lady, laughing. Outside could be heard a huge tramping of feet, the concerted breathing of hundreds, thousands, a mob, a storm, a heaving sea of Common Persons, and all were singing:

"Come on, children of the national unity!
The glorious diurnal period has arrived.
Let us move immediately against tyranny;
The bloody flag is hauled up!"

"My God!" cried Rav, "you don't understand!" as the
Lady—with un-Lady-like precision—whipped off her coiffure and
slammed it across the face of the nearest guard. Her real hair was a
good deal shorter. "Wonderful things—fifteen pounds' weight—"
she shouted, and ripping off the robe of night, tripped the next
guard, grabbed his sword, and put herself back to back with the exbodyguard who had another guard's neck between his hands and
was slowly and methodically throttling the man to death. The servant girl was beating someone's head against the wall. The Lady
wrapped a soldier's cloak around herself and belted it; then she
threw the jeweled wig at one of the peasants, who caught it,
knocked over the two remaining guards, who were still struggling
feebly, not against anyone in the room but against something in the
air, like flies in treacle. None had offered the slightest resistance.
She took the magician by the arm, laughing hugely with relief.

"Let me introduce myself," she said. "I—"

"Look out!" said Rav.

"Come on!" she shouted, and as the mob poured through the
Governor's famous decorated archway, made entirely—piece by
piece—of precious stones collected at exorbitant cost from tax
defaulters and convicted blackmailers, she cut off the head of an
already dead guard and held it high, shouting, "The Pee-pul! The
Pee-pul!" and shoved Rav into position beside her. He looked sick,
but he smiled. The People roared past them. He had, in his hands,
the pieces and board of their game of Vlet, and to judge from his expression, they were causing him considerable discomfort. He
winced as tiny lances, knives, pothooks, plough blades, and
swords bristled through his fingers like porcupine quills. They
seemed to be jabbing at each other and getting his palms instead.

"Can't you stop them!" she whispered. The last of the mob was
disappearing through the inverted pillars.

"No!" he said. "The game's not over. You cheated—" and with a
yell he dropped the whole thing convulsively, board and all. The

pieces hit the floor and rolled in all directions, punching, jabbing, chasing each other, screaming in tiny voices, crawling under the board, buzzing and dying like a horde of wasps. The Lady and the magician dropped to their knees—they were alone in the room by now—and tried to sweep the pieces together, but they continued to fight, and some ran under the dead guards or under the curtains.

"We must—we *must* play the game through," said Rav in a hoarse voice. "Otherwise anyone—anyone who gets hold of them can—"

He did not finish the sentence.

"Then we'll play it through, O Rav," she said. "But this time, dammit, you make the moves *I* tell you to make!"

"I told you," he began fiercely, "that I abhor bloodshed. That is true. I will not be a party to it, not even for—"

"Listen," she said, holding up her hand, and there on the floor they crouched while the sounds of riot and looting echoed distantly from all parts of the city. The south windows of the hall began to glow. The poor quarter was on fire. Someone nearby shouted; something struck the ground; and closer and closer came the heavy sound of surf, a hoarse, confused babble.

He began to gather up the pieces.

A little while later the board was only a board, and the pieces had degenerated into the sixty-four pieces of the popular game of Vlet. They were not, she noticed, particularly artistically carved. She walked out with Rav into the Governor's garden, among the roses, and there—with the sound of the horrors in the city growing ever fainter as the dawn increased—they sat down, she with her head on her knees, he leaning his back against a peach tree.

"I'd better go," she said finally.

"Not back to the Governor," said Rav, shuddering. "Not now!"

She giggled.

"Hardly," she said, "after tying him and his mistress up with the sheets and stealing her clothes. I fancy he's rather upset. You surprised me at my work, magician."

"One of *us!*" said the magician, amazed. "You're a—"

"One of them," said she, "because I live off them. I'm a parasite. I didn't *quite* end that last game with a win, as I said I did. It didn't seem fair somehow. Your future state would have no place for me, and I do have myself to look after, after all. Besides, none of your damned peasants can play Vlet, and I enjoy the game." She yawned involuntarily.

"I ended that last game," she said, "with a stalemate.

"Ah, don't worry, my dear," she added, patting the stricken man's cheek and turning up to him her soot-stained, blood-stained, paint-stained little face. "You can always make another virgin Vlet board, and I'll play you another game. I'll even trick the Governor if you can find a place for me on the board. Someday. A clean game. Perhaps. Perhaps it's possible, eh?"

But that's another story.

How Dorothy Kept Away the Spring

It had been a long season and a lonesome one, and Dorothy had often no employment but a sort of dreaming journeying. She wandered slowly upstairs and down, through the bare halls and the dusty, crannied places under stairs. She watched the snow whirl silently around the corners of the house and went into the kitchen to breathe on the windows' frost-jungles, but the housekeeper didn't want her there. Then Father would come into the hall and stamp to get the snow off his boots, and she would slide away and go sit under the stairs. There she would make up a long, elaborate daydream: that her dead mother had left something hidden somewhere around the house for Dorothy to find. It could take days and days of just looking and turning over clothes in her dead mother's closet, but of course she would recognize it instantly when she found it. Her cough kept her from going to school or seeing much of anyone. She would sit under the stairs and think a lot, and then, when it got dark and the five o'clock chimes rang from the bedroom clock, Dorothy would go down to supper.

*   *   *

He looked across the dinner table at his daughter, her round rimless glasses perched seriously on her nose. Her pigtails stuck out at an angle from her head. She had put red rubber bands around them as if she didn't care what she looked like.

"How was everything this afternoon, Dorothy?" he said. She stopped eating buttered carrots.

"Fine," she said. Her glasses slipped down and rested on her nose.

"Push up your glasses, Hon," he said. She pushed them up with one buttery finger and watched him.

"Next week I'll be coming home a half hour early each day," he said. "Won't that be nice? We'll see each other a lot sooner."

She stared at him over the rims of her glasses. They magnified the lower half of her eyes and not the upper. She looked like a goldfish, somehow.

"Mm," she said. She took another mouthful of buttered carrots and chewed them slowly. After dinner he read to her and later, at her bedtime, asked the housekeeper how she'd been all day and what she'd been doing. He insisted on tucking her in himself when she went to bed.

Dorothy woke up in the middle of the night and listened to tell if anyone was awake. She knew it must be the middle of the night. It was dark and the house had become a great windy cavern that whispered and creaked and magnified the scurry of mice in the walls into thunder. Dim light leaked in under the window curtains. Dorothy sat up in bed, holding the blankets around her. She stuck her feet out of bed. Then she stood on the cold boards with her braids piercing the dark and her nightdress stirring faintly around her bare feet. She padded across the floor and pulled aside the curtains. It was almost light outside because of the snow; the sky was only a mass of falling, drifting flakes that passed inches in front of her eyes.

On tiptoe, barefoot, with her nightdress blowing as she climbed the windy stair, she crept up to the second floor. She passed her father's bedroom on the way, very quietly. There was the hall radiator—she ran her hand over it; it was so cold that the freezing iron burned like fire.

On the third floor there were full-length windows that opened out onto the courtyard. Dorothy leaned against them for a few minutes, staring out at the falling snow.

In her dream she put a hand to the mutely lit glass, and the window opened with a rush of air. The wind gathered around her; it whirled, lifted her, and dropped her slowly miles and miles through the falling snow. Snowflakes fell on her and lay unmelted. She liked that. She began to run. She skimmed swiftly over a long white country road, past windy hills, between the huge muted monoliths of the forest trees, past quiet avenues of hedges, through fields muffled in white, past tilted, half-buried cottages. There was a park she had once visited, with outdoor picnic tables spread in white, and circles of trees, each still branch ridged with snow. She smiled and let the pale folds of her nightgown drift around her feet, immensely pleased, her feet scarcely touching the blanched earth.

They were there.

One was thin, as hollow as a mask behind, of cold and cordial silver. A silver bow and long arrows lay over his arm.

You are a Hunter, she said, her voice deliciously quiet in the spreading quietness. Aren't you? He nodded. The two others were not as great. The taller one was a traveler with a clown's nose and peaked hat. His face was foolish and sad. The third was a gnome, chunky and thick, hardly anybody.

You seem to be a Clown, she said wisely to the one. And you—to the other—are very Little, although I don't know your name. Is there anything else?

The Clown spoke and his voice was absurdly high, thin, and sad. It was also silent.

We are adventurers, he said proudly. The Hunter smiled, although without a face and lips to smile.

Yes, yes, added Little. We go to dethrone a Tyrant who lives on a mountain. He holds a Princess captive in his castle.

The Hunter smiled and lightly touched his bow.

May I come? Dorothy asked. The Hunter extended one hand. It touched hers and its cold burned like fire.

We have been waiting for no one but you, he said, and his voice echoed light and hollow in the clearing. Dorothy unbraided her hair and let it fall loose. It grew long and hung to her waist. She turned and saw her father working his way laboriously towards them. He wore arctic furs and goggles and sank in snow up to his knees.

Don't vanish into silences, Dorothy! he cried. Come home, come home, come home.

She threw a handful of snow at him and he dissolved into snowflakes, gurgling:

You'll catch your death.

They rose and glided North under the heavy gray sky. Dorothy's breath made a frosty cloud around her. It was as warm as a coat. The snow was warmer, like cream, like white Persian kittens, like white fur, like love.

He looked across the dinner table at his daughter, who was seriously drinking her dinner milk.

"I guess your cough is better," he said. "Isn't it? I guess soon the doctor will let you go back to school. Won't that be nice?"

"Yes, Daddy," she said.

"Well, winter doesn't last forever," he said. "Does it?"

"No, Daddy," she said. She put down her milk, leaving a large white mustache over her upper lip. "Daddy," she said, "when I go back I won't know anything. I'll be behind."

"My daughter behind?" he said. "Don't you worry about that. You're smart, you'll make it up in a couple of weeks."

She nodded politely and finished the last drop of milk.

Once the Clown picked a flower. It was all white: petals, leaves, and stem, an odorless rose. He stuck it in his pointed hat, and all the travelers sang a song they had made up:

> Our hearts fill
> With goodwill,
> Four strong,
> Marching along,
> Singing this song.

The rose sang with them in a shrill voice, only singing "five" where they sang "four" because it seemed to think it was one of them.

After a while the Clown dropped it out of his hat onto the snow, where it stopped singing and crumbled into a heap of snowflakes.

It died, said Dorothy. The Hunter shook his head.

It was never real, he said. But it didn't know that.

In the hushed white forest where the sky dropped slowly and perpetually, it was never day or night, only a muted gray, half like twilight and not at all like dawn.

Little asked Dorothy: Are you hungry? She thought and shook her head.

But she should be, the Clown protested, holding his own head anxiously to one side. The Hunter brushed a strand of hair away from Dorothy's face with one flat silver finger.

Not now.

After days the trees began to thin and dwindle, and soon they came upon an open plain where the sky arched like lead. This was a terrible place. Dorothy and the Hunter were not afraid, but the Clown and Little hung back and hugged one another—not, as they carefully pointed out, for fear—only for warmth to keep out the chill of fear.

The castle is up ahead! they whispered.

The Hunter strode lightly ahead, carrying his bow and arrows, and Dorothy walked in the downy brushings his feet left in the snow. She made angels and roses of them. The Clown and Little began to wail—not, as they quickly pointed out, for fear—only for noise to keep out the silence of fear.

At first the ground began to slope; then they were in hills; then the hills grew; there were palisades, cliffs, escarpments, rocks black as night, nights rocky as ravines, paths that could lose you forever, boulders that could come rattling down. On a monstrous rampart that humped itself nakedly in massive ribs and shoulders, at the highest point, over an immense abyss, was the Tyrant's castle. It hung half over a sheer drop. It gleamed blackly, turreted in midnight basalt. An obsidian-colored flag flew stiffly over it, stretched to tautness by the toothy winds of the mountaintop.

Here is the place, the Hunter said, his queer, chiming voice echoing even in the mountain pass. The Clown straightened his hat and smiled gently at Dorothy. I must look my best when going into danger, he said. A shrill wind hit them, lifting Dorothy's long hair over her head like a flag. They began to climb.

Her father found her leaning out of an upstairs window in a cotton dress, letting the cold wind blow around her. She was trying to keep a snowflake unmelted on her finger. He didn't scold her, but sent her to bed and sent the housekeeper up to take care of her. She lay in bed with her hands clasped across her chest, politely refusing to read anything. She said she was perfectly all right. She lay there all day. And thought and thought and thought and thought.

The door to the castle was brass; it swung open into a long hall when Dorothy pushed it with all her strength. They followed the hall until it opened up into a great echoing room, hung with tapestries that depicted the four seasons, and haying, and mowing, and other mythological scenes. At the very end of the room, on a throne of flint, sat the Tyrant, his head sunk in sleep. He was huge and wavering and mist-gray; Dorothy could see through him to the wall behind. A circle of steel went round his head; it was his crown. Quickly Little ran to a trumpet hanging on the wall and blew three notes. The Tyrant started out of sleep, and as he rose, as he woke, his face became terrible with rage.

Push up your glasses, Dorothy! he roared. The Hunter drew back the invisible string of his bow and broke the steel circle with a frosty arrow. The Tyrant sank to the floor and spread in a puddle of tears.

Hurrah! cried the Clown. We have killed the Tyrant.

Hurrah! cried Little. I blew the horn that woke up the Tyrant.

Hurrah! cried Dorothy. I pushed open the door that let us into the castle of the Tyrant.

The Hunter leaned against a wall and said: Look. The Princess is coming.

The Princess blew down a corridor and into the room. She was all of fog.

Thank you for saving me, she said in a damp, rushing voice like water falling under stone arches. I am very grateful to you.

The Clown dropped to one knee. The pleasure is all ours, lovely lady, he said. She patted him on the head, and a little cloud from her hand caught on his hat and trailed from it like a breath.

They walked out of the castle. At once the fierce, grinning wind lifted the Princess and whirled her away in ragged, torn streamers.

What a shame, said Dorothy. Little nodded.

She was beautiful, declared the Clown sadly. I never saw anyone so beautiful before. Two tears rolled down his cheeks.

They walked easily down the shrunken mountain, and the castle, although not very far behind them, became a toy no bigger than Dorothy's hand. Then it disappeared. Snow began to fall; pearly covered trees and bushes rose silently around them. The light paled to a moonstone gray.

Look! cried Dorothy: Oh, look at that! and her voice seemed to seep away and lose itself in silences. There was a lake ahead, set like an opal between the fringed, drooping trees. Dorothy ran, she skated, she dipped and spun over the cloudy ice, whirling in tighter and tighter circles until she dropped on her knees and bowed and bowed while Little and the Clown applauded frantically. Then she saw through the trees a faint light, a touch of color, the very smallest kind of change.

There was a light in the East.

The dawn! cried the Clown. No, the spring! cried Little.

The spring, the spring! they sang, whirling about, holding hands and dancing in a ring. The spring, the spring, the spring's a thing when birds all sing and ice goes ching! and bushes fling and vase is Ming and flowers ping and hearts go zing and love's on the wing and life is king!

Dorothy, on her knees on the ice, said, No, no! It isn't going to come. I won't let it. But they danced on.

You can't stop it, they cried. The spring, the spring, the flowery spring! The glint, the chime, the sky, the blue, the joy, the jay, the jam, the rue!

And after that comes summer, you know, they added.

Dorothy began to cry, there on the pond. The Hunter knelt down and put one arm around her. Its touch burned like fire. He said, in his no-voice, his voice that was all the voices she had ever loved: You don't have to.

Then they were all gone and she was standing barefoot in her nightgown in the courtyard of her home. The sun had risen in the East into a clear sky: the long spell of winter was broken. A face appeared at a second-storey window. Come in here! it called crossly. You'll catch your death of cold. Quickly Dorothy ran upstairs to her room. She climbed into bed and pulled the covers up to her chin.

"Yes, Daddy, yes, Daddy!" she called. "I'm in bed now."

But she knew her mother's secret. She had found it.

The next day Dorothy was very ill, the day after that she did not wake up very much, and the day after that she died. At her funeral there were bunches of violets, banked azaleas, and lots of hothouse gladiolus. It was like summer. Everyone said so. Dozens of people came to see Dorothy in her Sunday dress and many women wept.

In a pale forest, under still, white branches and a slowly dropping sky, Dorothy plucks a white rose for the faceless silver Huntsman. There's no place to put the flower but in his hands, for he's as hollow as a mask. Her long hair is knotted beautifully about one of his long arrows. Another pierces her heart. She smiles a little, rueful perhaps, happy perhaps.

I kept away the spring, she says to him. Didn't I? I really did it.

I kept away the spring.

POOR MAN, BEGGAR MAN

A strange man, with a black cloak wrapped about him and a fold of it drawn over his head to hide his face, with the easy, gliding step of one who no longer cares if his feet go over rough or smooth, a man who smelled the smell of cooking at a turn in the narrow rocky path, but to whom it meant nothing but a signal about what somebody else was doing, nothing more, this fellow—who was of a fairly ordinary and nonformidable appearance (though perhaps a bit mysterious)—slipped along the winding path outside Alexander's camp near the Indus River as if he knew where he was going. But he had no business being there, certainly not in the heat of the afternoon, though the vegetation around him cast the path into a certain tenebrous gloom. Light and shade spotted him. It was early in the Indian summer, and petals and yellow dust dropped on the path and on the leaf-mold to either side. He shook himself free. He reached an open place and continued, not looking round.

A quarter of a mile from the general's tent the path ascended, became rockier and more open; a guard lounged on a rock, absorbed in a bluebottle he held between thumb and forefinger. He did not see the stranger as he passed, nor did he return his salute. Muffled to the chin, the stranger passed servants clearing dishes from a board table set up in the open sunlight (for the general's tent commanded a view of the valley from an uninterrupted but therefore somewhat inhospitable height). He stepped inside the tent, bending under the canvas flap, his black cloak trailing. He found his man seated at a low table, calling for a map; he put one hand on his shoulder and then he said—quite diffidently—

"Come, I'm still a civilized fellow."

"Apollo guard us!" choked the conqueror, turning pale. The stranger laughed and shook his head, still with the inoffensive and friendly manners that had made him so popular and that had occasioned such grief when Alexander had murdered him at the age of twenty-eight.

"Your teacher, Aristotle, wouldn't like that," he said, shaking his head humorously, and he sat down on the edge of the table, closing his hand around a wine-cup.

"Take your hands off that!" said Alexander automatically, and then he said, his color coming back, "Take it."

"Oh, no, thank you," said his dead friend, smiling apologetically, "I couldn't, now. You have no idea what an inconvenience it is, to be dead—"

"Take it!" said the conqueror.

"Ah, but—" and his murdered friend put the wine-cup down.

"Well?" said Alexander. The dead man smiled, the mild smile of those who provoke and endure insult; he smiled, backing away. "I thought," he said, "that the novelty of my appearance—"

"Doesn't last."

"Ah, but you owe me—"

"What?"

The ghost wandered away a few steps, past the ray of brilliant sunlight that entered the tent through the front flap, brushing the canvas wall with his shoulder and causing not a ripple. "I remember," he said, "I remember." Alexander watched him intently in the half-light, the light that made of the conqueror, of his handsome face and bronze figure, a statue.

"Ah, what I remember!" broke out the ghost, with a genuine laugh. "I remember your amazing forcefulness when you got

drunk." The man at the table watched him. "And I remember,"
added the ghost, padding round the room, "sitting with my feet up
and my knees under my chin on some kind of marble shelf, like a
schoolboy, and watching you rant . . . ."

"I never rant."

"Rave, then. But you mustn't split hairs. My word, they tried to
hold you back, didn't they? And my sister was your old
nurse—what a scandal! I hear you shut yourself up for three days."
Here he paused in the darkest corner of the tent. "You know," he
said, coming out into the light, dragging his cloak carelessly off one
shoulder, "you know," he said, his whole face becoming clearer,
his brow rising, his eyes opening as they do in strong feeling when
the face is about to become a mask, "you know," (with an expression almost of amazement) "I do remember it quite well. I have
analyzed it a hundred times. I had no idea what hit me. I thought
the room had turned round and the floor had come up and thrown
itself against me. And then something hit me in the chest and I bit
my tongue, do you know, and I saw your face—"

Here Alexander broke into a roar of laughter that might have
been heard even outside the tent, but the tent flaps did not move;
they hung quite still.

"My dear friend," he said affectionately, "really I am very sorry,
but you know you might have come back four years ago. I feel for
you, I do, but I'm afraid time has rather worn the whole affair
away. You see—" and he pointed to the litter of papers on his desk.

"Ah," said the ghost wisely, "but *I* don't age, you see."

"That's too bad," said the emperor, putting his elbows on the
table and his chin in his hands, "and now—"

"Now?" said the ghost expectantly.

"Now be a good fellow and go away."

"No."

"Then *I* shall," but when the emperor pushed back his chair and
got up, he saw that the friend he had killed was somehow sitting in
it and fingering his papers and that he did not like.

"My, look at this," said his friend.

"Let that be!"

"You're going to India; how nice."

"Will you—!" and he snatched the stranger's hand, but the shock of finding it flesh and blood was too much for him and he started back, shouting, "Guards!" No one came.

"Ah, nonsense," said his friend quietly. He sat at the table as a secretary or accompanying philosopher sits and writes down a great man's words; his black cloak had slipped off his shoulders and lay half on the seat and half on the dirt floor, like a pool of ink. He picked up one document after another, carefully and respectfully. It had always been remarkable how this man could pick things up; his hand closed around a cup, a vase, a woman's hand, with such gentleness and such attentive curiosity that one might almost imagine inanimate objects feeling actual pleasure at his touch. Women had liked him, and he had evaded them.

"You're going to India," he said. He was looking at marks on a map. Alexander strode matter-of-factly to the tent-flap to get friends or attendants who would rid him of this annoyance, but the tent-flap hung straight as stone. He could not move it.

"What do you want from me?" he said between his teeth.

"We-ell," drawled the stranger.

"*What*?" shouted the king, losing his patience.

"You're growing afraid."

"Not I!"

"Yes, you are, and you'll do it."

"Do *what*!"

"Quietly." He studied the map. "Look at this," he said; "you're going to cross the Indus, you'll be another seven years away from home, your army will mutiny and by the time you establish another Alexandria—how many Alexandrias are there by this time?—at the Eastern edge of the world, your government in the West will have collapsed and you'll have to begin all over again. Good Lord, what an agenda!"

"Stop playing with me," said the king and he sat, with considerable dignity, on a low bench near the opening of the tent.

"Why not? You used to play with me," said the ghost reasonably.

"I used to."

"Precisely. You used to."

"Death hasn't steadied your character," said Alexander.

"Or sweetened yours!"

"Those who want to get kicked will get kicked," said the king.

"Yes, precisely," said his friend, blinking. "Well, what I want is this. I want you to turn back, go spend the next winter in Heliopolis, renamed from Babylon (what a change!), and withdraw your borders to the edge of Persia. You're a fool. You can't keep what you've got. As it is, the empire will fall apart three days after your death. You think you can put up a few carved pillars, appoint a satrap, and a place is yours. Nonsense."

"And—" said Alexander.

"And," repeated the ghost, looking a little bewildered, "and—well—there you are." Alexander rose to his feet. "I'm not done—" but a sudden breeze blasted the tent-flap into the air as if someone's violent enthusiasm had flung it skyward. Grinning cheerfully, though perhaps with a certain awkwardness, Alexander walked to his friend and embraced him.

"Would you believe me," he said, "if I told you that I had repented? Sincerely repented? Why, man, I saw no one for three days; they thought I would abandon them in the middle of the desert. So much grief! But you should have known enough to keep away from me." He patted, without shrinking, his friend's unnaturally solid back. "And the story about your sister was true," he said, "though embroidered a little, I'll admit. I was truly fond of her and hated to cause her pain. And you—" His voice thickened. "Well, you know—"

"Ah," said the ghost, helplessly blinking.

"*You* know," said Alexander tenderly. "*You* know." And then, without another word, only looking back with smiling and compassionate regret, he walked out of the tent.

Left alone, the stranger gazed thoughtfully after him for the space of a minute. Then, with extraordinary rapidity, he whipped his cloak from the chair near the low table, wrapped it into a small package, and flung it into the air. Watching it as it hung suspended between the roof and the floor, he laughed to himself, a noiseless fit that doubled him up. As soon as he took his gaze off the cloak, it fell like any other object, gracelessly unfolding itself in a scattered bundle like a wounded goose. He picked it up and put it on. *Now for the other one,* he thought, and he sat down on the bench near the canvas wall, quite composed. His name was Cleitus. He had been known in life as Cleitus the Black.

In Persia, in order to secure his political position, Alexander had married (and caused two hundred of his nobles to do likewise, although their sentiments on the matter had not been ascertained at the time) a Persian lady of aristocratic birth. Roxane, as his wife was called, had spent most of her childhood in a courtyard with a mosaic marble floor, either learning to read and write (which she despised) or chasing a striped ball with several other girls who kissed her hand in the morning and in the evening and said, "my lady." When she was seventeen she was surprisingly and suddenly married to a man famous, handsome, young, and formidable. Three weeks' absence from home made her desperately sick for her court-yard, which she had always considered a prison before, and in which she had longed to stand on a chair piled on another chair piled on a table so that she could see out of it and view the great world.

She came into the tent five minutes after Alexander had left it and two minutes after the stranger had seated himself on a bench.

"Eh!" she said, startled. He was down on his knees, bowing, before she could take fright and run. Then he kissed her hand, which comforted her because that was so familiar.

"Who are you?" said she, sensibly. He only smiled at her, as vaguely and disarmingly as a man who has never been anything else but a woman's bumbling pet, and he kissed her hand again. "I, madam," he said, "am called Theophrastus."

"What a foolish name!" said Roxane, giggling, for she had never learned to lie or be polite either.

"My lady," he said, suddenly affecting to look alarmed, "should you be here alone with me? That is—I mean—I believe—" Roxane tossed her head.

"Nobody follows me around," she said, *"here.*

"Nobody would dare hurt me," she added. "I suppose."

"Nobody with any heart would," said he. She colored.

"Madam," he said quickly, "I must find the emperor."

"I don't know where he is," said she, sitting plump on the bench. She looked interested and expectant. The ghost began to walk up and down like a man tormented in his mind by the urgency of something; he said, "Ah, but madam!" and then he shook his head to himself a few times and said, "Madam—"

"Why, what's the matter?" cried Roxane, who was entirely ignorant and hence unafraid. The ghost came and sat down beside her with his black cloak (looking rather foolish) dragging behind him.

"You know, madam," he said earnestly, "that your husband, his Imperial Majesty, *pai dios*—"

"Yes, yes," said Roxane impatiently, clasping her hands.

"Your husband," said the ghost, looking round as if afraid they might be overheard, "has no doubt told you, madam, that he intends to cross the river in a few days' time and for this he will need native scouts, guides, madam, to acquaint him with the towns and villages that may lie beyond." Roxane nodded, perfectly attentive. "Well now," continued the ghost, "and, madam, I tell you—I tell you, I am nearly out of my senses—these guides whom your husband has engaged now refuse to go anywhere. They have scattered to the four winds, madam." He looked at her apologetically, as if what he was about to say was too foolish to be believed and in any case utterly beyond her notice, and then he said, "They are afraid, madam, of the ghosts."

"Ghosts!" shouted Roxane, sitting bolt upright.

"Oh, yes, but it's nothing, some native foolishness, people walking about with their feet on backwards—"

Roxane sprang to her feet and began pacing nervously around the tent.

"If there are ghosts out there," she said, "I won't let him go."

"But his Imperial Majesty—" said the ghost, coughing faintly.

"Never you mind about that," she said; "I know what's what and I know—" She turned to him suspiciously. "What kind of ghosts?"

"Kind?" said the ghost, puzzled.

"Yes," she said. "Are they—are they—" (she whispered this) "bloodsuckers?"

"Uh—no," said the ghost, his wits scattered.

"Oh, then it's all right," she said, relieved. "You can keep away the other kinds, but *that* kind—" Suddenly she looked at him keenly. "You don't really know, do you?" she said.

"Of course I do," he said. She frowned. "No—you—don't," she said with emphasis. Her face darkened. "You're Greek!"

He admitted it.

"Ha!" she said, "you probably don't believe in them at all."

He protested that he did.

"No, you don't," she said, "I can tell. You'll tell my husband it's a lot of nonsense. I know."

"Madam!" he protested. "On my honor—"

"Greek honor!" she cried. "You'll tell my husband it's some Asiatic foolishness." She darted to him, grabbing his shoulders and furiously shaking him. "Yes, you will!" she shouted. "You'll tell him it's nonsense and then he'll go out there and then—" and she turned away and screwed up her face. She began to cry.

"Now, now, now," he said.

"He'll get killed!" wailed little Roxane. "He will! He will!"

"No, no, no," said the stranger, stroking her hair. She leaned against him, sobbing a little. Then she pulled away.

"I'm rather homesick," she said sharply, explaining her conduct.

"Of course, of course," said the ghost in the tone women had loved so when he was alive, "it's only natural, of course."

"You shouldn't pat my head," said Roxane, sniffling.

"Yes, of course," he said smoothly, "of course. But it calms you, doesn't it? and it does so distress me to see you upset."

"It makes my eyes red," said Roxane, blowing her nose in her long Persian sleeve.

"It makes you unhappy," said he, "and I don't like to see people unhappy, you know, though I have so few feelings myself." He smiled. "I had a wife like you once; she was much cleverer than I and she hated the court: a real intellectual."

"I'm stupid," said Roxane spitefully. "I believe in ghosts."

"Ah, but," said the man, as if he had made an astonishing discovery, "so do I!"

"Really?" said she.

"Ah, yes, I've seen too many not to believe in them. But the kind I believe in are not those Indians with their feet put on backwards or your Persian demons and afreets that suck blood but a kind—well, a kind—"

"A Greek kind?" asked Roxane, fascinated.

"No, I think a universal kind," he said with a slight, guilty laugh, stroking her hair. "The kind, you see— You see, when a poor wretch dies, some unfortunate idiot, many times he dies with an unfulfilled passion, something that tormented him all his life but something he never mastered or settled with. And this poor fool, he finds after his death that he's not one of the blessed dead that lie in the ground or end up in the fire and are gone, that's it, the lucky ones. Most of these men—and women, too, you know—most of them are nothing much, no force of character, you might say, so they simply blow about with the wind like old rags, drifting from place to place."

"Oooooh—yes—yes—" whispered Roxane.

"Now for most of us," he went on, cupping her face in his hands, "that's it, you see, but for a few—" He smiled enchantingly. "A few have too much feeling to stand for that; they want too much, and these are the dead you hear about in songs and stories, who come back to pay off debts or wreak vengeance, you know, or take care of their children. And some—ah, some! they have a driving passion, a force that won't let them rest. They have hard bodies like you and me. You can see them, too. And you can find them—why, anywhere! In the marketplace at high noon, in temples, theaters—"

"They don't cast shadows!" Roxane broke in eagerly.

"Ah, but they do," he said, "indeed they do and sometimes," (with the same slight, guilty laugh, picking up his cloak and cradling it in his arms) "sometimes they even carry their shadows around with them. They do all sorts of odd things. But they are poor folk, after all, you know."

"Why?" she whispered.

"Why?" he said lightly, "why, because they only live while their passion is unsatisfied, you see. And as soon as they get what they came back for, they die for good. But they *must* come back, you know, they can't help themselves. They want it so much. You know yourself" (here she shuddered) "what it feels like to go about wanting something desperately, don't you?"

"Oh, I do!" sadly.

"Well, there you are." He stopped, looked tenderly at her, and then, as if it were the natural sequence of his discourse, kissed her, pulling her up to him by the shoulders.

"Ah, that's wrong!" cried she, bursting into tears because she had a husband but nobody, really, and he—smiling—because she reminded him (perhaps) of three or four memories picked out of his memories of women or perhaps all of them, because he had loved and pitied everything living when he himself was alive.

"Little one wants to go home, doesn't she?" he whispered, holding her against him. "Little one's lonely? Eh?" kissing her hair.

"Yes, yes," she sobbed, pushing him away. As if she were coming out of an enchantment, she looked at him doubtfully, ready to run away.

"Madam," he said briskly, "if you would permit me—I mean to utter no treason against his Imperial Majesty, but a man of affairs, a man preoccupied with questions of state—a busy man, in short, why such a man may neglect those nearest and dearest to him without the least design. He may not even realize that he is so doing, his mind being preoccupied as it is."

"Ah?" said Roxane, bewildered but sure there was something good coming.

"In such cases," said the stranger, with a bland smile, "a short absence may be the best—ah, madam, forgive me offering you advice, but as an old friend of the family, as it were, I feel—"

"Well—" said Roxane, trying to look like a *grande dame*.

"I feel," he continued, "that if your husband could be presented —though not in reality, of course—with the prospect of losing you—if he could be made to imagine it, so to speak, he would at once realize the void, the gap, if I may say it, the absence in his life, and he would—with a rush of feeling, of repentance, as it were, though far be it from me—he would immediately regret that his business affairs had taken him so often and so far away from you."

"Well, ye-es," said Roxane.

"Many men," continued the stranger, with unction, "many men only realize their true feelings when those feelings are threatened, as it were. They—"

"Yes, but how?" Roxane broke in impatiently.

"How?" he said.

"How could I do it?"

He bowed (as best he could from a sitting position).

"How?" she repeated anxiously. "Come, tell me and do stop beating about it like that!"

"Madam has seized the thought at once," said the stranger admiringly.

"I always do," she said. "I'm very quick but really, if you won't—"

"A minute, a minute." He cleared his throat. "Could you not—" he said, and then: "There is an Indian village a few miles from this camp."

"Yes, indeed," said Roxane promptly.

"You have never been to this village," he said, "but you can go there easily enough. In daylight, of course. The path is wide and unmistakable. If you don't mind staying with one of the farmers—a comparatively rich and luxurious household, of course—"

"Pooh! I don't care," she said.

"Well then, that's that! Stay for a night and he'll go wild without you. And I wouldn't be surprised if he gives up this Indian project, too. You'll get a good deal more attention from him from now on." He spread his hands. "That's it."

"Oh!" exclaimed Roxane, then "Oh!" again in delight. She sprang to her feet. "I shall," she said to herself, "this very night. Thank you." She started to run out of the tent, exclaiming, "Yes—I must—" and then she turned around abruptly, saying, "Don't tell!" He took her hand and she cried, "Really!" quite unaffectedly, snatching it away with a disgusted expression. He bowed low—a real bow this time—and the princess rushed out.

Left to himself, the dead man appropriated two items of his former master's property: a pen and a piece of paper. With the appropriately serious expression he began to write a letter, a letter such as those written to husbands by adventurous and fleeting wives who are only too delighted to be runnning away with somebody interesting, but who write of the whole matter in terms of the deepest and direst compulsion. He was laughing soundlessly to himself by the time he had finished. Ah! that kiss had been sweet! *but only for old time's sake*, he thought. The static qualities of death oppressed him; he felt that mutability was mankind's only

hope, even though it took the flowers and pleasures of one's time.
Most terrible about the dead was the way in which they did not,
could not, could never, could never even hope to change. *Change*,
he thought, with unspeakable anguish. Outside the tent, as transparent to his sight as the sky, the sun was beginning to set. Little Roxane would be in her Indian village by evening, very curious,
very delighted, to see how the peasants lived and playing alter-
nately milkmaid and the great lady. He envied her. He envied Alexander, he envied every common soldier, he envied every dog, every
rat, every louse, on that inhospitable rocky eminence. They could
be hungry. They could be in pain. They might not walk through
the worst of Alexander's battles no more in danger than the rain
that rotted the bodies of the dead. Did men want little—or get
much? He could not tell. With the mild, ingenuous face and diffi-
dent manner that had made him so popular in Alexander's court, he
wandered about the tent with the letter in his hand. Dinners were
cooking all over the camp, three and a quarter miles of dinners.
The thought of so much human busyness caused him considerable
pain. He moved unsteadily and blindly against Alexander's campaign table, and then as the innocent maps and memoranda stared
up at him in the gloom, his brow cleared. He dropped the letter on
the center of the heap. Alexander would look for his lady in the
woods, not in the village, misled by the fanciful instructions of a
dead man, and in the woods—his blind face stirred with a painful
rage. *That damned fool!* The sentry who would find it would run to
him—not a moment too soon, that would be seen to—and Alexander, who knew perfectly well that his wife detested writing and
could not spell, would—! The ghost bent over in a silent fit of
laughter. Oh, the emperor would call himself an idiot, but he
would go! He despised his wife, no doubt, but he would go! He
would know it was a trap, but he would go! What had the Athen-
ian philosopher said? Ghosts hate crowds? Ah yes, that was it. *In
silence and in little company and most of all at night*— The fool!
Men were easiest to manipulate alone, in silence, and in the dark;
that was all. Even that great fool, that king of fools, that king of
kings . . . Laughing still to himself, the emperor's friend walked
towards the tent wall, his cloak folded over his arm. He could have

gone out any way he chose, but he chose to melt through the wall like a mist, astonishing anyone who saw him. No one saw him.

When Alexander received his wife's letter he was lying on a divan after supper, hearing one of his tame philosophers read him a discourse on the immortality of the soul. It did not please him. He had drunk moderately at table. He received the letter curtly, read it abruptly, and gave vent to his feelings with a roar of rage.

"My lord!" exclaimed the tame philosopher.

"Damn her!" cried the king.

"The immortality of the soul—" ventured the philosopher, trembling.

"Damn the immortality of the soul!" shouted the conqueror, his neck swelling. He began to put on his armor. He dashed to the wall, seized his shield, and rushed out, looking in again only to snatch up his sword from where it stood by the entrance to the tent. His face was scarlet and distorted, like a djinn's.

"And damn *you!*" he shouted.

They searched the area north of the camp, taking no chances; they shouted to each other; someone found footprints but they were not the proper size. Soon, through his own impetuosity and his soldiers' fear of becoming separated, the emperor and one of his philosophers, a historian, one Aristophorus, found themselves ahead of the search party. They were in a little glade.

"Rest yourself, rest yourself," said Alexander, and the old man, tottering to a fallen log, said, "Yes, my lord." He was carrying a torch. He took off his sandals and sat, his back hunched over, his beard pointing at his knees.

"Why don't they shout?" said Alexander suddenly. "I told them to shout."

"They will catch up with us, my lord," said the philosopher, rubbing his feet, "no doubt." Alexander repeated, "No doubt," and wandered to the other side of the glade, into which a faint radiance had already begun to creep from the rising moon. He peered into the darkness.

"I can't see any lights," he said.

"According to Aristotle," said the philosopher contentedly, "the eye sends out rays which are reflected by objects in its path, thus producing sight. But when the rays are reflected strongly by any object—and those objects composed of the element of fire are most vigorous in the exercise of this property—then other objects appear but weak and faint in comparison."

"Put it out!" said the young man, and as the old one only stared at him uncomprehendingly, Alexander seized the torch himself and thrust it upside down against the earth. Immediately the darkness around them seemed to rush in as if the circle of light had been snapped like a hoop; Alexander leaned between two trees at the edge of the little clearing.

"I can't—" he said, and then conscious that he had spoken more softly than before, "I can't see a thing."

"They will catch up with us, my lord," said the old man. With the moon rising and the firelight gone, something very peculiar was happening to the little glade: objects were melting and changing; they ran one into the other as if nothing in the universe were stable. The clearing looked like the bottom of the sea. Alexander walked rapidly back and forth for a few moments, then turned (as if the place were affecting his nerves) and stared at the old man.

"I'm afraid to talk out loud," he said, as if stating a fact, and then he said sharply, "Who are you?"

"What, my lord?" said the old man, startled, but his imperial master did not answer, only shook his head as a man does who has found a mote in his eye. He walked about again and then stopped as if the indistinct light and the masses of shade confused him; he said, "I hear no one."

"Why no, my lord," said the old man placidly, stroking his toes, "I daresay they have passed us by and we must wait until morning."

"Fool!" said Alexander. He stopped in the middle of the glade irresolutely. Then he said, "Get out of here, old man."

"My lord?" said the philosopher mildly.

"Get out of here!"

"But, my lord—!"

"Get out! That's a command! You'll find the others soon enough."

"Will you—" began the philosopher, but Alexander (who had drawn his sword) waved him imperiously away.

"Get out!" he roared.

"But, my dear lord—" (shocked) and then the king urged him with such fury that the old man flew out of the clearing with his sandals still in his hands. He saw the lights of the soldiers' torches at once, as Alexander had said he would, and they spent the rest of the night looking for the emperor, but they did not find him.

Left alone, and doubly uncertain of himself, Alexander turned back into the glade, only to see his friend lounging against a tree in the moonlight at the opposite end. The moon had risen, and it bathed the little glade in livid quicksilver; the king felt his nerves give way; he had an impulse either of love or of despair that made him want to bury his head in his friend's knees and beg—

"I like a light in which I can judge distances," he said grimly.

"There are no distances here," said the dead man. "Here things are very close together."

"My wife?" said the conqueror.

"Quite safe." They looked one another over for a few moments, the one erect and bristling like a dog, the other curved against his tree as he had curved against every surface, every command, every necessity in his short and easy life.

"Your fine world!" said Alexander contemptuously, indicating the clearing with a gesture that was almost—but not quite—a snap of the fingers.

"No," said the dead man, smiling urbanely, "yours. The real world. Like the bottom of the sea. As you look at my features, they seem to swarm and melt. They could be anybody's."

"Imagination!" with scorn.

"Ah, the imagination . . . the imagination, which the philosophers say gives color to everything." The dead man detached himself from his tree and moved noiselessly into the clearing, over grass the color of mercury. "My dear friend," he said lightly, "my dear, dear friend, you must remember that I am dead and so I look at things from a very special point of view. I know, you see, the torments of desire after death, desire too late to satisfy desire, and I want you to avoid the same fate as myself. You must not spend eternity longing for your wife and your cook and your mattress-maker, for you neglect them; you know you do."

"Bah! Don't want them," said Alexander.

"No?" With the same fixed smile the dead man moved towards him, like a walking corpse or a man in a dream.

"Keep away!" cried the king in horror.

"Why?" said his friend gently. "Because I have a white face? Because I look like a leper? My face is white, my dear friend, through an excess of passion. My movements are slow because I am dead."

"Damn you, what do you want?" cried Alexander, breathing hard.

"Want? The man who killed me."

"I never—never—!" cried the king passionately.

"Never? Never?" Color came flooding into the dead man's face, making it look black under the moon. "Never intended? Never meant? Oh, no, I daresay! No one ever intends to kill a pet! One wrings the poor bird's neck in a moment of sheer unthinking irritation, isn't that right? One kicks the clown and behold! the poor fool falls downstairs and breaks his neck. Bah! One shatters a vase, merely." They looked at each other for the space of a minute and then—as if the outburst had broken his mood and reassured him—

"I never disliked you," said Alexander sullenly.

"Oh, no!" in a tone half between a laugh and a sob. "Oh, no!" more quietly.

"No, never," said the king stolidly, and he went and sat on the fallen log.

"I'm not through," said his friend mildly. "Do you know what you missed?" He leaned over the seated man. "For one, your wife's sweet little tongue that I tasted some four hours ago." Alexander said nothing. "Ah, you don't care? You have glory?"

"I do," said the monarch.

"Yes, like the sunset, I suppose. All the color and light that belong to nobody belongs to you. Names! What else do you have: love?"

"We don't deal in that commodity," said Alexander with a flash of teeth.

"Ah! there you speak like your father. Your father whom your mother poisoned with the poison they use to drive rats mad, and who died blubbering over a servant girl who was the only one in the palace foolish and brave enough to give him a drink of water."

"One can avoid being poisoned," said Alexander, grinning again.

"Yes, one can," said his friend, "and I daresay if you avoid being poisoned or assassinated or stabbed in a mutiny—and you have been pretty successful so far—you will live to be an old man."

"You tire me out," said Alexander, rising.

"Ah! but wait—can you get by, do you think, at the end?"

"You've shot your bolt, man!"

"No, wait—listen—there's my wife. I think about her all the time, about the colors of her face and hair and the remoteness she had for me, and how I liked her the better for that, I think. Oh! don't you wander about when you're dead, remembering things like that!"

"I can remember what I've done," said Alexander, laughing, "which is more than you can manage, I think. Now! Let me go. I have no time for any more."

"No, no," said his friend softly.

"Ah, yes!" answered the king, as softly.

"Try," said the dead man. The king drew his sword. "Try." His friend was smiling charmingly; he stretched forth his neck as if to offer it to the knife. "I can keep you here," he said; "that's one thing I can do."

"For what!" harshly.

"You'll see."

The king began to laugh. He walked about the clearing roaring with mirth. The moonlight struck sparks from his sword-hilt and a line of silver blazed along the blade; he whirled his sword above his head like a boy going into battle for the first time; he struck the trunks of trees with it and laughed.

"I have something to show you," said the dead man quietly.

"What?" gasped the king, "what?" half out of breath.

"Something, dear boy." Alexander could not stop laughing. He sat on the log and roared, rocking back and forth. The moon must have gone behind a cloud, for the little glade grew darker and darker; in the gloom, in the midst of the indistinct mass of confused shadows, sat Alexander, laughing. He looked up and found, to his surprise, that his dead friend had come up behind him and now held him by the shoulders in a grip so strong and yet so light that he could not break it. He was forced to turn to one side; he tried to turn back and could not; he struggled impotently under the dead man's grip while his friend's face, so close to his own, moved not an inch, showed not by the slightest alteration in its expression that to control the warrior of the age was any effort for him, a soft and an always soft-living man.

"Look," he said, "look ahead," in a voice almost like love, and changing the position of his hands so that he held the king's face (that king whose arms now hung uselessly at his sides), forced him to turn his gaze.

Alexander gave a scream like the scream of the damned, like the yell of a hurt animal that has nothing to restrain it: no discretion, no prudence, no fear. He would have fallen to the ground if the dead man had not held him.

"There, there, there!" said the dead man in a soft, enthusiastic, urgent whisper, his eyes glittering. "There, look! look!" He grasped the king's shoulders with a vehemence that left marks; he shook him. "There's glory for you!" he whispered, and finally letting him go, retreated across the clearing, never taking his eyes off him, never moving his rigidly spread hands, blending into the stippled shadow and the uncertain light until one looking after him would never have known that there was any such person.

Alexander sat drooping on the fallen log as the old philosopher had before him. The moon was setting; morning was near. His soldiers, horribly frightened at losing him in the middle of the night, would find him at last, though he would not speak to them. He would raise his handsome face and say nothing. They would bring his wife to him (she had gotten worried and had sent a messenger back to the camp in the middle of the night), and he would look at her, say her name in a tone of surprise—and faint. Two days later the army, the Persian queen's handmaids, the king's philosophic retinue, and the royal couple themselves would pack all their gear and start on the return march to Babylon, now called Heliopolis.

The rumors were started by an Egyptian professor whose cataloguing system for the library at Egyptian Alexandria had been summarily rejected by the emperor. Alexander, he said, was mad and had been shut up. He was drunk all day. He alternated wintry midnight swims with bouts of fever. His wife had left him. "No, no," said Aristophorus heatedly, "the truth is—" and hurried away to attend to something else.

Egyptian Alexandria, Babylonian Alexandria, Alexandretta . . . one room of the palace at Heliopolis had a replica (about seven feet high) of a monument Alexander had caused to be built to the memory of his dead friend. The monument was a bronze tower, eighty feet high, with a platform at the top—"for jumping" Alexander had said disingenuously, watching Aristophorus twitch. He drank for hours at the foot of the replica, in a desultory way. He talked to it once in a while.

One afternoon in that part of late winter when a stone house—even in the Babylonian climate—becomes a place to freeze the living and preserve the dead, Aristophorus found his master asleep at the foot of the monument.

"You're drunk, my lord," said he sadly and disapprovingly.

"You're middle-class," said Alexander.

"That monument ought to be destroyed," said Aristophorus, weeping.

"It has charm," said Alexander.

"It's graceless!" (weeping harder).

"It's necessary." Alexander rolled over and fetched himself up on a step, blinking like an owl. "We want to honor our dead friend, Aristophorus." He discovered a wineskin under a heap of outer garments on the step. "Bravo!"

"My lord, my lord!" wept the old philosopher.

"My lord, my lord!" mimicked Alexander. He lay in the heap of clothes, idly. "You think I'm drunk, but I'm not." He sighed. "I haven't got properly drunk for years. I'm too used to it."

"Oh, my lord!"

"Bah! get out of my sight!" and when he was left alone, his face settled into an expression of perfect vacancy. The stone hall was covered with stately patterned hangings that gave the walls a spurious, slightly ridiculous dignity. There was one uncovered window. Alexander ambled tiredly over to it. It gave on a small court and a garden; someone was hoeing. As the king watched he closed both hands unconsciously; the sight of anyone working always affected him. The slave outside bent himself double, clearing and pulling; then he straightened and rubbed his back. A faint, disorganized sound, of which he was not aware, came from the king's throat; he lifted the wineskin to drink and halted halfway. He remembered, with satisfaction, wresting a cup from the old philosopher when the man would drink from it in a dramatic, despairing show that he too would sink to the king's dreadful level. Alexander laughed. "I'm sick," he said. He leaned on the stone windowsill, watching the sky and shivering. He thought, *The words they use for drunkenness. Smashed. Stoned. Blind. Hit yourself over the head with a rock.* Ah!—to fall— His shivering increased. He thought again, with pleasure, that he was sick. *Wipe it out,* he thought. He leaned his head in his hands. They worried him about his wife; who would protect her? they said. Yes, that was right. . . . Slipping to his knees, he leaned his back against the clammy stone wall with a kind of comfort. The dead man had said once—what had he said? "Comfort, above all." But that had been when he was alive.

"My dear lord," said someone. Alexander opened his eyes. "Go away," he said.

"My lord, my lord—" said the old philosopher.

When he opened his eyes again he saw that Aristophorus had gone. He knew that he was sick, and it alarmed him. He dragged himself to his feet and started towards the monument. *Oh, my dear, my dear,* he said passionately to nobody in particular. *My dear, my dear, my dear . . .*

The late afternoon sunlight, wintry and wan, came through the uncovered window and made a square on the floor. He lay on the floor. He opened his eyes for the third time (when the drowning man goes down) and saw the face he had expected to see.

"You're dying," said his friend, and there were tears in his eyes. Alexander said nothing, only lay on the stone floor with his mouth slightly open and his eyes vacant. His breathing was quick and shallow. "Clown," he managed to say. "Jackal. But I kept you around."

"I've kept *you* around. Doing nothing. For the last four years."

"Ah!—ah!" cried Alexander, for the floor was sinking and bellying under him. "Help!" he cried. Crouched over him, his nurse's son, his harpy, his old friend, watched him intently. "Courage, man!" he cried, "courage! It only lasts a moment! Keep your head clear."

"Call my wife," said the king, with an effort. The dead man shook his head.

"Oh, yes," said Alexander grimly. "Oh, yes."

"Never," said the other. "I don't share."

"Roxane!" cried Alexander, and then before his friend could stop him, "Roxane!" so that the walls reechoed with it. There was the sound of light steps in the passageway. "You cruel fool!" whispered the dead man angrily, and he rose to his feet and darted to her, barring the way. She carried her eight months' pregnancy in front of her like a basket, hurrying along the hall with little breathless steps.

"My dear," he said, "my dear, it's nothing, nothing. Go back. Please go back."

"Good heavens, it's you," said she matter-of-factly.

"Yes, love, go back," he said, "go back. Go rest." He held out his hands, smiling tenderly.

"Oh, no," said the queen wisely, "there's something; *I* can tell," and she pushed past him. She began telling her husband that he really must go to bed; then she stopped, puzzled, and then a little intake of breath announced that she had seen the dying man's face. The dead man trembled; he stood at the window where the king had stood, but saw nothing. At his back the princess gave a little scream.

"My dear," said the dead man, turning round (she was kneeling at Alexander's side) "my dear, he'll be quite well, I promise you," (but she seemed not to hear him) "my dear, I promise you—" but she rushed out, crying different names out loud. She stopped at the doorway, looking right past the dead man as if she were looking through him. Her face expressed nothing but surprise, although she was wringing her hands.

"My dear," he said calmly, "what you see is a delusion. The man is not suffering. At the end fever is not unpleasant, I assure you; the body sinks but the mind floats like a piece of ash, and you will only make your husband's last moments needlessly unhappy if you cry and wring your hands and behave in an unconsidered and haphazard way."

"Aristophorus!" screamed the princess, "Aristophorus!" and she rushed out of the room.

I am beginning to fade, the dead man thought, going back to Alexander. His attack of trembling hit him again and he knelt by the dying man, taking the unconscious face in his hands.

"King," he whispered urgently, "King." Alexander opened his eyes. "Listen to me."

"No," said the dying man. His friend, cradling the conqueror's head in his hands, smiled with a radiant and serene joy. "Live," he whispered. "Live. Live."

"Can't," said Alexander brusquely, trying to shrug. He closed his eyes. Gently the dead man let his friend's head down onto the floor; he stood up; he moved away. Roxane had come back in with friends, philosophers, doctors; they crowded round the emperor while his friend (whom nobody saw) wandered out of the room into a passageway and down the passageway into another. In the garden (he looked out of a window) the gardener still hoed and weeded last year's dried stalks. The dead man had carried Alexander's wineskin with him and a cup he found near it; he poured himself a drink and sat down on the floor by the window where the pale sunlight came in. Then he stood up. "You butcher!" he shouted, "you bully, you egotist, you killer in love with your own greatness!" and then he said, "How I loved you, how I admired you!" raising the cup in one hand and his other empty hand to the ceiling an attitude of extreme and theatrical grief. His arms sank; he sat again on the floor. *Now I die too*, he thought. He thought, with a certain amusement, of that night in the Indian forests near the river and what he had shown the great Alexander. Like the demons in the old stories he had shown him all the world; he had shown it filled with Alexandrias and Alexandrettas as numerous as the stars, with carved pillars set up in the East as far as the kingdoms of Ch'in and Ch'u, farther than Han, satraps ruling the undiscovered continents on the other side of the globe, tablets commemorating Alexander in the lands of the Finns and the Lapps, in the hands of the Alaskan Eskimos, empire up to the Arctic Circle and down into Africa, over the Cape and through the other side, Alexanders here, Alexanders there, a fulfilled empire, a safe empire, a satisfied dream. And then two words: *What then?*

Legend has it that great Alexander wept because there were no more worlds to conquer; in truth, he bellowed like a bull.

No one, thought the dead man, *feels more despair than a man who has been robbed of his profession. Luckily I never had one.* A sound from the room he had just quitted hit him and made him catch his breath. How terrible to die, he thought, how terrible! He took a drink from the wine-cup and noted that his hand was shaking. From the next room came a sharp cry, little Roxane wailing for her man. The dead man, whose heart seemed to have stopped, sat motionless while his face became clear of all expression, taking on the beautiful, grave melancholy of all faces whose owners are absent, temporarily or otherwise. Gently and carefully he put the wine-cup down on the damp stone floor, with the concentrated gentleness of all the times he had picked things up only to put them down—cups, flowers, jewelry, paintings, and women's hands. He thought of all the things he had touched and never owned, of all the women he had liked and avoided. The one man he had admired so passionately and so passionately envied was dead. Nothing was left. He thought, as if thinking of a picture, of his wife—a dissatisfied Sappho who had written verses and left the court to live with some businessman. He doubled over, not in laughter this time, but as if Alexander's blade, which had long ago stabbed through his vitals, once again tore him. The dead forget nothing. The blade had ripped apart the intricate webs that kept him alive, it had startled and hurt him, it had broken his heart. Silently he bent over and fell to the floor. He stretched along it with a kind of sigh, as if going to sleep, and the moment he closed his eyes, he disappeared. The wine-cup stood alone on the floor. An attendant who had heard the news of the king's death ran excitedly through the room and out into the garden.

"Something has happened!" he shouted to the gardener. The gardener threw down his hoe, and the two talked together in low whispers.

"It'll be hard on us," the gardener said, shaking his head. The attendant clapped him on the back. "Don't forget," he said, "we stand together." He added generously, "I don't forget my relatives." The gardener nodded solemnly. He picked up his tools, the attendant helping him. Together they disappeared into another part of the court. The sun (for it was now late afternoon) moved a little; the square of light on the floor altered its position somewhat and touched the standing wine-cup with a spark of gold. Nearby lay the wineskin, on its side but closed by some considerate hand—or so it seemed, for the floor remained clean. Nothing moved. Everything remained as it was. It was exactly as if nothing had happened.

NOTE ON "Poor Man, Beggar Man": It is riddled with inaccuracies. Cleitus the Black was one of Alexander's generals whom Alexander actually did kill in 328 B.C., as Cleitus became incensed at the *proskynesis* (Asiatic knee-crawling) Alexander demanded of his associates. Alexander was drunk at the time, Cleitus' sister had indeed been his old nurse, and from that day on Alexander exempted Macedonians from the Persian court etiquette of *proskynesis.*

However, Alexander did cross the Indus in 326 B.C. It was the Beas or Hyphasis River that his army refused to cross; after three probably rather unpleasant days, Alexander consented to return to a more Westerly portion of the world.

Even more at variance with my story, Alexander had not—in 326 B.C.—married Roxane. She was a Sogdian, to be exact, and he married her in 324 B.C. at Susa, so that she could not possibly have been with him at the historically crucial moment when he decided to penetrate no farther into India. In fact, Alexander also married Darius' daughter Barsine in 324 B.C., the year in which he returned to Babylon. He died of fever on June 13, 323 B.C. He was thirty-three years old.

In character he was far from the blunt-minded bully my story suggests; in historical fact, my Alexander and my Cleitus, put together, would have made up a much better facsimile of the historical Alexander.

Perhaps that is the whole point of the story.

—Joanna Russ

Old Thoughts, Old Presences

I. DADDY'S GIRL

. . . their sons' and brothers' need to debase so totally all that was previously sacred (Nature and Women) in order to experience themselves as divine, in order to found a civilization based on their own sacredness.

—PHYLLIS CHESLER,
"The Amazon Legacy"

My mother's country: the body and garden of the Great Goddess, fair, ornamental, tended; I can wander forever in Her lap under the sun of Her face, in a cultivated place like the Botanical Gardens of my childhood where everything is suffused with the divine personality, regal, wide, and lovely. Everything's here—pineapples from Java, Norway pine, greenhouses like tropical igloos, the long wide lawns, camomile meadows veiled with hair, lawns that look like—and are—the dancing-grounds of angels.

The fatherland is another place.

If Mother is Being, Daddy is *nada*, the flaw, the crack at the center of the universe, the illusion that implodes as you look at it, the glittery thing you thought was real but it's made out of nothing: seduction, emptiness, cold, the brightness of rooms without air. Terrible energy radiates from this. It's the state of being falsified. I have a friend called Linda and Linda lives in this world, not I; last autumn Linda and I were riding into the fatherland inside the big blue bell of a snowstorm—that light is a sign of sorcery.

"Visit me?" says Linda. "I'll get a babysitter. I'll get divorced. I'll get an abortion." Linda and I were riding on talking horses who put their heads together and said nasty things about us; in all that whirling whiteness there was not one kind word. Linda rode bad sidesaddle. The familiar signs of the road swam by, humped shapes buried indistinguishably under snow: murder, adultery, incest, suicide. This is fairy-tale country. "I wonder what we'll find," says Linda. She, not I. Linda is what the French call *rondelette*; she's young, foolish, and sinfully pretty. She wipes the magic snow off her sandals and the cleft between her breasts; her shoulders and bosom are bare. She's all female. In my father's country I can never remember the motherland because my father's country has what's called *invalidation*, so although I know where I'm going I don't know why, or rather the reason I do know has a very hollow ring to it and I think I may have forgotten, i.e. confusion in the middle of the snowstorm.

Am I going there to be a governess?

Snow settles thickly on Linda's horn-rimmed glasses.

When I was very young—eleven or twelve years old—I walked into that light and recognized in it my personal destiny. I walked into my eleven-year-old's bedroom and saw the air turn blue between the frosted windowpanes—Jack Frost at work. It was very, very cold. My destiny is waiting for me outside this whirling glass ball. Up ahead is a flagged courtyard where I will get off my horse, blowing on my fingers and wishing I were a man; I'll gather up my skirts and crinoline and the little box that came with me from Miss Swithin's; I'll tie the crackling ribbons of my bonnet. Menstruation, Victoriana, marriage, anemia, women's troubles. I mustn't. Nursing my dead father. So many paintings in which a woman adores a dead male divinity. Pictures of domestic unhappiness. Hatboxes. Emily Brontë owned a square carnelian brooch, which she kept with manuscripts in a blue box. There are times Linda makes me throw up because she has no mind at all; I don't mean that she's mindless, actually, but her amazing bare buttocks are somehow always triumphant over her face; my poor friend has just a faint glaze of consciousness like the stuff they put on a ham, a constant innocent surprise (she's very trusting), a perpetual temptation to forcing her. And she has enormous stamina; she can live through anything—beat her with a padded coat hanger and minutes later she's fresh and rosy. I have been through so many dramatic scenes with Linda; she's in a pretty gingham dress (neat but provocative) which they tear off, they put her into a stupid affair of velvet tags and leather straps which lets her body hang out all over; they hold her down, pulling her legs apart, and every man in the place rams himself into her (it's a treat) with ecstatic ohs! and ahs! (she, not I) bruising her, violating her, hurting her, using her, swilling up her round, round, round, jiggling, wretched parts with their exquisite slight taste of stupidity. She, not I.

She has no sexual thoughts. This is very important to understand. She's a dish of ice cream. Divinity hits her between the legs and dazes her. When she's in her bafflement, when the syrup of sacrifice rises from the modest temple (she, not I) in Linda's vagina and totally obscures her brain, then you can "have" Linda. You can even pretend to talk to Linda. I've done it myself, at least in imagination, beating her like a gong, as the saying goes, bursting with itchy, nervous, unhappy desire (that's the kind of appetite for her, isn't it?) and enjoying her thoroughly, crying out hot wench, hot wench, but if her temple is convulsed in ruin and horror, that still was not she. None of it gets into her head.

She has some vague feeling for jewelry.

(In my dreams I keep trying to get under the surface of the sea but can't; the waves miss me or the water dries up as I run into it, or I pretend I'm in it but know I'm not or the summery sea takes one look and revolts into a reverse tsunami because it's not my personal destiny to get wet. I even row on dry land, in fact between the white lines painted on a parking lot, quite hopelessly.

(I have a secret taste for vomit.

(Linda means "lovely." Doesn't it?

(I want to breathe water and go home.)

When we reached the courtyard I saw that this time the scene of my personal destiny was to be a castle, a huge home. Fields canceled, gone quite suddenly, replaced by a human habitation: the interaction of snow with stone, snow with glass. If you are born without the sacred totem, what do you do, what do you do? This basso profundo daydream dreamed by so many in the public prints that it must be true. The servants took my horse and I strode over the flagged yard (snow whirling into the flames of the torches on the wall, making them sputter), flicking my gloves against stone, wrought iron, massive oak, slapping my gloves with one hand against the palm of the other. I'm tall and ugly. I don't bother about what happens to Linda. Perhaps this place is a Home, although it's miles from anywhere; no need in that case to put iron bars on the windows. I used to escape from places like this nightly, met once by Linda (who in my dream was wearing Garbo slacks and an enormous sun-hat) in some sort of outbuilding, a shed or something. Somewhere in this very complicated blueprint is an apartment I know well: a pretty, middle-class place nicely decorated, with the living-room floor (well-varnished and polished) buckling drastically over a sort of wooden hump, as if there were something heaving up from underneath, and a shack or lean-to built on the back with all sorts of gardening and carpenters' tools rusting away in it because it's so wet, the walls running with water and the floor covered with slime. The darkness here is, as usual, absolute, more an abstract condition or state of mind than the real thing. I follow a servant up the raw stone stairs—and we need servants, otherwise how could we be magnified—although I'm quite used to doing the floors myself on hands and knees. It (the servant, the thing, the person, the hunchbacked what-do-you-call-it) leaves me in a firelit room where the walls sweat moisture, it's so cold, and I sit down on a bench before that visual flame which warms nothing but the pupils of my eyes. There's a book on an inlaid table set right on the stone floor, a little book with a medieval enameled cross on the cover; I pick it up and read:

like a wastebasket

Who or what is like a wastebasket?

There's something in this book I don't like, so I put it down—you know, something that shocks me although I can't remember what. I don't like reading about such things: love, pain, a constricted unhappiness.

I had always wanted a man's griefs, his passions, his boredom, even, to be emptied into me.

There's something outside, beyond the archway of the door.

Refusing to feed my hidden vanity, my sulkiness, my individualism, X neglects everything I demand; he takes my head in his hands kindly but impersonally, because I'm only a means to a sensation, after all

How can things be so vivid to the eye and so absent in every other way?

The two of them X and Y, fussing over me, but really through me or past me while standing me against that very expensive office desk, communicating with each other by means of my abused body like two executives talking into the dictaphone or over the secretary's head, casually enjoying a bit of fluff, so to speak, and my poor mind caught between, the victim of a little bit of vanity (my own), to be removed without mercy if I show the slightest symptom of having any sensations, so I must be as blank as the telephone or the rug

What's the good of not reading the book if I can't help reading the book?

No tears of shame or joy. No sounds. I'll let it out inside, the only place they like it. As X, who is one zero, shoves me one way and talks over my dumb breasts to another zero, Y, who in my mouth

I know I'm foolish. Ashamed to be caught daydreaming.

You know, I'm obsessed with the servant problem—I mean getting hunchbacks to serve us, cripples, idiots, the insane, women— all kinds of unfit persons. Persons below the law. The trouble is, there's no one else. (There really is someone outside this room; I've fallen in love so often with unseen presences that I can tell when they're going to pop up; I mean of course a man outside the room with a torch, which makes his radiance precede him, and who has come to tell me I don't know what, that I ought to be rescuing Linda from something or other (the second thing she's good for).

And I remember walking on the battlements here in clothes I'd stolen, men's clothes, isolated like a god in my own fancies, distorted and magnified by the fog in which everything became glitteringly visible. Everyone who saw me desired me. Although no one desires me or loves me now, someone exists in the fatherland whose very name would make my heart stop; I'm afraid even to look up from this bench on which I sit. A tree trunk. A pre-Columbian sun god. A masked suit of armor, fretted with gold. The characteristic emotion of the fatherland is that feeling called by men *anguish*, by women *love*, and here in my little room in my tower, lit by a cold fire, reading, terribly nostalgic, remembering, dead, quite insane, a reincarnation of a Victorian ladies'-maid, I underestimate myself, I put my head in my hands, I long with all my soul to be staked, immolated, torn to pieces, suicided, to be stabbed repeatedly, to be repeatedly impaled. Tears of desire and anguish, although I am so tall and so friendless and so ugly. They were all unattractive, those legions of unloved sisters and fatherless girls, spinsters without hope, sick women in crinolines who nursed their fathers through mortal illnesses and never even got into pornography books. I think I'll get out; I could easily fool the guard outside the door, that hunchbacked rochester or watson or whatever-you-call-it (they're all over the place), who can be fooled by the crudest male impersonation. I will be so damned nonchalant, so recklessly brave, so brilliantly intellectual even in my page's costume (an alto). And Linda takes the heat off me, if only for a little while. So I'll get up and go. Looking for love.)

I was quite alone through all this, of course.

Stone stairs: each riser a different thought. Sometimes I saw three soldiers playing dice for my heart, sometimes a woman I know, a friend of mine, brushing her little daughter's hair. Such different scenes. The halls of this château are lit by naked, unfrosted light bulbs or sometimes with oil-dip lamps, or torches, or candles. To go traveling for love makes you a very vulnerable pilgrim. I thought that on the stairs I might meet Him, or that He might be walking down a passage, and these conjectures made me sick at heart. Girl in snowstorm, running away from castle. Girl in jungle, running away from verandah. Girl in moonlight, running away from mansion. That terrible presence that knocks you down. Fate. Kismet. I saw a great many things.

In one stone room myself as a five-year-old playing cards alone; the child turns, revealing that Its face is covered with ice or metal, some kind of mask or (horrible!) It grew that way.

A butcher shop set up inside the stone walls of this castle, with the meatcutter in his bloodstained apron winking energetically at me to show that he's jollying me along, he likes me. What do you want, Honey? I bet you read books, ha ha. I bet you go to school. I know you don't mind my talking to you like this. Hell, she doesn't mind. Don't look so down, Honey. I'll take care of you. He winks spasmodically like a demented machine, he can't stop, and the other women streetwalkers lean against the walls of the room in various attitudes of dislike and boredom. They've seen it all before, they don't care. His murderer's hand on mine.

A woman in a long skirt combing out her daughter's hair. A big brown-and-white dog lies snoozing by the stone fireplace and the amber Persian cats curl up in a chair by the embroidery frame. It's very quiet. The woman catches sight of me and smiles as if she knew something but won't tell me what it is; she looks up at me, amused; she'd rather be silent as my mother was while combing out my tangledy child's hair, as my cousin complained about having to be still while my mother's sister combed the snarls out of her long curly red hair, as someday I will set my daughter between my knees and comb her hair. We know something.

A man all in black reading in a room full of books, shelves set right into the stone walls; he's turning the pages under a shaded electric lamp. Dry, sensible, and competent. Who are you? He's amused: "I have the same name as you but I'm the lucky one."

It's hopeless. I'll never find Him. And I need Him so desperately. Right in the middle of the empty lit-up corridor my palms sweat with fear, I get dizzy, my throat dries up; the very air is glittering with a dry, horrible desire. I'm nobody. I'm nothing. It's so humiliating to be me. I want to be taken out of myself, life is unbearable if I'm not, so I yearn for water, for Him; I almost lie down right here on the stone floor of the corridor; I want to curl up and die. The corrida of the horridor. His absence: malicious and prying. A sterilization, a lack of sound. I remember what it was like to be without Him at sixteen, knowing that romance danced all around me but that He wouldn't come, that somehow I blighted it, that I had a bad touch. Night after night I've fled down these halls, out of my mind with fear, trying to get out when I should have been trying to get in, carrying my shameful parts with me, of which the worst was: *I don't really want to be here.* They're right when they say it's the most important thing in your life. *I'm no better than the others.* I don't want to miss it, so I start running, like all those girls on the covers of paperback books who are running from mad wives in attics or dead wives in closets; I go zipping through the halls of the fatherland and, in my blindness, with a dry grin of terror and repulsion *am catapulted through a crimson velvet drape into a scene of wild sexual license, everyone masked, naked, faceless, impersonally powerful except for the boys and girls spread-eagled, bent over, who are being pierced hard or worked at hard and who are not being consulted. Their anxious, pathetic, pained little faces. Perhaps my ambidextrous smile will save me.*

Don't you want to be—?

Yes, I said (but do I have to go through all this?).

Made solemn by suffering, with my anxious little monkey-face all pursed up, I offered to him my delicate little bits of skin, my nether face, the quizzical palms of my hands, all my small thoughts. He battered them to pieces. I put my face in my hands and wept. This dreadful mechanical business, shes on their backs, hes on all fours, so much human misery. I wouldn't mind if it was just a solid and dependable prick; I wouldn't mind if I could hold on to it and come one two three four five times just like that. I don't want this edgy, subtle love that pierces to the marrow of my bones. Over my head I heard: I like boys; it's tighter. He took it out before I was ready and I wriggled like an eel, though I didn't want to; another appeared and I came. Have I violated etiquette? They fucked me in the ass and it hurt badly. Part of my clothes are gone, so I walk through it all in my long black aphrodisiac stockings and no pants, my dumb bush of hair showing dejectedly in front. It's a blight, desire in the secret parts everyone can see, my nether lips preparing to speak, stirring slowly, the tongue beginning to swell. There are denominators between me and the door. I took weak hold of a boy I did not know, but nothing happened; I think he will

change in a moment (as I shake him pettishly by the shoulders),
he'll go limp, his flesh will flow and change, he'll turn under my
hands into a young woman, her face slender, her eyes violet-dim,
little rolls of plumpness under her breasts and around her thighs.
Chubby Linda.

I'm embracing a mirror.

For heaven's sake, put your clothes on! she says.

Dreaming of being kidnapped by pirates (I was eleven).

Movies.

Love comix.

The way it was: Dad helping Mother across the street because
she was so weak and stupid she might get killed. His picking up jars
by their tops and then blaming her for not screwing them on tight
enough. His turning to me at the dinner table after he had finished
all his food and saying, "Don't eat so fast. You'll get an ulcer." I remember a woman in a restaurant at the next table from us who had
fresh flowers twined in her and her two little daughters' hair (honest) and a husband who said nothing. The matriarch talked endlessly to her two little girls because the three of them were so sensitive and beautiful and her husband obviously wasn't; she pointed
out to her admiring girls how pretty and stylish Mother and I were.
The man sat there and said nothing: the indispensable, crucial lay
figure.

That's what I am. That's what I'm for. Am I even that?

I think the Man I'm looking for, the Governor who controls this
castle, will be somewhere at its highest point. He doesn't own it, He
haunts it. I think I own it. I want to look up at Him imploringly and
timidly; I want to say, "Do you need me?" I want to say, "Let me
do something for you." We'll sit together in front of the fire, I with
my dreaming head on His knee, and I'll be necessary to Him. All
these thoughts are clichés, but that's life. I'm going up a sort of cir-
cular stairway, the treads of which are metal and therefore slippery. I could lie and say that the stairway is full of ghosts, but they
were exhausted long ago; everything like that has already happened. I've been making my nightly pilgrimage for years, and now
only the reality is left.

With one exception: I think the ghost of my father is haunting
these stairs. I can remember him so well—I can remember so many
things. Queer to think that in those days he was younger than I am

now. When I was five he took me out in a canoe and picked wild orchids for me. He made fishing flies by hand with a jeweler's loupe and tweezers, working on bits of tufted fluff as delicate as thoughts. He had bright eyes and a big nose (like mine), which I thought was beautiful. I made a shrine for his photograph with cardboard backing and two candles when I was twelve. He forgave my mother for being a woman because she was also a saint, but I betrayed him; I grew up. He liked to talk about history and epidemiology. When I was a little girl I believed that it was he who made the sun come up every morning; I didn't believe it off my own bat but because he told me so. He gave me a Dumbo doll when I was four (that's the Disney elephant made out of gray plush) because we both had big ears and we would both learn to fly.

You know who's behind that door.

I want to see what he'll say to me this time. He always says something interesting.

I open the door and there he is, with his jeweler's loupe in his eye, working with tweezers and a needle and thread.

He looks up unsympathetically. "Don't touch anything."

I wait. Petulant and bitter, a little old man with exophthalmic eyes and the white sideburns and whiskers of the Emperor Franz Josef, my father works with his bits of thread. He is, in some way that I don't understand, a failure. He's embittered by the world's refractoriness, by his mother's strength, by the treachery of his daughter. He looks up and says crossly, "I don't like the way you sit. Your thighs are too fat."

That's first. He's muttering to himself, something about A Beautiful Blonde who drove the wrong way down a one-way street. Ha ha. He's really nobody. He lives here, in my head.

"You," he says sulkily, "have been chosen to be Commander General of the whole universe." He lifts his lip cruelly in a smile, gloating over what comes next. "But you're not going to get the job.

"Do you know why?"

I say nothing.

"You're not going to get the job," says my father with immense self-righteous pleasure, *"because they can't provide bathroom facilities for girls!"* He starts laughing like a crow that used to live next to us in the country, the pet of the people down the road; it would get terribly stirred up and would hop around its cage with a hoarse, loud caw, trying to eat the bars or worry at them with its beak, excited and gratified over things none of us could understand. Who knows what makes a crow happy or sad?

And that's my father.

My God, but it's *cold* in the fatherland! Bitter cold even inside the castle; I had to wrap myself in my cloak, and when I met Linda on the next landing down (long past that door, now shut) the wind outside flung a gust through the trefoil window that covered us with stinging snow. It stuns you; it makes your ears ring. Linda must have had an experience like mine; she crossed her arms and beat them against her chest to keep warm. "Oh, fuck it," she said bitterly. "Oh, fuck it, the hell with it. It's not worth it."

"Where'd you get the fur coat?" I said. (That was one swell fur coat.)

"Stole it." She coughed, breathed on her glasses, and then polished them on the lapel of her fur—bear, as I remember. She jerked a fist across her throat to indicate what she's done to somebody (or maybe only what she'd like to do), then staggered comically around the landing with her tongue stuck out and her eyes crossed. "Blotto," she said. We kissed goodbye because we were going separate ways. "Will you write?" we said, "Oh, do write." Down the freezing halls of the fatherland—or man's land—where rime spreads in poetic, furry stain over the stone floor, out between the bars of the back gate, around the edge of a vast, dark, frozen pond, and crawling on our stomachs through a hole in the last stone wall where Linda lost her fur hat. There was a blizzard you could not face into, now that the magic was gone, trees that lashed at you, and the iron-hard furrows of the potato fields of my father's country where maidens in the springtime (which never comes) may gather (if you'll excuse the expression) very small potatoes indeed.

How did I get out?

I said, Goodbye, Goodbye.

I walked through the door. The door to the motherland can be a door in a construction fence that leads nowhere, a door inside a closet that leads to a hidey-hole, a door in the brick front of a house on a street in a town in any part of the world. The trick is to get inside oneself. The Great Goddess puts me between Her knees and combs my hair night and day. Striding over the crests of the grassy hills with Her panthers, She causes the grass to stretch precariously between its grasping toe and its one drinking eye, trying to be with Her; trees lean towards Her, disheveled with desire. As the fish is in the sea and the sea is in the fish, so we live and move and have our being. It's colorless in the swimming mist, clear and thin-drawn, here where it's infinite, as color comes back to things from Her bright face. Her pine-cones, Her spear, Her sandals, Her twisted snakes. Time runs differently in the two places, and as my father creates around Him perpetual night, so Her days and nights naturally progress, and now Her sun rises clear of the hills. Linda rises too, nymphlike, from the grass, embodied out of a stream, hung about with watches, knapsacks, wallets, extra socks, canteens, and collapsible drinking-cups, all the trophies of travel. "Have I had adventures!" she says. "It took me ten years to get home." She pitches a tent, washes her socks, builds a fire, shears a sheep, ploughs a homestead, delivers a baby, sets up a collapsible typewriter, digs a field toilet, and holding a wetted finger up to the wind, accurately predicts the weather for the next twenty-four hours. "Have I got things to tell you!" she says. Delighted, I settle down on the grass and prepare to listen. It's going to be a long, leisurely feast. She Herself is listening, one vast, attentive, radiant Ear bending over the hills. We're in Her lap this pale, fresh, chilly summer dawn.

At last.

II. THE AUTOBIOGRAPHY OF MY MOTHER

I'm an I.
  Sometimes I'm a she.
  Sometimes I'm even a he.
  Sometimes I'm veryvery I.
  Sometimes I'm my mother.

I was visiting friends in Woodstock; you may find it surprising that I met my mother there for the first time. I certainly do. She was two years old. My mother and I live on different ends of a balance;

thus it's not surprising to find that when I'm thirty-five she's just a little tot. She sat on the living-room rug and stared at me, with her legs bent under her in a position impossible to anyone but a baby. Babies might be lobsters or some other strange form of life, considering what positions they take up. A little light tug at the ornamental tassel of my shoe—not apologetic or tentative, she feels both modest and confident, but she has small hands. "What's that?" she says.

"That's a tassel." She decamped and settled her attention on the other shoe. "And what's *that?*"

"Another tassel." This baby has flossy black hair, a pinched little chin, and round pale-green eyes. Even at the age of two her upper lip is distinctive: long, obstinate, almost a chimp's. I think she thinks that every object has its own proper name and so—without intending to—I made her commit her first error. She said: "That's *a tassel.* That's *another tassel.*" I nodded, bored. She's of the age at which they always take off their clothes; patiently, with her own understanding of what she likes and what's necessary to her, she took off all of hers: her little sailor dress, her patent leather shoes, her draggy black cotton stockings. It's only history that gave her these instead of a ruff and stomacher. She practiced talking in the corner of the living room for half an hour; then she came over to me, nude, without her underwear, and remarked:

"That's a tassel. That's another tassel."

"Uh-huh," I said. Pleased at having learned something, she pondered for a moment and then switched them around; declaring:

"That's *another tassel* and that's *a tassel.*"

"No, no," I said. "They're both tassels. This is a tassel and that's a tassel."

She backed away from me. I don't think she likes me now. Later that night I saw her scream with excitement when her father came home; he held the tail of her nightshirt in one hand and her brother's in the other; they both played the great game of trying to scramble away from him on all fours. My mother shrieked and laughed. Even at the age of two she's addicted to pleasure.

It'll ruin her.

You get stuck in time, not when you're born exactly, but when you "sit up and take notice," as they say, when you become aware that you have an individuality and there's something out there that either likes you or doesn't like you. This happens at about eighteen months. It isn't that you really prefer some other time, you don't know anything about that; you just back off (still crawling, perhaps), not shaking your head (for you don't know about that, either), just wary and knowing you don't like *that staircase* or *those visitors* or *this parent.* But what can be done about it? You're stuck. It would be the same if you could travel through time but not through space.

Like this story.

At a Chinese restaurant: that is, a big room with a high ceiling and dun walls, like a converted gymnasium. Sepia-colored screens in front of the Men's and Ladies'. There is a fan of crimson coral over my mother's head and the chairs are high-backed and plain, the ultimate in chic for 1925. My mother is nineteen. When I was that age I discovered her diary and some poems she had written; they didn't mention the restaurant but here she is anyway, having dinner with her best friend. I've looked everywhere in them to find any evidence that she was abnormal, but there's none. Nobody hugs anybody or says anything they shouldn't, and if there's any morbidity, that's gone too. My mother's written remains are perfect. At that time I wasn't born yet. I'm not even a ghost in her thought because she's not going to get married or even have children; she's going to be a famous poet. It was known then that you had to have children. It was a fact, like the Empire State Building I saw every morning out of the corner of my eye at breakfast (through the kitchen window). When you looked at childlessness in those days you didn't even realize that you had made a judgment, an inference from one set of conditions to another, you just *knew.*

I sat down imprudently at my mother's table.

Now I'm not as pretty as she is (I don't look a bit like her with my big behind and my buck teeth) but I'm much better dressed, and having been able to arrange my entry to suit myself, I can turn on to the full that bullying, leering, ironical boldness I adopt so easily with women; I place my well-cut suede coat, my smart gloves, my modernique pearl earrings, and Dior scarf directly in the track of my mother's green, beautiful, puzzled, nearsighted eyes. My mother didn't want me to sit next to her—she wanted her friend to come back. Strangers alarm her. When my mother is not with a good friend her spirits flag, she becomes vague, she loses control of herself and stares around the room, not because she wants to look at things but because she's diffused and anxious; it's a way of not meeting anyone's eye. She ducks her head and mutters (mannerisms that won't look so cute at fifty-nine). I want to protect her. Years later I'll hold her elbow when she crosses the street, suffer with her when she can't breathe in a crowd, but this is before she's perfected any such tricks, so I can only bare my teeth at her in a way that makes her uncomfortable. She essays a smile.

"Do you come here often?" I say, and she draws on her gloves; that is, she wanted to draw on her gloves, began to move her hands as if she would do so, then didn't. She looked guilty. Mother has been taught to be nice to everybody, but she doesn't want to be nice to me. Last week she wrote a romantic love story about a girl whose mouth was like a slow flame. When I'm eleven I will get felt up on my rear end in a crowd and will be too ashamed to run away. It may occur to you that the context between us is sexual. I think it is parental.

"Would you care to step outside?" I said politely. Mother demurred. Sitting there—I mean us sitting there—well, you might have taken us for cousins. I picked up the check and she suffered because she didn't know what to do. Her friend, who will never get here in time, forms in my mother's memory a little bright door. I dropped two anachronistic quarters on the tablecloth and then put my French purse back in my navy-blue suede bag, an easy forty-five dollars which she has never seen, no, not even in dreams.

"Do you mind if we chat?" I said. "Shall we have coffee?" and went on to explain: that I was a stranger in town, that I was new here, that I was going to catch a train in a few hours. I told her that I was her daughter, that she was going to marry eventually and after two spontaneous abortions bear me, that I didn't usually ask for favors but this was different.

"Consider what you gain by not marrying," I said. We walked out onto Columbus Avenue. "All this can be yours." (Be the first one on your block; astonish your friends.) I told her that the most sacred female function was motherhood, that by her expression I knew that she knew it too, that nobody would dream of interfering with an already-accomplished pregnancy (and that she knew that) and that life was the greatest gift anybody could give, although only a woman could understand that or believe it. I said:

"And I want you to take it back."

We were both eleven, on roller skates, skating towards Bronx Park with our braids flying behind us, but my mother was a little younger and a little slower, like my younger sister. I called her "Stupid."

In the first place I never borrowed it, in the second place it hasn't got a hole in it now, and in the third place it already had a hole in it when I borrowed it. I was going to show her all the kingdoms of the world. I wanted to protect my mother. Walking down Columbus Avenue in this expansive and generous mood—well, my mother didn't know what to make of me; like so many people she's puzzled by a woman who isn't beautiful, who doesn't make any pretense of being beautiful, and who yet flaunts herself. That's me. I asked my mother to tell me her daydreams, daydreams of meeting The Right Man, of being kept by an Older Woman, of inheriting money. Money means blood in dreams and blood means money. The autumn foliage in the park, for example, because the sun hadn't quite set. My mother is wearing a shapeless brown cloth coat that conceals her figure. It's very odd to think that this is 1921. Overheard: I thought it would be different.

I told my mother that when women first meet they dislike each other (because it's expected of them) but that's all right; that soon gives way to a feeling of mutual weakness and worthlessness, and the feeling of being one species leads in turn to plotting, scheming, and shared conspiracies. I said that if we were going to be mother and daughter we ought to get to know each other. As we walked on the stone-flagged park paths my mother's soul flew out from under my fingers at every turn, to every man who passed, a terrible yearning, an awful lack, a down-on-your-knees appeal to anybody in the passing scene. She didn't like my company at all.

"Do you know what I want you to do?" I said. "Well, do you?"

"Well, do you?" my mother echoed earnestly, looking up at me with her nymph's green eyes.

"Look here—" I said.

("Look here—")

I suppose you expect me to say that I listened to her artlessly simple chatter, that I confided in her, or that next she will be a big girl and I the little one, but if you expect me to risk her being older than me, you're crazy. I remember what that was like from last time. I told her all of it—the blood, the sweat, the nastiness, the invasion of personality, the utter indecency (except in middle age, except with money), and she only looked up at me as if she knew things, that girl. She didn't like me. The palisade looking out over the river. The mild October air. We stood arm in arm, like chums, watching the wakes of the boats in the water. She said I couldn't understand. She said with complete conviction:

"You were never young."

My mother, a matron of fifty but for some reason shrunk to the size of an infant and wrapped in baby clothes, is lying in her cradle. Swaddled, her arms at her sides, furious. Frowning—this is no way to treat a grown woman! She is about to wawl. I could leave her there and she'd die—dirty herself, starve, become mute and apathetic—she's just a baby. Maternally I take into my arms my fifty-year-old mother because you can't leave a baby, can you? and cradling her tenderly to my breast I start dancing around the room. She hates it. Screaming and red-faced. Maybe she wants a different dance. I change into a waltz, rocking her softly, and right away, my goodness, the little baby is rocked into quiet, she's straightening her corrugated little brows, unwrapping the snaky moist curls that come finely from under her cap, smoothing her sulky little mouth. I guess she likes waltzing. If I didn't take care of her, how would she ever grow up to be my mother? It would be infanti-suicide, to say the least (if not something worse). When she stops crying I'll put her back into the cradle and sneak off, but there is command in that steely little face, those snapping little eyes, she stares up at me like a snapping turtle, making plans, telling me with her expression all the terrible things she's going to do to me when I'm the baby and she's the mother and I know she did them because I was there. *You keep on rocking me!* she says.

So we keep on waltzing around the room.

When I was a chid—
a child—
When I was a chidden child—

I came into my right mind at a certain age, I think I inherited it, so to speak, although they didn't allow me to use it until I was already fairly cracked. Coming home from the dentist at sixteen on winter evenings with the sky hot-pink and amber in the west and the wind going right through your coat; it's discouraging to find automata in the living room. Cars shooting by to cheery dinners, homey lights from the windows above the stoop. Mirages. Inside, a steamy kitchen, something horrible like an abstract sort of Frankenstein's monster made up of old furniture, plates, windows misted over. My mother, who is with us tonight, is also sixteen, and going this time under the name of Harriet (I think) which is a false name and no kin to the beautiful, imaginary playmate I had when I was four, who could fly and would write me letters with hand-painted stamps on them (canceled). After coming all the way in the cold, to be in a room with no living persons in it. To be distressed. To feel superior. To hold myself in good and hard, to know what's possible and what's good for me. Little Harriet Shelley watches wide-eyed the intercourse of a real human family.

AUNT LUCY: No one would tell you the truth about yourself, Harriet, unless they loved you very much. I love you and that's why you can trust me when I tell you the truth about yourself. The truth is that you are bad all through. There isn't a thing about you that's good. You are thoroughly unlovable. And only a person who loves you very much could tell you this.

UNCLE GEORGE: Tell me all your troubles, but don't say a word against your aunt. Your aunt is a saint.

My mother sits listening to the radio, learning how to sew. She's making a patchwork quilt. Does she dislike her family? She denies it. She's not really going to grow up to be a poet. My mother has a mind like a bog; contraries meet in it and everything becomes instantly rotted away. Or her mind is a peat bog that preserves whole corpses. The truth is that I haven't the right to say what's going on in her mind because I know nothing about it.

She goes on sewing, gentle, placid, and serene, everything she should be. I told her that she could have any color car she wanted as long as it was black, but even this failed to shake my soundless mother; One's Personal History Is Bunk, she might have answered me but didn't; she didn't even move away down the couch because my mother is not even mildly stubborn. Perhaps if she were not so polite she would say, "I don't know what you're talking about," but no, she's perfect, and when she raises her great, wondering, credulous, tear-filled gaze, it's not for me but on account of bad Mr. X in the kitchen, who is telling stories to Uncle George about the women who have jobs with him, for example, that their asses stick out:

MR. X: —— —— —— —— —— ass.

UNCLE GEORGE: Mr. X is only joking, dear.

MR. X: That's right. Don't be so sensitive. How can you go out and get a job someday if you're so sensitive? I don't have anything against the ladies who work with me. I think they're fine. I think you're fine, even though you're so sensitive.

AUNT LUCY: See? Mr. X thinks you're fine.

MR. X: I think your aunt is fine, too.

UNCLE GEORGE: He thinks your aunt is fine, too, because he *likes* ladies.

AUNT LUCY: See? Mr. X is generous.

UNCLE GEORGE: Even though your aunt Lucy is a fool.

To cut out those noises people emit from time to time. To be hard and old. To retreat finally. To be free.

"My parents love each other," says my mother, shaking out her work, malignancy in its every fold. She's a wonder. She really believes. I used to think I knew the form of the ultimate relation between my mother and myself but now I'm not so sure; there's that unbreakable steel spring in her accepting head; no longer can I come clattering up the King's highway on my centaur/centurion's hindquarters (half Irish hunter, half plough horse, gray, fat, lazy, name: Mr. Ed), and I no longer look down from my wild, crazy, hero-assassin's eminence at the innkeeper's little daughter in her chaste yet svelte gingham (with its décolletage) and her beautiful, spiritual, dumb eyes and her crumby soul.

"Do you," I said, "do you—tell me!—oh, do you—believe me!— *do you*—**Do you—believe all that?**"

"Yes," she says.

O if you only knew! says her face. Her hands, resting on their sewing, change their import: Life is so hard, hard, hard. An unspoken rule between us has been that I can hate her but she can't hate me; this breaks. (A day in the longed-for life: for once when my mother is carried across the crumbling battlements on the screen the audience laughs, they hoot when she wrings her hands, when she obeys her father's prohibition they howl, when she is seduced they screech, when it starts to snow and the hero walks on her face with his lovely black boots it's all over, and by the time she commits suicide, *there is nobody there.*)

"I think," says my mother thoughtfully, biting a thread, "that I'm going to get married." She looks at me, shrewdly and with considerable hatred.

"That way," she says in a low, controlled voice, *"I will be able to get away from you!"*

(When she was little my mother used to scare her relatives by asking them if they were happy; they would always answer, "*Of course* I'm happy." When I was little I once asked her if she was happy and she said, "Of course I'm happy.")

Something that will never happen: my mother and I, chums, sharing secrets, giggling at the dinner table, writing in each other's slambooks, going to the movies together. Doing up each other's hair. It's not dreadful that she doesn't want me, just embarrassing, considering that I made the proposal first. She would beam, saying sentimental things about her motherhood, anxiously reaching for my hand across the table. She was not wicked, ever, or cruel, or unkind. We'll never go skating together, never make cocoa in the kitchen at midnight, snurfing in our cups and whooping it up behind the stove. I was never eight. I was never eleven. I was never thirteen. The mind I am in now came to me some time after puberty, not the initiation into sex (which is supposed to be the important thing), but the understanding that everything I had suffered from as a child, all my queerness, all my neuroses, the awful stiffnesses, the things people scorned in me, that all these would be all right when I was an adult because when I was an adult I would have power.

And I do. I do.

Power gave me life. I like it. Here's something else I like: when I was twenty-nine and my mother—flustered and ingenuous—told me that she'd had an embarrassing dream about me. Did she expect to be hit? It was embarrassing (she said) because it was incestuous. She dreamed we had eloped and were making love.

Don't laugh. I told it for years against her. I said all sorts of awful things. But what matters still matters, i.e. my mother's kicking a wastebasket the length of the living room in a rage (as she once bragged to me she did) or striking her breast, crying melodramatically, "Me Martian! Me good! You Jupiterian! You bad!" (as she also did). Bless you! do you think she married to get away from me? I wasn't born yet.

It's immensely sweet of her to offer to marry me, but what I want to know is: do you think we're suited?

Don José, the Brazilian heiress—wait a minute, I'm getting them muddled up, that was the other one where I was the Brazilian heiress, this one's Don José and he's *Argentinian* and an *Heir*—anyway, his cruel smile undressed her with his eyes, I don't think I can go on writing like this, she said. Are you not woman enough to know? And the unfortunate sadist tossed his typewriter out the window. That is what they called working-girls in those days. My mother will never forgive me. For what? cried the incautious maid with the almond-blue eyes. Thank you, sir, I shall make the bed, she sobbed. Only do not lay me in it; that will crease the counterpane and I will be fired. And your children, his mustache twitching, I have sworn to have them, have me first, no, have a shashlik; there is blood on my dress.

Blood!

I have murdered the butler.

(A lively game of bed-to-bed trash filled the evening air as the charming little summer-camp Mädchen disemboweled the myth and passed it gigglingly from hand to hand. Salugi! Gesundheit. Thank you very much.)

What Every Woman Knows.

It is quite possible that none of this happened or has value; still I wish life could have been different for my mother. But we're all in Tiamat's lap, so there's no use complaining. In the daytime we stand on Her knees, looking up at Her face, and at night She hides Her face so we get uneasy. Our Father Witch (in whom I used to believe) is very jealous of his name or it's a secret or it's too ugly (or maybe he hasn't got any), but you can call Tiamat in any language you want; she broadcasts Herself all over the place and She doesn't mind kiddies pulling at Her skirt; call her Nyame and Tanit, call her 'Anat, Atea, Tabiti, Tibirra. This is what comes of remeeting one's mother when she was only two—how willful she was! how charming, and how strong. I wish she had not grown up to be a doormat, but all the same what a blessing it is not to have been made by somebody's hands like a piece of clay, and then he breathed a spirit in you, etc., so you are clay and not-clay, your ingredients fighting each other like the irritable vitamin pill in the ad—what a joy and a pleasure to have been born, just ordinary born, you know, out of dirt and flesh, all of one piece and of the same stuff She is. To be my mother's child. (Your pleasures and pains are your bellybutton-cord to the Great Mother; they prove you were once part of Her.)

I asked, Why couldn't my mother have been more like You? But She didn't answer. I felt something coming from Her. Times She doesn't like me—I don't always like myself—but we're still the same stuff.

Change my life! I said.

Sorry, won't. Her fog veiled Her face (that is one of Her moods), and Her towns (which are the rings on Her fingers) grew ugly. Tiamat is talking. She spoke through me as in the Bible, that is I spoke, knowing the answer:

Am I my mother's mother?

On winter nights, when my mother and I were twelve, we would go out together with chocolate cigarettes and pose under streetlights like little prostitutes, pretending that we were smoking. It was very glamorous. Now we do it in our cheap dresses, our tight shoes; my mother has waited for The Man all her life, that's why she had no time for me. In the beauty parlor, on the street, in the nursing home, waiting for The Man. We lean on each other, very tired, in our makeup, a sad friendship between us. We even hold hands.

Will you be my best friend? she says.

I say yes.

Will you live with me?

I say yes.

Will you sleep with me and wake with me?

I say yes.

Will you marry me?

I say yes.

All you need is love.

The Zanzibar Cat

HOMMAGE À HOPE MIRRLEES

Duke Humphrey, bearded and humped, had died six hundred years before but not really, so that the people of Appletap-on-Flat were understandably frightened when he began to reappear in the outlying districts with (it was said) a demon cat from Zanzibar sitting on his hump and telling him what to do. Shepherds had seen him laughing and loitering at dusk; little boys watching cows at night had heard strange sounds of war; armed men were perceived to issue from the shadowy depths of wells; and more than one young girl had run terrified into a cottage at twilight with tales of which no one could make either beginning or end, for the Duke (they had always said, as a joke) was armed in more ways than one. For a while the Mayor of Appletap-cum-Cumber, which is the principal city of the whole

---

Hope Mirrlees's fantasy, Lud-in-the-Mist, *is full of symbolic place-names, fairy fruit, and references to Fairyland. Ms. Mirrlees's novel does not describe Fairyland—so I did, half in affectionate parody, but the other half very seriously indeed.* —J.R.

plain, merely humphed and the Vice-Mayor declared, "They have eaten of that fairy fruit which makes the treason lissomer," but as no one in the whole Flat had seen fairy berries—which look like candles or Christmas-tree lights or chandeliers, but never, never like honest vegetables—for ten generations at least, the explanation tended to ring a little false. Besides, as the old remembered and the young were beginning rather reluctantly to appreciate, the Duke's depredations followed an all-too-familiar pattern—so the maids and matrons of Appletap-cum-Cumber, their husbands, their fathers, members of the learned professions, gaffers and gammers and even little children (in short, the whole population of the town), repaired to attics, storerooms, and old libraries, to ponder the lessons taught on vellums worn with age, on tapestries falling to loose thread, on old miniatures, scenes painted on fans, and the buckles, medallions, and party favors of another age. Some said the Duke had come to claim his own again, and was Evil, some that he was giving Appletap-on-Flat one last chance, some even that he did not exist, and some (down by the wharves at the mouth of the Cumber and this was the oddest opinion of all) that the Duke had an interest in the importation of fairy berries, and that these ought to be seen back again in the Flat, and that by marching against the Duke, Appletap-on-Flat was arming itself against nothing less than all of life and all of death and would doom itself—unless the Duke prevented—to an existence that was Flat indeed.

For arm they did. After much prodding by the guild representatives and professional councils (especially the Law, which considered itself to be most insulted by the whole irregular affair), the Mayor of Appletap-cum-Cumber organized a militia, to proceed through the counties, gathering strength as it went. Ladies and non-participating citizens were to be strictly excluded, but the fact was that nobody could be kept out; and the whole of Appletap followed the army to the town gates. Half of Appletap followed it for the rest of the day, the other half cut out by suppertime, and when the sun came up over the Meaning Mountains, no one was left but the Miller's daughter, a shy, brown-haired, plain-faced young miss who had become separated from her parents and was afraid to go back alone. No one bothered about her much. As the army marched—or rather, straggled—North, for the people of Appletap-

on-Flat were not military in their habits, the Miller's daughter went
with them. She sewed a button for a soldier, a plain farmer from
the hills, who said, "Thank 'ee, miss." She salted the porridge of
another soldier. She helped gather sweet-smelling branches for the
evening fire built by a third. In the twilight the Meaning Mountains
began to look somewhat sinister—great serrations and saw-toothed
gaps against what a little shepherd lad called "a bleeding sky." Nor
did the foothills, called The Merry Marches, lighten anybody's
spirits, name or no name. Nor did (everyone added) the common
knowledge that beyond the Meaning Mountains lay Nobody-
Knows-What, Don't-Say, and Avoid-If-You-Can (they would do
anything to keep from calling it by its proper name). By the time
the militia had passed the next day in ragged single file up The Dis-
mal Downs—long, tumbled ridges of stones and thorn—there was
not a man among the grim farmers of Appletap-on-Flat, the solid
burghers of Appletap-cum-Cumber, or the few queer foreign sailors from the low dives by the Cumber (allies of the Duke, some
whispered) who believed that he would ever return from beyond
the Mountains alive.

And nobody did, except the Miller's daughter.

"I only have escaped alive to tell you," said the Miller's daughter.
Everyone listened attentively.

By the evening of the second day (she continued) the going had
got pretty bad. Thorns tore at them and they stepped on stones that
turned underfoot as if they had been living things—and maybe they
were, for half the army was limping. If you think soldiers can't fall
and go arse-over-teacup, you're wrong. The Miller's daughter had
fallen down so many times it would be cruel to count them, and her
gown was ripped in dozens of places. She was missing her parents,
too, and sobbed a little, even though the soldiers had made a kind
of mascot of her. Even a country girl can't walk as fast or as far as a
man, and the soldiers weren't willing to leave somebody behind
with her—not that I think she would have consented to stay, for
the light was draining out of the sky and the sky itself turning a
most peculiar greenish-black, and above the Downs where the stars
should have been coming out there was nothing at all: not light nor
haze nor stars nor moon. The ground, too, seemed to shift under
their feet as they marched, not that anybody fell exactly, but the

feeling of it changed; so that now it seemed to be tilted to one side and now to the other, and sometimes you didn't know if you were walking uphill or downhill. It was altogether most unsettling. And then it got darker still and there was (for everyone) an overwhelming certainty that a precipice lay only a dozen steps away, and then only six steps, and then three, and at last it was the hardest thing in the world for anyone to take a single step, for each man seemed to be on the edge of his own cliff, so (as one man) they stopped.

There was a light shining in the distance.

As they watched the light grew, a kind of friendly light, actually, the sort you might see through trees in the middle of a forest at night, and although there was no forest on the Downs and never had been (which was not a pleasant thought), still it was better to see a light through trees than no light at all.

"By damn, these be trees!" said one of the foreign sailors.

"They be not natural trees, neither," complained a burgher who had just been hit in the face by one.

"The light is growing stronger," said the Miller's daughter.

If you have ever watched a magic-lantern display or the kind of shadow-pictures countryfolk make before the fire in winter in the outlying districts of the Cumber, you may have seen a hazy dot broaden to a blur, the blur to the flickering lines of a fire, and the fire suddenly waver and clear like a curtain to reveal a castle, or a painting of the Cumber, or a portrait of the maker's favorite niece. Thus the light in the woods grew from a dim glow, only glimpsed through the tree-trunks, to a far-off star, and as the struggling militia of the Cumber pushed through the trees, to a spreading glow of fire and finally—as if the forest had become transparent and the trees had suddenly turned to veils—resolved itself into the light of an hundred torches playing on a fretwork of stone, an hundred torches set in the niches of a lofty castle close embowered in trees; and in front of the castle stood an hundred mailèd knights, their faces obscured and their arms folded on their chests. No one in all of Appletap had ever seen even three armed knights in one place at one time before.

Or twelve five-star generals or fifteen Messerschmitts or thirty Herrenvölker, said a voice. No one recognized it, but it belonged to the Miller's daughter. The men of Appletap pressed in through the outside gate of the castle as if they and the knights and the trees and indeed the whole scene itself had been bewitched asleep; and when the gate closed behind them they climbed the broad stairs, and from there they crowded under the castle archway, and from there into a long gallery, and from there up stairs and down, round about, through rooms, past old tapestries, into courtyards and out, under faded banners, through draughty passageways, until the enchantment dissolved and they woke up to find themselves in the longest, broadest, oldest hall of all.

There was the Duke. He needed no servants. Behind him stood his men-at-arms, but whether there were one hundred or fifty or five or thirty million or none at all, nobody could tell; for when you looked away, then you saw them, and when you looked right at them, they weren't there.

The Duke was a very evil man. He had a fair, silken beard and a beautiful face. He sat on the ducal throne in the leaping light from the fire at the end of the huge hall; the foreign seamen swore there were leopards in the shadows behind him, doubtful creatures half-formed, partly men and partly beasts, like shadows from the fire. To some the Duke looked handsome in the face but deformed in the body, to some straight in the back but crooked in the mind. There were, however, two things about him that none could deny: one, that he wore the suit of apple-green brocade in which he had always been pictured so that everybody knew it was he, and two, that on his shoulder, in a little striped pool, lay the Zanzibar cat.

Who has come to make war against me? said the Duke very softly, and the Zanzibar cat, dainty and taloned, rose on his shoulder, stretched itself, yawned pinkly, and settled again. It had no tail.

Then it grinned like a man.

This is the fifty-nine-thousandth cat in Zanzibar, said the Duke. *I have counted them.*

No one from Appletap stirred.

O Appletappians! said the Duke (and the humorousness of it seemed to please him). *Do you know against whom it is you come to wage war? I have counted the cats in Zanzibar, I have numbered the waterspouts over the Red Sea, I am all-life-and-all-death, I am the shadow inside the shadow, the shadow that makes the light, the light that makes the shadow, I am tender and cruel, I am he whom they call the Altogether Persuasive One, I am as hard as a thrust in*

*the groin and as diffused as water, and you cannot keep me out of
your little world by your fences and your names and your books
and your short memories and your Rules for the Behavior of Young
Misses.*

Now, said the Duke, *I am going to strip away the walls of this
castle; and you must know that you are on the edge of Fairyland,
which is the name you keep avoiding, by the way, on the very
edge, to be exact, and when the walls of this castle disappear, the
wind which always blows from that place will strike you, and as
you will no longer be protected by these walls of mine, that Fairy
blast will kill you. It's a cheap way to be rid of one's enemies and
very much to my taste.*

"Not bloody likely," said someone in the crowd. The Zanzibar
cat horripilated like a bottle-brush. He arched himself on the
Duke's hump and spat a ghastly *gah!* like any ordinary cat. There
was a stir in the crowd as the Miller's daughter pushed through. She
did not look, to those who looked at her, like the same girl she had
been, sweet as a lamb and so shy she could not hold up her head.
She looked possessed. She looked, in fact, (as they blinked and
rubbed their eyes) not at all like a young girl of twenty but like a
woman twice that age, and a spinster too, and a hard one too, as
hard as nails, or maybe a many-times-married woman, because the
effect is—curiously enough—much the same. All this came out in
her face gradually as she walked the length of that courtly hall, and
as rooms seem to listen to what's being said in them and to conform
themselves to it, so the hall shrank as the Milleress walked down it
until it seemed to the army of Appletap-on-Flat that they stood in a
smoky tavern on the edge of the Merry Marches where a desperate
and infamous gambler sat in front of a half-spent fire and that the
gambler was the Duke. Some even fancied that the Milleress looked
rather like a landlady, a comparison that evoked painful memories
in many. The Duke's cat, still threatening, had nevertheless hidden
behind the Duke's neck. He plucked it into his lap and stroked its
fur. It settled, though cautiously.

It is very much to my taste, he repeated, *and accords well with
my fancy. I will do it now.*

"You will not," said the Milleress. The room shrank a little more.

Do you really think, said the Duke very, very gently, *that you
can exist without me?* He smiled like a humane man. The pet on his

lap looked up with a puckered brow, with a little human face of protracted woe. It said quite clearly, "O master, the silence of those infinite spaces is terrifying to me." The men of Appletap gasped to hear a cat speak (for it had never happened before that *they* remembered), but the Milleress did not flinch and she said nothing, only she stood with her arms folded, quite silent and unmoved, and in this silence there was the attitude of a person who expects to be paid. The Duke tilted his head, as if he were listening. Then the cat said in its little voice:

> "The bad picture
> Leads me on.
> What to do?"

The Duke shook it. It was evident that he did not like what he had heard. The cat gave a mew in a voice like a little girl's. It stood up in his lap and cried rapidly, "You see, all this nonsense is very exotic, until your grasp of life begins to deepen and glow beyond the common, I mean here and now is your America, I mean every time I cut an onion, that is like cutting my throat, isn't it, and there was a man who heard about the fifty-two enzymic reactions occurring constantly in the human body and who grew so perturbed in mind at the thought of them and so terrified because one of them might fail, that he hanged himself, and that is what I mean by hell. Do you see?"

Furiously the Duke flung the animal from him. It landed on the floor on its back and lay there weeping in distress. The Duke made as if to stumble up from his throne, but the Milleress stepped forward (whereupon the room shrank again), and the animal writhed to its feet and streaked back to its master's shoulder. The woman recited stolidly:

> "Nor life nor death were not
> Till man made up the whole,
> Made lock, stock, and barrel
> Out of his bitter soul."

Very pretty, said the Duke, rising, and considering that the people of the Flat had always seen him painted as one who has a faint mocking smile, the expression on his face was really extraordinary, *very pretty and very apt and quite enough, though I rather wonder where you got it, as I had always understood that the crown of an Appletap girl's education was making swans in butter-pats under the direction of some benevolent old hag. But understand, my girl,* (and here his eyes gleamed dangerously from under his half-lowered eyelids) *there are the fairy berries, which leave you with longings nothing in this world can satisfy; there are the dwarves; there are the anthropophagi and men whose heads do grow beneath their shoulders; there are worlds which twist the very structure of the human mind so horribly as to make Fairyland look like a child's picnic, though the airs from Fairyland can kill you, and I, who am lord of it all, can poison with a touch, can heal with a touch, can leave you grieving your life long, can show you hells and intimacies you never dreamed of, and I—who am shortly going to kill you—ask you again: Do you think that you, or any other human being, can bind me with your petty rules or loose me with your fences of custom and habitual blindness and comfort? I am lord of it all. Can you—or any other human being—keep me out?*

"Keep you out?" said the Milleress flatly. "I think the question is, can I keep you in." And again the walls shrank. The room was no bigger than a burgher's parlor. It was an Appletappian's front room. It was impossible that the entire militia of the Flat should be able to fit inside it, but somehow they all did. The Duke's head had sunk on his chest, for the Devil is never so dangerous as when he appears to be asleep. As in a small parlor or a small cave that is lit by firelight, so that everything appears through a haze or screen of flame, thus the whole room seemed to be full of fire. The Duke, now hunched on the bare ground beneath his own deformed back, sat with his face hidden by flames; the Milleress stood burning in her flesh; the Duke's pet curled up behind a wavering screen of fire. There was nobody else in the room; there was nothing but flame.

Then I don't exist? said the Duke, or someone.

You exist, said she.

Why?

Because I made you up. And seizing him by the beautiful fair hair, in all that burning, she drew his head up and back so that his face was next to her own. They were twins. Passively—or scornfully—Duke Humphrey stared at the men of Appletap, and nobody could tell whether the Miller's daughter had gotten to look like the Duke or whether the Duke had gotten to look like the Miller's daughter. She kissed him on the mouth: mirror meeting mirror.

O my dear, she said, *I wanted so much for you to exist.*

But let us at least call things by their proper names.

And at those words the Duke disappeared. The burghers of Appletap-cum-Cumber, the farmers of Appletap-on-Flat, the foreign sailors who come from lands beyond the Cumber and who can therefore be presumed to know more about these things than other people, all these watched the Duke disappear and were very, very shocked. He disappeared the way a dream does: first the vividness went out of him so that although he had the same coloring, you knew he wasn't real; and then he went in patches like a construction falling apart, this one, for instance, which is going to do so in a very few minutes, and then he was only the impression of an impression, the memory of brocade, a ruff, a cat sitting on a hump, and after that the memory goes too and all you have is the vague feeling that you had hold of something a minute ago, and then you only remember that you remember that you remembered. It's no use going to count the cats in Zanzibar because, if the truth were known, just between you and me, there are no cats there.

"Do not," said the Miller's daughter, "go around looking for the kingdom of Heaven as if it were a lost sheep, saying wow, here! and wow, there! because the kingdom of Heaven is inside you."

"Who are you," said the people of Appletap-on-Flat, all kneeling down instanter, "who speak not as the scribes but with authority?"

She said:

"I'm the author.